MW00899222

Shattered Jade

Carol Ashley

This is a work of fiction. Names, characters, places, and incidents either are the product of the author's imagination or are used fictitiously. Any resemblance to actual persons, living or dead, events, or locales is entirely coincidental.

Copyright © 2022 by Jane Carol Ashley.

All rights reserved. No part of this book may be reproduced in any form on by an electronic or mechanical means, including information storage and retrieval systems, without permission in writing from the publisher, except by a reviewer who may quote brief passages in a review.

Book design by Kent Mummert, MFA

ISBN 978-1-4583-1247-1

Published by Lulu Press, Morrisville, North Carolina
Lulu.com

Printed in the USA

DEDICATION

I want to dedicate this book to my sister-in-law, Paula Carter, Cynthia Leavelle, Dianne Rainey, my original editors, my proofreaders, and to the members of my writing and grow group– Renelle Folse, Carole Ford, Jodie Harris and Ollie Voelker–who encouraged me to keep on writing.

Transformed by Terror

A shot followed by a scream penetrated the darkness that engulfed her. "Put him in the trunk. He didn't have it on him. Check the car and the girl's purse. He might have put it there," a raspy voice said. She heard the door open and the sound of movement all around her.

"There's nothing in here but the woman, and she's unconscious. Do you think we should shoot her? We don't know what she saw." That sounded like another voice.

"She might have seen the car right before we t-boned them, but she was out cold before we took him. Even if she did see something, her story would be incoherent after that blow. It looks like she doesn't believe in seat belts." The raspy voice grew faint; then she heard a car drive away.

The semiconscious woman was slumped in her seat. Slowly, she completely regained consciousness. When she sat up, her reflection in the mirror on the visor showed a large knot where her head had banged into something. No wonder her head was pounding! She looked down from her forehead to her eyes, nose, and then her mouth. It was the face of a stranger.

She looked for a purse. Who was she? Maybe if she could see her driver's license, it would help her remember. At least she would know her name.

There was no purse in the car. Raspy Voice had said something about a purse. Now she remembered that the other one had asked if he should shoot her. They were looking for something after she heard a shot. Did they kill the person who was driving? Maybe not; why would they load a dead man into their car or whatever they were driving? If that man lived but wouldn't answer their questions, or told them the thing they wanted was somewhere in the car, what would they do to her? They knew where she was and what the car looked like. What if they came back?

She had to get away, but where could she go? Would the police take seriously a report given by a woman with no name, about a missing victim she couldn't identify or describe who had been shot over an unknown missing object? They would think she was crazy. Of course, they would believe she had been in a car accident and suffered a blow on the head. That would explain her wild story. She had better get away from here as fast as she could. For all she knew, she herself, might be involved in something illegal.

When she got out and slid behind the wheel, she saw a thin package between the console and the passenger's seat. That gap had been covered by her skirt. This must have been what they were looking for. It wasn't very large, but it must be valuable from the way those men acted. In case she might need it to bargain for her life, she put it into her blazer pocket.

As she drove, she tried to think through what had happened. If she was to be safe, she had to organize her thoughts and come up with a plan. They just shot someone and thought about killing her. She had to go somewhere to disappear and find some way to support herself.

What skills did she have, if any? What a foolish question; no matter what she could do, no one would hire her without the proper documents and recommendations. Why worry about documentation and recommendations? Right now, she needed a name. Just then she passed an exit sign for Grace Garland. She wondered if that was one town or two. Not that it mattered; it would do for a name if anyone asked.

Farmland separated by miles of forest seemed to fly past her window as she sped down the road. She'd better slow down. One thing she didn't need was to attract the attention of a vigilant highway patrolman or local sheriff. A woman with no license, who couldn't tell them where she was going, would surely seem suspicious.

When the low fuel warning began to go off, Grace continued to drive until a metallic noise announced she had not only run out of gas but might have destroyed the fuel pump. She abandoned the car and started walking.

The day was bright, and the sun burned her unprotected skin as the hot pavement radiated heat through her thin-soled high heels. Still, she couldn't walk on the grassy roadside. The three-inch heels sank into the soggy sod and made walking almost impossible.

Car after car passed as Grace forced herself to keep on walking. At least the tags on their bumpers gave her a clue to her location. A disproportionate number had Alabama tags.

Finally, a rusty, red pickup pulled over on the shoulder. A woman called out, "Lady, do you want a ride? I won't ask if you need one. You look like you're about to drop. Hop in; I promise I'm just a harmless old lady."

Grace didn't need to be coaxed. She climbed into the cab. "Thank you so much, ma'am. I was about to drop."

"You don't need to ma'am me. I'm just plain Lovie, Lovie Millburn. What's your name?"

"I'm Grace Garland."

"That's a pretty name. Are you kin to the Garlands over in Rainbow City?"

"I doubt it. I'm not from around here."

Lovie looked at Grace for a while, observing every detail. "I didn't think so. You sound Southern but not Alabama Southern." She paused and then added, "You don't have anywhere to go, do you, girl?"

"Why do you say that?"

"Just look at yourself in the mirror. It's written all over you. Your husband hit you and gave you that goose egg, didn't he? You got mad and lit out walking and hitching rides to get away from him. Am I right?"

"Close enough, but why do you think it was my husband?" Grace asked.

Lovie smiled and pointed to Grace's hand. "That's easy. See that pale ring of skin where your wedding band should be? That told me almost everything I needed to know. Just tell me, did you throw those rings in his face before or after he hit you?"

Grace looked at her finger; the evidence that she had worn a ring was clearly there. Maybe it was a wedding ring. Was she running away from her husband or running off with someone else? She looked up and simply said, "I'm not sure. That blow to my head made me forget a few things." At least that much of her story was true, she thought.

"Knocked some sense into you, I'd say. No woman needs a man so much that she has to put up with that kind of stuff." Lovie gripped the steering wheel with one hand. "Where are you planning on going, and what are you planning to do once you get far enough away from your old man?"

That was a question Grace had been asking herself. "I don't really know; it happened so fast. I left without my purse, so I don't have any money or credit cards. I don't even have my driver's license, and I can't go back to get anything now. There has to be a way to make enough money to live on without my social security card and identification, but the only thing I can think of is illegal."

"My mama's second husband, the devil who raised me, used to say he could 'keep her in line with his fist.' She put up with it because of us kids. She didn't think she could support her family on her own. You had the guts to leave; she didn't. I couldn't help her, but maybe I can help you.

Grace smiled at her. "Thank you. I appreciate that."

"My husband and I have a bunch of relatives who live with us from time to time. We have a big family, but there's always room for one more. You're welcome to stay with us if you don't mind sleeping on a cot in the storage room. As for earning some money without your social security card, you can help us. Our family hires out to pick vegetables on some of the farms around here, and I clean a few houses from time to time. It's just day labor, no contracts or paperwork. We figure there're a lot of things Uncle Sam doesn't know, and one more won't bring down the government. Like I said, there's always some relative staying with us. I could tell them you're a distant cousin if anyone notices a new girl."

Grace smiled and said, "You seem to have all the answers. Are you sure your husband won't mind?"

"Don't get me wrong, Grace, he's a good man; he couldn't be better. He's just a little slow. I make the decisions in the family; things run smoother that way. It will be fine with him."

Grace never had suspected angels were dumpy, aging blondes who drove beat-up red trucks, but Lovie qualified for a halo and wings. The two women drove the rest of the way making plans for Grace's new life.

Grace was relieved when they left the main road. No one would follow her down the rutted, dirt road. At the end of the road was a dilapidated trailer with several junked cars in various stages of disrepair. A silver-gray sedan was parked behind them. Two men engaged in conversation were leaning against it.

Lovie sighed and said, "Oh, no, it's the pastor. This is going to complicate things. I hope Billy Ray won't mess things up by asking who you are. Put on these sunshades and pull this ball cap down over that goose-egg. We don't want the men asking questions."

Grace did as she was told. She and Lovie climbed out of the cab and walked over to join the men.

Lovie put on her best fake smile and extended her hand to the preacher whose unruly, sandy hair and boyish smile always made her think of a well-dressed farm boy who'd be more comfortable in jeans and a work-shirt than a sport coat and dress pants. "Hello, Brother Bax. It's good to see you. I guess you're here to visit with my wounded husband."

"Yes, I heard that Billy Ray was injured while he was working on the Hall place. I'm glad to see him up and around even with that cast on his leg."

"You know Billy Ray. As long as he can hop around and hold on to something he won't use those crutches," Lovie said, noticing Bax's interested look at Grace. There was no way to avoid introducing the pastor to her, so like a child she crossed her fingers behind her back and lied. "I want you to meet my second cousin Grace. She's going to be working with us for a while. You remember Grace, don't you, Billy Ray? Of course, she was just a little thing last time she was here."

Billy Ray looked a bit confused but nodded at the stranger, having correctly read Lovie's look that conveyed the message he better remember her. "It's good to have you back, Grace. Family's always welcome here."

Bax Alford looked at the slender, olive-skinned brunette. She didn't look like any of the Millburn relatives he'd seen.

"Grace, this is Reverend Baxter Alford, the preacher at our church. He's been real good about looking in on us when we have trouble. He takes the pastoring part of the job as seriously as the preaching part."

She held out her hand and said, "I'm pleased to meet you, Reverend Alford."

"Just call me Brother Bax, Grace. Everyone else does." She liked the way his hair fell over his forehead. He seemed like a nice guy. They chatted for a while, and then Bax looked at his watch.

"I better leave. I have several more families to visit. Take care of yourself, Billy Ray. Call me if there's anything I can do for you. I doubt if you'll be ready to take up offering this week. I'll get Sylvester Bush to do it for you. Good-bye Miss Lovie and Miss Grace; I hope to see you two ladies in church on Sunday even if Billy Ray isn't up to coming."

Lovie and Grace walked into the house after the preacher's old sedan disappeared around the bend. Billy Ray hopped along behind them grabbing first one thing and then another for balance. He caught up with them at the kitchen table and dropped into a chair.

"Spill it, Lovie. When did we get a new cousin I've never seen in all my born days? You made me lie to the preacher. I just hope there's a reason for all these lies."

"I'm sorry, Honey; I would have told you everything if the preacher hadn't been here. You picked up on my story about my cousin and said just the right thing. I do owe you an explanation. This is Grace Garland. Her husband hit her, and she left him. I'm helping her get on her feet. "Grace, take off the shades and cap."

Grace did as she was told. Billy Ray winced when he saw the knot on her head. Her forehead and eyes were dark and swollen.

"I told her she can stay in the storage room and work with the family for a while. I hope you don't mind, and I pray that God understands why we fibbed to the preacher."

"Lovie, you did good. We can't let this little lady be treated bad by her old man. Your mama would be proud of you. "Welcome home, Cousin Grace."

∽

That night before he went to bed, Bax made an entry in the
journal where he recorded the private prayer requests of his
church members, his visits, and observations of things that
caught his interest. Bax was considering that woman, Grace, he
had met that day. As he shook her hand, he had noticed how
soft it was. Her nails were manicured and much too long for
farm work. He'd also seen the look Lovie had shot her husband.
Something was going on here that Lovie didn't want him to know
about. He wrote his thoughts.

> *The new cousin who has moved in with the*
> *Millburns is nothing like any of the others. She is dark,*
> *slender, and dressed like a doctor's wife on the way to*
> *a luncheon at the country club. Her shoes have seen*
> *better days—probably thrift store finds. The strangest*
> *thing about her outfit was the faded Bama cap pulled*
> *down so far the bill touched the big sunglasses she*
> *wore. There was bruising behind them, but it could*
> *have been just a shadow. Still, Miss Lovie was up*
> *to something again. Was Grace a battered wife, a*
> *working girl who was hit by a pimp or john, or maybe*
> *just a careless cousin who walked into a door? There*
> *was no telling.*

He always thought of Lovie as the neighborhood's own
Mother Teresa. Sometimes she could stick her nose in where
it didn't belong, but her motives were always beyond reproach.
She might never achieve official sainthood, but, like Mother
Teresa, her love of all those who needed help was unlimited. Her
methods, though, might be questionable.

TWO
_____

Dave

"Joe, get our school boy out of the trunk. He's sure to be awake by now," Mitch ordered.

Joe opened the trunk. David Fontaine, curled into a fetal position, blinked his eyes in the bright sunlight and moved deeper into the trunk. Joe grabbed his arm and pulled him to a seated position. "Get out; you're okay. The only thing that touched you was the breeze from the bullet when it missed your arm. Now be smart, professor; tell us where our package is," Joe said as he pulled the man to his feet.

"I don't have it. It was in the car. I stuck it between the seat and the console. I didn't know it was yours. A friend asked me to take it home for him," David said.

"Yeah, we know...Professor Tony Berry. What did he tell you about it?" Joe asked.

"Nothing much. He just told me to take it and put it in a safe place, and not to mention it to anyone, even my wife. He said he'd get it later."

"Did he tell you what it was?" Mitch asked.

"No."

"Joe checked the car and didn't find anything. Are you sure you're telling us the truth?"

"Yes, why would I lie to you?"

"He might be telling the truth, Mitch. I checked the console, under the seats, the trunk and even the woman's purse, but I didn't look between the console and the passenger's seat. She was kind of slumped over that way."

"Go back to the car and check it out again. Don't overlook anything this time. If she's in the way, move her," Mitch ordered.

"What if she comes to while I'm searching?" Joe asked.

"You know what to do; take care of her. We don't want her to have bad memories."

"Don't hurt my wife! Please don't hurt Anastasia!" As Dave watched Joe walk away, the reality of the situation hit him. Whether or not they got the package Tony had given him, if they found her, they would kill her.

He realized that they hadn't been concerned about using their names around him. These men were planning to kill him, so they weren't worried. They would be sure he would never be able to describe them or tell their names. He hoped Joe would find what he was looking for, but not her. Ana was his. He couldn't let them find her.

The cabin where they had taken David was only five miles from the place they had rammed the car. Joe was back in less than fifteen minutes.

"The car and the woman are gone!"

"Then we'll find her. She can't have gone far, but there is no telling what direction she drove. Fontaine, you're going to call the police and report the wreck. Tell them she was unconscious when you went for help. Then before they have time to get here, call back and report your wife as missing. Add that you are afraid that someone stole the car and drove off with your unconscious wife, or that she came to and may be driving a damaged car and in need of medical help.

"If they ask why you didn't just use your cell phone to call 911, explain that the phone lost signal. That happens all of the time in these foothills. If they ask about the people who let you use their landline, you are to say you saw this cabin in the distance when you were walking back for help. You got to it just as the family that had rented it was packing to leave. They let you in to use the phone. You went back to your car. When you found your wife and car missing, you went back to the cabin. They were about to leave and told you to pull the locked door closed when you finished your call. If you're asked about the family, pick a real family to base their descriptions on. That'll help you remember details if you have to retell the story," Mitch said.

David nodded.

Joe said, "Don't try anything; we won't be far away. We'll know if you don't do as we say. That near miss was just to get your attention. You'd have been useless to us if you couldn't talk. If you cross us, I won't miss again. And after you're dead, I will find your wife and kill her." Dave couldn't let anything happen to her. No one would ever know what she meant to him or how much of his life he had invested in her. He would have to figure out a way to escape. But for now, the wisest thing to do was call the sheriff's office and tell their crazy story.

Joe dialed 911 and handed Dave the phone. He and Mitch listened, counting the rings until someone answered the phone. "This is David Fontaine; I want to report an accident."

David proceeded to tell the story. After the near verbatim account, he answered a few of the sheriff's questions and hung up.

"You did a good job, professor. Now we'll wait a while and call back. If you do as well with the second call, you get to stay alive," Mitch said.

Thad

J ames Thaddius Brownlee had been in law enforcement for sixteen years. In that time, he had learned to recognize a cock-and-bull story when he heard one. There were the tell-tale signs of one all over the story Professor David Fontaine had told on the phone. It just didn't make sense to him, and as he had learned from the eminent legal scholar, Judge Judy, "If it doesn't make sense, it's not true."

He walked to his chief deputy, Francisco Shaw's desk and said, "Fran, I'm going to check on a missing person report. Fontaine reported a wreck a few minutes before he called in reporting his wife as a missing person. Since Eugene is already on his way out there to investigate the wreck, I won't need you this time."

Thad pulled up to the crossroads where Fontaine said the accident had occurred. Eugene was talking to a disheveled man. The husband clearly looked worried; no, it was beyond worried. The way he moved when he got up and approached the cruiser seemed almost frantic.

Thad got out and approached him. "Professor Fontaine, I'm Sheriff Thad Brownlee. Can you tell me more about the wreck and your wife's disappearance?"

"It's just like I told you on the phone. We were returning from a conference in Tennessee. When we got to this crossroads, a car came out of nowhere and crashed into the passenger's side of our car. It was a hit and run. My wife was knocked out cold. I went for help because my cell wouldn't work, and when I got back, my car and my wife were missing. I went back to the cabin and called you. That is all I know."

"What did the car that hit you look like?"

"I'm not sure. Everything happened too fast…light, maybe white or silver. I don't know the size, make, or model. It was a sedan of some kind. That's all I can say."

After he looked around the scene of the accident, Thad said, "Eugene, make some pictures of the tire tracks. It's clear there're tire prints on the shoulder of the road and marks where someone scratched off away from the area where the impact took place, but none to indicate the driver tried to stop to avoid hitting you. I called a friend who is an engineer to come out and take some measurements so he can make calculations that will give me more information."

"Are you talking about your forensics people?" Fontaine asked.

"No, this is a small, poor county. We don't have access to all of the things you have seen on TV, but John and his calculator, along with Eugene and his camera, do a pretty good job."

"What did you say were the names of the people who helped you?" Thad asked.

"I didn't ask, and I'm not sure they said. It wasn't a time for formal introductions. They were just nice people who let me use the cabin they'd rented and then dropped me back here to meet you and went on their way. They said they had a plane to catch."

"There's John now. When he finishes with his measurements and I get all the pictures I need, I'll take you into town. There's a motel you can stay in, and I have a friend who sometimes rents his extra car to people he knows he can trust not to drive it off into the sunset. Since you are a respected college professor, and I'm giving him my word that I'll track you down if you take it, I'm sure he will be glad to rent it to you until we find your car, or you get another."

Thad still had an uneasy feeling about David's story. Yes, phones did lose signal in the area sometime, but the coverage here was unusually good. There were towers for several of the major carriers in the vicinity. And why did he say the family dropped him off after the second phone call when earlier he said they told him to lock the door when he finished his call?

Thad knew the only cabin David could be talking about was old man Wilson's place. If he had ever rented it out, no one in the county would believe it. Wilson was a man who enjoyed his privacy. Having strangers using his cabin and his things just didn't fit with what he knew about the man. There was no doubt in his mind that Fontaine was lying. He would find out why.

After they'd finished their work and John had driven off, Thad said, "I'll drive you to the motel now. My friend will bring the car around in the morning."

"Thanks, Sheriff, I appreciate all you have done. I'm so worried about my wife I can't think straight," David said as the two men left the scene of the accident.

Thad thought that was the first thing Dave had said that he completely believed. He wished he knew what was going on. Instead of going back the way he came, Thad drove past the Wilson cabin. "Is that the cabin where the family let you use their landline?" he asked David.

"Yes."

"Was it the Wilson family that helped you?"

"I told you, I don't know. They were just a family: husband, wife, and little girl about seven."

Thad dropped David at the Sleep Tight Inn and drove back to his office to begin planning his search for Anastasia

Fontaine. The first thing he did was call Hank Wilson, the county curmudgeon.

Thad counted the rings. Wilson never answered before the ninth ring. The sheriff thought Hank hoped the caller would give up and leave him alone. After the ninth ring the answering machine acknowledged the call. A recording of the old man's unfriendly voice said, "You know what to do."

"Mr. Wilson, this is Thad Brownlee. Pick up. This call is part of an investigation."

Wilson picked up. "I don't know what in the blue blazes you could be investigating that would involve me. Stop wasting my time and the county's money!"

"Don't hang up, Mr. Wilson. I'm checking out a story. A man told me he was with a family of three, a husband, wife, and seven-year-old girl, in your cabin today. That didn't sound like any of your family, so I thought I would check to see if you rented the cabin to any family like that."

"I don't know who that man is, but he's guilty…at least guilty of lying. I don't even let my sons and their families stay in my cabin."

"That is what I thought. I need to check out your place. If he was telling the truth, then someone must have been there without your permission."

"No one goes there without my permission, not even you! I'll meet you there in half an hour," Wilson said as he slammed down the phone.

True to his word, Hank Wilson drove up to the cabin in thirty minutes. He got out of his truck, slammed the door, and walked to join Thad at the cabin's door. "Well, get on with it. Investigate!"

"I already have. See these marks on the door jamb? It looks like your door has been jimmied. If you'll open the door, I'd like to look around."

Wilson opened the door, and the men went inside. "Does anything look out of place?"

"Let me look around," Wilson said, going from room to room carefully checking each.

"Mr. Wilson, don't touch anything. We may want to dust for fingerprints. Someone broke into your cabin; if anything is missing, we don't want to destroy the evidence."

"The only thing I see is one of the bottles on the shelf behind my bar is in the wrong place."

"How can you be so sure? People just put bottles back on the shelf. It's not like the library's Dewey Decimal system."

"Sheriff, you don't know me very well. Some people may just put things anywhere, but the doctors say I have OCD. If things aren't in just the right place, it drives me crazy. I do have a system of sorts. There is a place for everything, and that bottle is on the wrong end of the shelf."

"Thank you for your help, Mr. Wilson. I'll get my fingerprint kit from my car and dust for prints. I'm not sure what's going on, but so far I have a missing woman, a lying husband, and a misplaced bottle in a cabin with a jimmied door."

"You're welcome to dust for prints, but I understand that it makes an awful mess. I expect you to clean up after yourself."

"We don't do that as a rule, but I understand enough about OCD to know how upsetting it could be. I'll send someone over to clean up the powder when I'm through."

Thad didn't tell Wilson that the jimmied door wasn't the only evidence his investigation had turned up before the old man got there. He had seen tire tracks in the soft earth near the woods that looked like the ones at the site of the wreck. When he got back to his office, he would compare the two sets of prints and send Fran to make plaster of Paris casts of the both of them.

Thad had one more thing to check out. Was there a family of three who had to leave to make a flight? He was sure this was another lie, but a good lawman checks everything.

Grace

Grace entered her new life with the Millburns. Their trailer was small and rundown but immaculately clean.

"I know it's not much, but you're welcome to share what we have. There're three small bedrooms. One, of course, is mine and Billy's. Bubba, our second son, got divorced from his wife and had to move back into what we call the boys' room. The kids know they're always welcome to move home if they need to. Baby Girl, she hates when I call her that, but I can't remember to call her Becky. As I was saying, she's never left home and lives in the room she shared with her sister before Sister married and moved down the road. I'm afraid the only place left for you is the laundry room."

Grace looked into the small room. The hot water heater was in one corner. Hook-ups for a washer and dryer were there next to it; however, the appliances had long since worn out. Grace had seen them in the front yard prominently displayed beside a rusted-out Ford Fairlane that was older than sin. The narrow space would be her home, at least until she had some answers and knew what she should do next.

"I know it's kinda small, but we can fit our twin-sized blow-up mattress in here. I've slept on it in here myself when Billy Ray had a bad case of the flu last year. It's pretty comfortable."

"Thank you, Miss Lovie; this will be fine."

The next morning Grace awoke to the sounds coming through the thin walls. The Millborns were having a noisy family breakfast. Lovie was right; after a few minutes of worrying about what was ahead for her, exhaustion combined with the soft air mattress put her into a deep, dreamless sleep.

Lovie knocked on Grace's door. "Grace you're going to miss breakfast. You'll need to eat if you are going to help with the pea picking. One of the farmers over the mountain called last night after you went to bed. His peas are at peak, and he needs all the hands he can get."

"Sure, I'll help. But don't you think I'll stick out like a sore thumb in this outfit?"

"I've already thought of that. Sister is bringing over some of her jeans."

Just then Sister walked into the claustrophobically small room. "I heard you talking about me, Mama. Hi, Grace, here are some work clothes for you. They might not be a perfect fit, but they'll do. These are my jeans and sneakers, but the tee shirt is one of Bubba's."

Grace tried on the things Sister brought. When she looked at her reflection, she laughed. "Your things fit, but the shirt is really big on me."

"I did that on purpose. We are picking peas today. We don't pick by the hour but by the job. Today we are picking on two farms. You will need to use both hands to pick fast enough to get through with the first job in time to get the second one done. Let me show you a trick that will let you use both of them.

"Catch the front hem of the shirt in your teeth. The big shirt becomes a picking sack. Pick with both hands and fill your shirt; then dump them into a bushel basket at the end of the row. Then start over. You'll be surprised how much time you'll save."

The two women climbed into the blue van Sister's husband, Louis, and Bubba had resurrected from its junkyard grave and drove toward the first farm they were to pick.

"The rest of the family is probably already there," Sister said as she pulled into a convenience store with gas pumps out front. "They'll just have to start without us. I need to get some gas. Louis forgot to fill the tank. If you get hot while I pump the gas, remember this heat is nothing compared to the heat in the pea patch."

As she waited for Sister to pay for her gas in advance, Grace overheard the man at the next pump talking to the driver of his car as he filled the tank. She heard only a few words, but they sent a chill through her body.

"She can't be far from here. He was a fool to think he could..."

They could have been talking about anything, but she knew it was about her and the person who had screamed. She recognized the raspy voice. They were looking for her. What had happened to the screamer? They said he was a fool, not is a fool. Was he dead?

Grace pulled her straw hat low over her face and got out of the car. When she entered the convenience store, Sister was still in line to pay for her gas.

"I need to go; don't ask why; I'll see you later," Grace said softly as she walked past her and toward the ladies' restroom. Then she detoured to the employees' only door that took her to the rear exit and kept walking until she reached the edge of the woods. Slipping deeper into the woods but keeping the road in sight, she walked toward Lovie's house.

Was she over-reacting? Raspy Voice hadn't been interested in the frumpy woman in the baggy Bama tee shirt and straw hat. He was probably well on his way by now, but what if he had recognized her? There was no reason to hang around. If he hadn't recognized her, he didn't need a second chance; and if he had, how could she keep from leading him to Lovie's family?

FIVE
_____

Tony

Aftercalling the small liberal arts college where the Fontaines worked, Thad called David at his motel. "Professor Fontaine, this is Thad Brownlee. I just got off the phone with the head of your department. Were you aware your wife isn't the only faculty member who is missing?"

"No, who else is missing?"

"Professor Anthony Berry was expected back Friday afternoon. His wife went to the airport to pick him up, but he wasn't on the flight. First, she called his cell phone and got no answer, then the hotel. The desk clerk said he had checked out after the conference ended. Next, she contacted Dr. Williams, the history department head, to find out if he had rescheduled their meeting, since the professor wouldn't be able to get back in time if he took a later flight or another mode of transportation. As of this afternoon no one has seen him or heard from him," Thad said.

Dave sounded perplexed. "That's not like Tony at all. When I talked to him while we were checking out, he said he was on his way to the airport. I can't imagine his getting sidetracked. He's one of the most dependable, methodical people I know."

"That's what Dr. Williams told me. He has been missing more than twenty-four hours and Mrs. Berry has filed a missing person report. Is there anything you know of that could tie these two disappearances together?"

"If you are implying what I think you are, you're crazy! You know Ana disappeared after a wreck. I don't know how or why, but I do know it wasn't planned so she could run away with Tony!"

"I didn't mean that; but it's strange that two people who taught at the same small college should come up missing about the same time. What do they have in common?" Thad asked.

"There's nothing, except we all went to LSU. Of course, they both are connected to me; Tony and I teach history at the same college, and Ana is my wife."

"Dr. Fontaine, one last question, when was the last time you saw Tony Berry?" Thad asked.

"I ran into Tony at the front desk Friday afternoon when we were checking out of our hotel after the conference. We made small talk about the merits of the presentations, shook hands and left. That was the last time I saw him. Before you ask, I haven't heard from him either. We're just co-workers, not close friends. I'm not surprised he hasn't called."

"Isn't it uncommon to check out at the desk? Almost everyone pays with cards when they check in," Thad said.

"That's right, but we both had charges we questioned. I guess we assumed the conference fee would have covered everything, but we were wrong."

"You didn't walk out together?"

"No, he left through the front door to get on the shuttle to the airport. Ana and I took the elevator to underground parking. Is that all?"

"Thank you for your help. I'll get back to you if I have any more questions."

Dave hung up the phone and wiped the perspiration from his upper lip, then turned to face the two men who were standing behind him.

"You didn't really think we would let you live when you know our names and can describe us. Come on." Mitch waved David toward the door with the pistol he held on him. Let's take a ride in that limo you rented. Hey, I just thought this will be like a real funeral. You're going out in style in a rented limo." He laughed at his own morbid joke.

Mitch slipped his gun hand into the pocket of his windbreaker, pointing the concealed weapon at Dave's back as he walked him to the car. "You get to drive. I'm going to sit next to you, so you don't do something stupid to tip off other drivers.

"Crank her up and take a left at the stoplight. Joe's going to follow us a few cars back. I don't want anyone to remember seeing our car anywhere near this albino brontosaurus." Mitch's attempt at humor was unappreciated by his victim. "Come on, laugh at my little joke. This thing is huge, white, and a relic of the past! Look on the bright side: you won't have to worry about your wife anymore. The cops will track her down for us, thanks to your cooperation. When they do, we'll find our little package and continue with the plans your friend Tony interrupted. Oh, you didn't know good old Tony set you up, did you? It took a little persuasion, but he told us which way you were going and what you were driving. We were able to overtake you by driving like the devil and not making any stops."

David couldn't help remembering how he'd often told Ana he'd rather make history than teach it to a room full of kids who were only in his class so they could check off one more requirement for graduation. Now it seemed he would get his wish; he was about to become a sad footnote in this backwoods county's history.

❧

The next day the usually easy-going Bubba Millburn charged into Thad's office and pounded his fist on the sheriff's desk. "He stole my baby!"

"What are you talking about, Bubba? You don't have a girlfriend to steal."

"Not a woman, my limo! David Fontaine, that professor you vouched for, stole my car. When I took it over to the motel the other day, he paid for two days. He said he would leave the keys at the desk today; but if he needed it longer, he would leave a money order for another day. I went to his room thinking he might not have gone to the desk yet, and I'd save him the trip. When I knocked on his door, the maid came out. She said he had checked out. I looked around the parking lot on my way to the office but didn't see my car. So I checked the desk, and the clerk said he had paid with a credit card. When the maid found he had not slept in the bed last night, they assumed he'd moved on and got the room ready to rent. So, here's my problem: no keys, no money order, no limo, and no Fontaine. Sheriff, you know I wouldn't have trusted a stranger like I did if you hadn't said you'd vouch for him. You know that car isn't just my ride; it's my hobby and my pay check. I race it at the dirt track and rent it to kids for weddings and prom nights. It's even been used in a few funeral processions. Now it's gone."

"Calm down; maybe he found another place to stay. I'll check around; and when I find him, I'll get him to pay in advance for the rest of the week."

Bubba wasn't convinced he'd ever see his modified limo again, but he nodded and said, "I just hope you find him before I do. He'd better not have done nothing to White Lightning. We have a race coming up Saturday." He walked out the door and climbed into his mother's rusty red pick-up and drove away.

Thad was worried. He had just gotten off the phone with his counterpart in Baldwin County when Bubba came in. The two Alabama sheriffs had been on a conference call with the sheriff of Hamilton County, Tennessee. Sheriff Goldsmith had given Thad and Sheriff Ford as much background information on Anastasia Fontaine and Anthony Berry as he had.

Thad picked up the phone and called the sheriff's private number. "Goldsmith here."

"Bob, this is Thad Brownlee. I think we may have another missing person from your county. David Fontaine has checked out of his hotel. He had been told not to leave town until I gave him the go ahead. Do you know if he's back down your way? A fellow up here thinks David might have driven off in a car he rented from him."

"No, I haven't heard of it if he's back. I'll have my deputies check his home and the college. What does the car look like?"

"You can't miss it. It's an old, white limo with the license plate number 70HAHA and purple number seven magnets on the doors, the hood, and the trunk. Of course, he might have taken the magnets off, but you still shouldn't have a problem spotting it."

"You're kidding me, right?"

"No, I'm dead serious. Bubba races it at the dirt track on week-ends, and the tag's his idea of a joke."

"You're right; it shouldn't be hard to find if he drove it up here."

"Bubba's probably overreacting. I've never seen a grown man so torn up over a car. He blames me for letting David Fontaine steal 'his baby.' I'm sure Fontaine is driving it around here and just forgot his rental time was up. I thought I'd ask you to keep your eyes open."

∽

The sheriff was right; it wasn't that hard to find.

"Boss, some kids just found Bubba's limo on Pine Mountain Road," Francisco Shaw said as he put the phone down.

"What about Fontaine?"

"No, the car was empty."

"Let's check the car out. Call Bubba and let him know we found his car."

The sheriff and his deputy rode to the northwest corner of the county. As soon as they neared the dead end of Pine Mountain Road, they saw several buzzards circling an area to the west of the parked car.

Francisco Shaw shaded his eyes and watched with morbid fascination as the scavengers circled above. "It could be a dead animal," he said.

"Yes, it could be, but we both know it's not. I'd say call the coroner, but we'd better make sure before we bother The Handmaiden. You know how she hates to get a call before noon."

"Why do you call her that?" Fran asked, as the two men walked through woods that turned the ground into a maze of roots, limbs, and undergrowth.

"I used to call her 'The Handmaiden of Death;' she hated it so much that I shortened it, not that she likes it any better." Sheriff Goldsmith was right; the ancient racing limo wasn't hard to find. They came into a clearing; a flock of buzzards, busily employed in clearing away carrion, reluctantly took to the sky.

"Is that him?" Fran asked.

"Well, it sure isn't an animal. With no face, that's all I'm sure of. Call 'the Maiden'... call Dr. Harris."

As soon as Thad got back to his office, he called Goldsmith. "Bob, this is Thad. We've got a body."

"Is it Fontaine?"

"I can't be sure. Animals and buzzards got to him long before we did. But it appears to be him. The body has the same build and hair color as Fontaine, and the limo was parked nearby. We may have two missing and one dead faculty member from your jurisdiction. Can you talk to friends and co-workers of the three of them and see if anyone was aware of anything unusual going on with the Fontaines or Berry?"

"I've already started. I called the college this morning. Most of the faculty and staff were on campus getting ready for the next semester. No one I talked to knew anything except that the three of them all went to a conference in Chattanooga last week. Berry and David Fontaine, both history professors, participated, and Mrs. Fontaine just went along for the ride. Thad, you didn't tell me how he died."

"We don't know. The coroner is working on that now, but I think we can rule out suicide. We found fresh car tracks on a dead-end dirt road near the limo. Someone was out there with him."

"Keep me posted, and I'll let you know if I find out anything at this end."

Brownlee hung up. "Fran, I'm going to lunch. Let me know if you hear anything from our lady coroner."

He got in his car and noticed his gas tank was almost empty. Instead of going straight home for some of Bren's good cooking, Thad pulled up to pump four at Wilber's Grocery and Gas. He got out and lifted the nozzle when he glanced at the car parked on the opposite side. I must be imagining things, he thought as he put the nozzle back and walked behind the other car to get a closer look. On the ground behind the silver sedan, he saw the familiar tread with a tear printed on the pavement with water.

The car had driven through a puddle left over from an unexpected shower. The print was quickly drying in the noon sun, but the image was unmistakable. He took out his cell phone and made pictures of the print and the car tag; then he sent them to Fran. If the driver got away and the tracks evaporated, he would still have the pictures.

The sheriff walked into the store and went to the counter. "Morning, Miss Della, did the driver of the sedan at pump two come in to pay in advance, or did he pay with a credit card?"

"A man came in a while ago and got in line behind several other people. Some were buying groceries, so he had a little wait. He was next in line after Mrs. Foster, but when I finished with her, he was gone. Since the car was at the pump, I figured he must have gone to the restroom, but he hasn't come out yet."

"I think I'll check. He could be sick." Thad walked to the back and knocked on the men's room door. When there was no answer, he asked, "Are you all right?" When there was still no answer, he tried the knob to see if it was locked. Just as he suspected; it wasn't, so he opened the door. He had known it would be empty.

Thad pulled out his phone and called Fran. "Did you see the pictures I sent?"

"Sure did. It looks like you've found our man. Where is he now?"

"I have no idea. He must have seen me checking out the car."

"Fran, get one of the fellows on patrol to come watch the office for a while. Eugene would be a good choice. Put on those civvies you keep in your locker, drive your personal car over and park at Main Street Cleaners so you can keep an eye on the car at pump two at Wilber's. I'll leave as soon as I see you pull in. Call me if anyone gets in the car, and follow him if he drives off."

"Sure thing, Thad."

"You'll notice the left rear tire, a Nexin with a tear. You're right; he was our man," Thad said as he hung up.

As soon as Fran was in place, Thad went back to his office and called Sheriff Goldsmith.

On the second ring a young sounding woman answered, "Sheriff's Office."

"This is Sheriff Thad Brownlee in Eastabuchie County, Alabama. I need to speak with Sheriff Goldsmith."

He had to wait only a moment when the familiar voice of Bob Goldsmith came on the line. "Hello, Thad. Is there a new development in the case?"

"You could say that. I sent a picture to your cell phone about an hour ago. I think you'll be interested. The quality isn't that great, but you'll recognize it. Give me your fax number and I'll fax it also so you can have a hard copy for your files."

"Let me get my cell out. I've been in a meeting and haven't checked my calls."

Thad waited while the other man pulled up the picture.

"You found the car! Have your techs found anything interesting?"

"Not yet, I still have one of my deputies watching it in case our man comes back. I doubt that he will. He may have spotted me when I snapped these pictures. As soon as we go over the car, I'll send copies of what we find."

"Good work, Brownlee. I'll be looking for it."

"More like good luck," Thad muttered as he hung up.

Fran watched the car from a distance for two hours. He was positive it had been abandoned just as Thad suspected. Finally, he called his boss. "Thad, no one's come near the car for more than two hours. What do you want me to do now?"

"Stay there until I get back with the finger print kit. We'll vacuum it and dust for prints before we have it towed to our impound lot. Wilber's lost enough business on pump two for one day.

"I ran the tag. The car was stolen in Tennessee about the time Tony Berry went missing."

"I'll bet my Bear Bryant autographed picture we'll find trace evidence of him and Fontaine in it. The killer might have been careful enough not to leave anything behind that would tie him to the car, but we can always hope."

I won't take you up on that bet not just because I believe you're right; but even if you're not right, I'm just as sure you wouldn't honor that bet!" Fran laughed at his own joke.

"You know me pretty well, don't you?" Thad said joining in. When he hung up the phone, Thad stopped laughing. He could kick himself for being so obvious, blowing his unbelievably good luck by not thinking and starting to document his findings too soon. If he had only finished pumping his own gas, he could have waited for the man to come out. It was a rookie mistake. He knew it, and so did Fran and Bob.

The News

"Remember old man Bardwell who lived over on the other side of the bend? He died last week, and now his kids have Colitis," Bubba told his sister, Becky.

"How in the world did their dad passing cause the kids to get colitis?"

"It was in the will, all legal-like."

"Everyone knows you can't will another person a disease, Bubba!"

"I never said Colitis was a disease; he's a mule. The old man named him that because he is such a pain in the butt, Colitis is the pain, not old man Bardwell, at least not now that he's dead."

Grace had been with the family long enough that such conversations no longer seemed odd to her. In fact, she hardly listened. She was thinking about the men she had seen at the gas pump and wondering what, if anything, she could do. She had toyed with the idea of talking to Brother Bax about recognizing the voices.

Bubba's and Becky's older brother Junior and his son came in. Junior said, "Grace, there was a picture of a woman on the TV this morning. She looked enough like you to be your twin except she had long dark hair, not short blond hair like yours. She's a missing person named Mrs. Anastasia Fontaine."

"Fontaine! That's the name of the fellow who took my limo. Come to think of it, he was looking for his wife, and now he's missing, too. Well, he might be dead. Sheriff Thad called me this afternoon and said they found White Lightning in the woods near a body. He's holding my car to check it for evidence. Do you think the county'll pay me rent for the time they are using it?"

"I wouldn't count on it, Bubba," his little sister, Becky, said.

"I didn't think so, but I'm gonna send the sheriff a bill, just in case."

A cold shiver went through Grace's body. They had killed him, and they would kill her if they found her. What chance did she have with her picture plastered on TV? The newspaper would be sure to print it in the morning edition. Everyone would be looking for Anastasia Fontaine. The haircut and color change wouldn't fool people for long. Lovie and Sister had helped her change her looks, so her husband would have a harder time finding her. When they saw the picture, they would know for sure, as she did now, that Anastasia Fontaine and she were the same woman. They might believe that her husband abused her, but they would think it was their duty to tell the sheriff he didn't have to worry about poor Mrs. Fontaine; she was safe with them.

Brother Bax was a minister; surely anything she might tell him would be held in confidence. He might be able to help her get away.

Grace wasn't noticed as she left the room. Bubba was working out a fair rental rate to charge the sheriff's office for the use and potential damages to his limo. His siblings and nephew were laughing at his ridiculous scheme as she borrowed a bicycle and rode down the dirt road. When she got close enough to see the church, she got off the bike and hid it in the tall grass just beyond the well-manicured shoulder. Leaving it, she walked the rest of the way to the church.

Bax heard a soft knock on his study door and was surprised to see Grace when he looked up. His secretary hadn't closed it when she stuck her head in to let him know she was leaving for the day. "Hello, Miss Grace. I must say this is a pleasant surprise. What can I do for you?"

"Brother Bax, I'm in deep trouble. I need help and don't have anyone else to turn to. First of all, I lied to Lovie, so I can't go to her now. I have to get something terrible off my chest."

"Grace, before you go any farther, I need to warn you that what you say to me is not the same as the sacred act of confession in which everything told to a priest is held in confidence, no matter what. I will do everything in my power to keep what you tell me between the two of us. But you should know, in this church if you tell me that you did something illegal or plan to do something that puts you or someone else in danger, it is my moral responsibility to protect life and uphold the law. These are the only reasons I would break my silence. If you're comfortable with this, then by all means tell me your problem; and I will help any way I can."

"I'm not going to kill myself or anyone else, but someone wants to kill me!"

"What! Who wants to kill you?"

"I don't know. That's just the problem. I don't know anything! I have amnesia. When Lovie found me, I was badly bruised from a wreck. She put two and two together and got nine, and then came up with a story based on my appearance." She took off the sunglasses and ball cap so he could see the bruises that were beginning to turn from black and purple to a yellowish-green. "I went along with it and let her think she'd saved me from an abusive husband. I didn't even know if I had a husband. I even picked my name from an exit sign."

"I had guessed as much. I grew up near an exit for Grace and Garland, Alabama. It's lucky you weren't driving the other direction or you might have seen the exit sign for Hope and Hull first. Grace Garland is a much prettier name."

"I feel so guilty for deceiving Lovie and her family."

"There must be more to the story. I know you don't think the Millburns are going to kill you for not being honest with them."

"You're right; of course, I don't. You see, I was knocked unconscious when the car hit us. Just as I was coming to, I heard a shot and a scream. Then there was the sound of someone moving around in the car. A man said, 'It's not here. Should I shoot her?'"

"Do you know who was shot?"

"I think maybe I do know now. I'll get to that in a minute, but first I need to tell you what happened the second day I was here. I went to the convenience store with Sister to get gas before we went to the pea patch. There was a man pumping gas at the pump across from the one Sister parked by. He was talking to a man in the car.

"I heard that same voice that I heard after the accident say, 'He was a fool to think he could,' and 'they found the,' and 'She can't be far from here.' They are still looking for me.

"Today Junior said my twin's picture was on TV with her husband. They're missing. I am apparently Anastasia Fontaine, and my husband, David, must have been shot at the scene of the accident by those two men. A man's body was found near the car Bubba had rented to David Fontaine." She shook her head in confusion. "But that doesn't make sense does it? I heard the shot and scream a day before David rented the car, and I'm sure he would have told the sheriff if he had been shot. If he wasn't the victim, then who was? It's all so confusing. All I know for sure is I'm in danger, and my picture is being broadcast. Someone will remember seeing me. The news will cover what the witness said, and the men will find me if I stay where I am."

"Grace, why don't you just call the sheriff? Just tell him what you've told me. I can call Thad and ask him to come out here and talk to you if you are afraid to go to his office," said Bax.

"No! No police. I don't know why, but I know that would be a mistake. Wouldn't that be the very thing those men looking for me would think I would do? They will be watching the sheriff's office. He could lead them to me. I'm sorry, Brother Bax; I guess I've wasted your time as well as mine. All I want is a safe place to hide. It's not right to put the Millburns in danger. For the record, I have not told you I was planning to kill myself or do anything criminal, so I guess my secret is safe with you." Grace got up from the pastor's couch and started to the door.

"Don't go, Grace; I guess I should call you Anastasia now. I might be able to help you find a safe place to hide until you feel safe. My wife's parents had a small lake house that isn't too far from here. We used to use it several times a year after they died. I still keep it stocked with canned goods and frozen food. There is nothing to connect you to the house. If you think you would be safe there, I'll drive you over. There are some of my wife's clothes in the chest in the bedroom. I think they will fit you."

"Won't your wife mind?"

"No, it always made her happy to help someone in need. She died two years ago and left the house to me. I will ask one favor; please don't let anyone see you out there. All I need is for the whole town to start gossiping about the preacher keeping a pretty lady out at his lake house."

Grace gave him a mischievous grin. "Thanks for your help. As to your shameful secret, you know I'm not a priest; and this isn't a confessional. If you don't do anything illegal or put me in danger, I'll do everything in my power to keep it in confidence."

Bax laughed and said, "Touché; you have a wicked sense of humor! I'm glad to see a bit of your real personality, not the frightened victim or the pretend cousin."

"Oh, I'm still a frightened victim, but now I feel a little braver. Maybe there is something to 'the truth will set you free.' I feel less afraid now that you are helping me."

Bax took out his keys and said, "I'll bring my car to the back entrance. You get down on the floor of the back seat. That should keep anyone from seeing you with me and connecting you to my cabin."

When he pulled into the covered drive-through, he popped open the trunk and took out a hound's tooth blanket. She lay down on the back floorboard. Not wanting to take any chances, Bax covered her with the blanket he kept for football games on cold nights.

They drove for what seemed longer than it really was. Grace began to think he was being too careful; she could hardly move. Her cramped body yearned to stretch and get her blood circulating again. At last, she felt the car slow to a stop. They were there.

"I'll go turn on the water heater," he said as they got out and he unlocked the door. "I always turn it off when I'm not here. A cold shower wouldn't be a very warm welcome."

"It's a good thing you're a preacher. You wouldn't make it as a comedian."

"That's just what the deacons tell me when I try to add a little levity to my message. He opened the door to a closet and fiddled with the water heater. "Everything is just like I left it. You'll find bedding in the hall closet and towels and bath clothes on the shelves in the bathroom. There isn't any fresh food, but there are canned goods and some frozen meals. I'll bring bread, milk, eggs, and fruit tomorrow. What fruit do you want me to buy?"

"Oh, I don't care; maybe grapes, but I'd love some almonds. That's funny, I don't remember a thing about myself, but I know I love almonds."

"Maybe you are starting to remember."

"I hope so. Well, maybe I don't. What in my past could make someone want to kill me?" She looked pensively at her hands. "I really appreciate all that you are doing for me. I'll be looking forward to your coming tomorrow and to those wonderful, salted almonds you're going to bring!" she said as she walked Bax to the door.

"I'll come by after I finish Wednesday night's prayer meeting. I'm putting you on the prayer list. Don't worry, I won't name you. An anonymous prayer request for healing and guidance should be enough to cover your problems." Bax waved as he got in his car and drove away.

SEVEN

Lovie

Lovie came back from visiting her sister Pearlie in Huntsville. "I'm home," she called out. There was no answer. No one came out of one of the back rooms to welcome her. It's just as well; she would have time to hide the birthday present she bought Billy Ray. That man could find anything. She never got to surprise him.

She went back to the truck and pulled out a package from under the seat. Now, where could she hide this? She looked around at the cars that littered the yard and shook her head. He might decide to take a nap in one of those. Then she saw the rusted out washing machine. Perfect.

Lovie worked her way around discarded treasures and opened the lid. She was surprised to see a slim package wrapped in brown paper. *It looks like somebody had beaten her to this hidey-hole. She wondered what was inside.*

She pulled the package out, felt its weight, and shook it the way a young child would a Christmas present. When she started putting it back in its hiding place, it slipped from her hands and landed on a pile of assorted pieces of scrap iron the boys had collected to take to the salvage yard.

When she bent down to get it, a part of the wrapping caught on a sharp corner of the iron and tore. The half-exposed package showed the same kind of strange writing she had seen on TV. What in the world was this? It looked like the writing on the posters those Middle Eastern demonstrators were waving. It was pretty, more like art than spelling, but what was it doing in her washing machine?

She didn't know what to think about her strange find, but she knew what to do. She took it to the kitchen and found a brown paper bag she had saved. After smoothing out as many wrinkles as she could, she rewrapped it. *There, it was good as new.* She carefully folded the torn paper to save for future use.

Lovie returned the package to the washing machine, went back to the house, walked over to the TV and turned it on. With everybody being gone, she guessed it was the only company she would have. The old set came to life; she flipped channels trying to escape the infomercials that seemed to have taken over the airwaves.

Suddenly a picture of Grace appeared on the screen. They were calling her another name, but there was no doubt in her mind that the woman the police were looking for was Grace Garland. The woman had the same mass of long dark hair she and Sister had dyed and cut to change Grace's appearance. The man on the news was talking about a dead man found out near Wooten's Branch Road. It was believed to be David Fontaine, a college professor, who had been searching for his wife. Anastasia Fontaine had gone missing after a car accident.

"The little stinker lied to me! He didn't hit you; you were in a car wreck!" she screamed at the picture on the screen.

The TV, her only companion, didn't comment on her outburst but continued to talk about David Fontaine. "The body was found early this afternoon not far from the limousine Fontaine had rented after his wife and car disappeared following a hit and run accident."

"Miss Grace Garland, or whatever your name is, you're going to have some explaining to do when you get home!"

Lovie, exhausted from her long drive, continued to watch the news until the soft purr of the sports reporter and the meteorologist lulled her into a restless sleep. Dreams of Grace killing her husband while Arab demonstrators waved their placards caused her to scream out, "Don't kill him, Grace!" The sound of her own voice woke her.

"What's wrong with you, Lovie?" Billy Ray said as she opened her eyes to see the whole family standing around her… everyone except Grace.

"Billy Ray, we have to go to the sheriff. There is no doubt in my mind that the woman on TV was Grace. The poor girl I thought I was saving from an abusive husband turned out to be an art teacher at some college down on the coast. The news said they suspect the body found near Bubba's limo was her husband. Stop and think about the time she picked to hightail it out of here. Was she in trouble, or was she the trouble herself? I can't help it; in my mind I see her shooting her husband. Maybe the part of her story about abuse was true, and he found her. She could have thought it was self-defense; maybe it was. I think she killed him and ran away."

"But Lovie, this is Grace we're talking about. I think your imagination is running away with you. I can't believe she could do such a thing."

"What do we really know about her, Billy Ray? She lied to us; that's the only fact I'm sure of. On top of everything else, I found a strange package she must have hidden out in the washing machine. It's in some strange language. It isn't even written in our alphabet. I want to turn it in to the sheriff. It looks like the writing the people in the Holy Land use. She could be a spy for some country over there. Get the truck cranked up while I get the package. We're going to the sheriff's office, like the good citizens we are, and give it to him. I think he will be interested in what I have to say."

As they drove to town, Lovie built her case against Grace. Billy Ray just shook his head and thought his wife had jumped to her conclusions like a duck jumping on a June-bug, maybe with even less thought. He liked the woman and thought his wife was all wrong, but he said nothing. He knew who buttered his bread.

Lovie charged into the sheriff's office followed by Billy Ray. "Fran, we need to see the sheriff right now!" Lovie demanded.

This uncharacteristic behavior got the deputy's attention. "That's impossible, Miss Lovie, he's out of the office right now. I'll call him and let him know you need to see him as soon as possible. Maybe I can help you."

"You do that; call him. I need to tell him in person that I know who killed that Fontaine man."

"Now, Lovie don't be..." Billy Ray got no farther with his protest.

"Tell him what I said. I may not be educated, but I'm not dumb."

Before Fran could reach for the phone, Thad walked into the office. "What's going on, Miss Lovie? I could hear you from outside."

Lovie handed the package and said, "I think Grace is that missing Fontaine woman who killed her husband."

"Hold on, Miss Lovie, who is Grace, and why do you think she killed David Fontaine? We don't even know if he's dead."

"I saw a woman walking down the highway the other day. She looked beat up and tired so I gave her a ride. Her story was that she ran away from an abusive husband. I wanted to help so I let her stay with us. Now, she's missing, and her picture is on TV. Mrs. Anastasia Fontaine is none other than Grace Garland. I should know. I cut that long dark hair of hers and helped dye it blonde so her husband wouldn't recognize her. Now she's gone, and I found that strange package in my washing machine. I think she killed her husband and is tied in with a bunch of foreigners; maybe she's a spy."

When Sheriff Brownlee opened the package Lovie brought to him, a sheet of hotel stationary fluttered to the floor. He picked it up and started to read.

"What does it say, Thad?" Lovie asked.

"I'm afraid I can't tell you, Miss Lovie. This is evidence, and I'm going to have to study it awhile. Thanks for bringing it in," he said as he walked the couple to the door.

As soon as the door was closed, and the Millburns were out of sight, he called his deputy. "Fran, get in here. You have to hear this."

Fran came back from the back room. "What's gotten you so excited?"

"This," said Thad as he held up the sheet. "Sit down and listen."

Fran perched on the edge of his desk as Thad started to read the letter.

> *I don't know who put this in my briefcase. As you know, I studied several Middle Eastern languages in order to read primary sources for my dissertation. When I opened the package, I could easily read the salutation, "Brother, the time is near," but the rest made no sense; it must be a code. Someone slipped it into my case while we were talking to the fellow you knew at LSU.*
>
> *All I could figure was that the message must have been meant for Dr. Simpson. When he died suddenly, the day before the conference, as co-author of the paper, I was tapped to do the presentation. There wasn't time to reprint the agenda. The first time the person who put this in my briefcase found out I wasn't Dr. Simpson was when Dr. Hudson announced the substitution when he introduced me.*

That ominous first line scared me to death! If you're reading this, I may be dead already. When the person who put this in my briefcase heard the introduction, he knew he had to get it back. If I know you as well as I think I do, you will ignore what I said about not opening this envelope. I hope if I don't show up in a day or two you will read this and get it to the FBI. I'm counting on you!

Take care of Jane for me. Tell her I love her...and be good to Ana. Tony.

"Wow, Thad, this is bigger than we ever imagined. What are you going to do now?"

"First, pull on gloves and make copies of this. We know Miss Lovie's, Tony Berry's, and my fingerprints are all over these pages. We don't need to add any more. Then make copies while I call the FBI and hope they don't think I'm a crackpot."

Thad picked up the phone book to look for a number for the Birmingham office. He had never had to communicate with the agency and couldn't believe he was reporting a possible terrorist plot.

Fran carefully copied the pages and prepared to put them back in the wrapper. When he picked up the brown paper, he noticed the reverse side sported the logo of a local grocery store that still gave the choice of paper or plastic. As he worked, he realized that Lovie must have rewrapped the papers. He couldn't believe this case had its roots in their small hometown. Thad might want to check with Lovie to see if she still had the original wrappings

The Cabin

The next night after church service, Bax drove back to his cabin and parked in his customary place. As he walked past the kitchen window, he saw Grace at the stove with her back to the window. For a moment it was like coming home and seeing Elizabeth busy in the kitchen. Both women were about the same size and had a cap of short blonde hair. Grace was wearing his wife's shorts and Delta State Fighting Okra tee shirt with the mascot Beth had nicknamed the Pugilistic Pod, Bax forced the memories of his dead wife to the safe place they needed to stay, if he was to be any help to the young woman who came to him in desperation. He knocked on the back door.

"Hello, Brother Bax, I hope you haven't eaten. I just microwaved a frozen teriyaki chicken dinner for two."

"As tempting as that sounds, I can't eat another bite. We have a church family dinner before the service every Wednesday. I'd like a cup of coffee, if you don't mind. I brought a can of coffee, filters, sugar, and cream, as well as the things we talked about last night." He put the package on the counter. "Grace? Anastasia? I really don't know what I should call you."

"Just keep calling me Grace. I know her, and Anastasia is a total stranger to me."

"What if I call you Ana-Grace, a good, old Southern double name like Billy Ray's?"

"That would be all right. It even sounds a little familiar. Bax, I didn't tell you everything yesterday. I know what those men are looking for. There was a thin package wrapped in brown paper hidden between the passenger seat and the console. I took it with me."

"What was in it?"

"I don't know; it's still wrapped up. I was afraid the package was the reason the men shot someone, so I hid it."

"Ana-Grace, that package is the only clue we have to who those people are. The sheriff might be able to…"

"You promised you wouldn't tell anyone if I wasn't involved in any criminal activity or going to commit suicide. I can't identify these people. I have no idea who they are, or even if they killed that man. I just remember a voice that came from someone who decided not to kill me."

"You can't run and hide for the rest of your life. Not handing over the package is withholding evidence. That package could help the sheriff find out who those people are. Maybe no one was killed, but they did kidnap your husband, and the body at the morgue could be his. I understand that you don't remember David Fontaine, but you must have loved him and will again when your memory returns. Could you live with yourself if you did nothing to help catch those people after what they did to David?"

"I know you're right. Go get the package. I hid it in the junked washing machine in Lovie's yard. That seemed to be a place no one would accidentally find it. You can take it to Sheriff Brownlee, but don't tell him where you got it. Just say someone made an anonymous call telling you where you could find a package connected to the disappearance of the Fontaines. That's the best I can do. You just don't understand how afraid I am of those people."

"I'm not sure the sheriff will be convinced that the package is important without knowing the background story, but I will do what you say. Maybe later you'll be willing to come forward."

As Bax drove the fifteen miles to the Millburn's trailer, he ran the facts he knew over and over through his mind. Grace was right; she hadn't done anything illegal. She was a victim; still he didn't think she was telling everything she knew. Admittedly what she knew was next to nothing—a voice heard while she was semiconscious; however, she had recognized it at the gas pump. Though she had led him to believe she didn't look at the man, she must have stolen a glance from the safety of the checkout line when she talked to Sister. He knew he would have. It would have been human nature to want to know who was after her. Could she describe the man or the car?

When he rounded the curve that led to the house, he was relieved to see no cars or any signs of life. He got out of his car, walked to the door, and knocked. After a third try, he relaxed. No one was home to question why the preacher was prowling around in their junk collection. The old washer was easy to find between the junked cars and the flowerbeds that Lovie had planted to beautify the ground between the rusted yard art. He lifted the lid and found nothing. Had Ana-Grace lied to him or had someone found the package before he had gotten there?

&

Bax hadn't been gone long when Grace started re-evaluating her dependence on this kind man. Bax has given her a place to stay, food to eat, even clothes to wear; and he had asked nothing from her but the truth. She hadn't been totally honest with him. Her memory was beginning to return.

She looked in the mirror and laughed at the strange mascot on Beth's shirt. Even she knew okra was a slimy, flaccid vegetable. It was great for gumbo but silly as a mascot.

As soon as the thought came, she could see a stadium filled with a sea of purple and gold. Mike the Tiger was there. As quickly as the image came, it vanished. What could that mean?

She went to the bedroom and turned on the television to watch the local news before eating a light supper. The lead story was still about the three missing faculty members. First, Tony Berry's picture appeared. A feeling of calm came, assuring her that he was a problem-solver who had protected her before. Surely nothing bad could have happened to this kind man.

This time, when she saw her picture on the screen, she forced herself to stay calm and listen to the reporter. She was thinner now, and her hair was different; but she would easily be recognized.

Then David Fontaine's photo replaced hers. The reporter's words became an unintelligible white noise as fear and anger flooded her mind. The vivid memory of a house totally consumed in flames pulled her back into her past. How much of her life was destroyed that night—the night after her graduation from St. Elizabeth of Thuringia! How could she have forgotten all that had happened? How she wished she could forget it all again!

Anastasia had to get away, but this time she knew where she must go. She went into the bedroom closet, found a small duffel bag, and stuffed it with jeans and tee-shirts, and a few other items from Beth's trunk. Then she saw a small box. When she opened it, she gasped and emptied it into the duffel.

Just as she was about to leave the closet, she saw the blond wig Beth had worn after the chemo treatments robbed her of her own short hair. It felt wrong to steal all these things that Bax had kept so long after Beth died, but she really needed everything she was taking. Anastasia put on the wig and adjusted it until it looked right.

She stopped in the kitchen long enough to write a note and went back to put it in the empty jewelry box, and grabbed a key from the hook in the pantry on her way out. One thought caused her to pause before leaving. Bax won't understand. He will hate me for what I've done, but what choice do I have?

The sun was just above the tree tops as she went into the storage shed. Behind two kayaks in the back was a dusty motorcycle she had discovered the day before. Ana guided it between the collections of treasured possessions and detritus that populated the shed until she reached the shelf near the door. She took the pink helmet down and put it on over the shoulder-length blond wig she had taken from the closet. With the face shield down, and the long blond hair peeking out from the bottom of the helmet, she was unrecognizable.

Earlier Anastasia had used the laptop and printer at the cabin to print out a map. She carefully cleared the history in case Bax should check. Following the directions Google had provided, she rode the motorcycle around the river bend and down the foothill until she reached I-59. Then she headed south toward her destination, South Louisiana.

Bayou Gauche was a long way to travel, but she knew she would be safe there. Her picture wouldn't have been on the New Orleans TV stations. There were enough home-grown problems to fill their news reports. No one would be interested in a missing art teacher two states away. Only David would connect her with that small fishing village in St. Charles Parish, and according to all the news reports, he was probably dead.

Ana rode until she was too hungry and too sleepy to continue. She saw a small gas station just off the interstate. She pulled off, filled the gas tank, and bought a box of granola bars and an energy drink with some of the money she found when she emptied the jewelry box. When the false bottom fell out, an envelope with Christmas cash written on it tumbled to the floor. Beth must have been squirreling away money for months. There were three hundred-dollar bills and a fifty as well as a Christmas list with an amount earmarked for Bax, the church Christmas offering, and a child in Africa she had agreed to sponsor. She was still short of her goal when she died two years ago.

Ana continued down the road about a mile and found what she was looking for. There was a bridge over a dry creek where she parked the motorcycle and walked down to the stream bed. The drought that had plagued this part of the country had given her a blessing—a dry, secluded place to hide the bike and a place to spend the night. She made a bed in the tall, dried grass that bounded the rocky creek bed.

The next morning Ana got up before sunrise and continued putting as much distance as she could between herself and Eastabuchie County, Alabama. When she saw the city limits sign for Meridian, Mississippi, she gave a sigh of relief. She was almost halfway home.

NINE

Lovie's Revelation

The sermon wasn't coming together as easily as he had hoped. Bax had all the points and scriptural references down, but the illustrations that help the congregation to apply it to their daily life weren't quite right. He got up and paced around the study a few minutes praying for inspiration. His library had a collection of books with well-known illustrations, some folksy, some more sophisticated, but none rang true for this particular sermon.

Bax went to the coffee maker and poured his third cup of coffee. When he returned to his desk, he was no closer to a solution. He studied the table of contents of his favorite source again, rejecting each candidate for the last time before returning the book to the shelf.

Bax sat back down, took another sip of the black brew, then picked up his pen and tried once again to come up with an original illustration. He was about to add his attempt to the pile of rejects in the trash can when he heard an impatient knock. He looked up and saw Lovie through the glass panel in his door.

"Miss Lovie, come in. Can I help you?"

"I need to talk to you about Grace, or whatever her real name is. She may not have killed her husband, but who knows what else she's done. Why would a nice, married college teacher run off like that while her poor husband and his friend are missing and might even be in their graves? I think she has a boyfriend somewhere. I'll bet he was behind whatever happened to her husband. I was reading in Psalms about the evil angels that run around. You don't think she's one, do you?"

"No, I don't, but we all have the seed of evil in us. None of us are angels; that's why..." He didn't get to finish his sentence.

"I mean fallen angels like those who followed Lucifer. That's what gave me the idea about Weight Watchers. I think she needs to join up."

This time Bax interrupted Lovie. "You've lost me, Miss Lovie. What do you mean? She may be a lot of things, but overweight isn't one of them."

"Not Weight Watchers, the church! I've been thinking that becoming a Christian is a lot like joining Weight Watchers."

Bax couldn't believe he was having this conversation. "I can't say I've ever heard that comparison in all my years in the ministry."

"Well, it is. First, someone tells you about a meeting where your life can be changed. Then the speaker lays out a plan and encourages you to attend meetings regularly to learn more about that plan. If you fully understand and make a full commitment to that plan, changes happen, and you become a lifetime member. The biggest difference between the two is Weight Watchers charges a big first-time fee, and with Christianity, Jesus paid the joining fee."

"When you explain it like that, it does seem a little like a modern parable. I'm still pretty sure most of the major denominations wouldn't adopt it. I'm glad to see you're thinking on loftier subjects these days and have stopped worrying about Grace being a murderer."

"Oh, I'm not finished with her yet. I'm just going to change the way I go about getting even with that lying sinner. Instead of cursing her under my breath every time I think of her, I'm going to pray for her."

"That's wonderful, Miss Lovie!"

"I'm going to pray that she gets what she deserves, and maybe then she'll see the light." She rose heavily to her feet. "Thank you for talking with me, Brother Bax. I feel so much better."

He was so stunned that before he could recover and try to guide her to a more Christian attitude, Lovie had left his study.

One thing was sure; Ana-Grace could use all the prayers she could get. God would have to weed out the mean-spirited ones.

Bax went back to his desk and began to write. "The prayer of a righteous man availed much. How many times have we read James 5:16? Yet we sometimes lack the dedication to our prayer life. It could be so much more effective if we were as committed to our prayer log as members of Weight Watchers are to their food log. Every day they check off the things they have committed to eat, then list and count points for everything they eat. If we could be as devoted to our prayer life, committing to pray for our world, nation, leaders, friends, and family every day, our prayers would, to paraphrase James, really count. We would see results. Just as the faithful dieters see the pounds drop off, we would see prayer after prayer answered."

He got up and walked out of the study, thinking Lovie might be on to something.

Brosia

na rode down the only road on the narrow peninsula. The picturesque fishing village, less than an hour from New Orleans, was the counterpoint to the exciting city. No music was pouring out the doorways luring tourists into one of the many bars, restaurants, or specialty shops that fill the quarter. Only the sounds of nature punctuated by occasional voices or a distant hum of a motor could be heard. No beautiful historic buildings were found here. There were just weather-beaten houses and fishing boats on the narrow strips of land on each side of the road. If she had only one word to define this place, it would be haven.

She stopped the motorcycle in front of the house she'd regarded as her home since she was seventeen. She thought as she looked at the small house that had been flooded more times than she could remember that some things never change. Ana got off the bike and walked to the door. It was unlocked; no one here would bother with that. They were like family, and you don't lock out family.

Ana let herself in and walked back to the kitchen. Her Aunt Brosia was standing at the stove sipping gumbo from a kitchen spoon to see if it passed the taste test. "Thea, I'm home."

The old lady turned around and stretched out her arms to the woman who was like a daughter to her. "Anastasia, my darling, it's wonderful to see you! It's been so long." The two women hugged, and then Brosia asked, "Where's David?"

"I don't know. He's missing and might even be dead." The old woman gasped, and Ana continued, "Now some men who want to kill me are after me. I need some place to hide where they would never look for me. I don't think anyone will find me here. David, Tony and Jane are the only people who would think I might come here."

"Oh, Baby, how horrible! But I don't understand. How did all this happen? The burners didn't find you, did they?"

"I doubt it. That was a lifetime ago. I'm sure they've forgotten about their oath by now, even if they find out I survived."

"Their kind never forgets."

"I hope you're wrong. I don't even want to think about that time if I can help it."

"You said David might be dead. That's awful! Why do you think that?"

"I was semiconscious after our car wrecked, but I heard two men talking while they kidnapped him. I ran away as soon as I was fully conscious. For a long while I couldn't remember anything, not even who I was. It must have been a concussion."

"Don't you know? Didn't you go to a doctor?"

"No, I didn't even think of doing that. I should have gone to the police, but I didn't know who David was, what the men looked like, or even what really happened. I didn't think they would believe me. Somehow David got away from his kidnappers and went to the sheriff looking for me. He rented a car from a local man because I used our car to escape. Later a man's body was found near that car. They haven't identified the body yet, but it's believed to be David."

"I can't believe it. How could such a thing happen to that dear man? Why do you think they are after you? Surely, they must have mistaken him for someone else. Who would want to kidnap David?"

"I don't have the answers to your questions, Brosia. All I know is that when I was at a gas station a few days ago, I recognized the voice I heard when they kidnapped David. The man said enough that I know they're still looking for me. I ran to this place and to you, the person who rescued me before. "You understand you might be in danger if you take me in again, and I'll understand if you can't. I'll find another place where no one knows me."

"Don't be ridiculous; this is your home. When Sully brought me here when we first got married, I felt isolated. I soon learned to love the peace and beauty of this place, and he became all the family I needed. When he died, the loneliness returned; grief was turning me into a bitter, withdrawn woman. After the burners came and Raymond brought you to me, you became my family. Don't you know there's nothing you could ask that would be too much or too dangerous if it would protect you?"

"I love you, Ambrosia Leblanc! You may not be able to give me immortality the way ambrosia gave it to the gods in the myths, but you've saved my life twice."

"Now, let's not get too sentimental, and don't call me Ambrosia. You know Sully thought Ambrosia Leblanc sounded like a stripper's name. I'm just Brosia or Thea Brosia to my favorite niece."

The two women laughed. "Go get your things while I put fresh sheets on your bed and air out your room."

Tracks

T had reached for his phone, "Sheriff Brownlee here," he said. "How can I help you?"

"Sheriff Brownlee, I'm Howard Knox. I own Opportunity Knox Pawn in Birmingham. I was reading the newspaper story about the missing couple over your way–the Fontaines. Well, it made me think about a guy who pawned a ring here the other day."

"What made you think the man was connected to the Fontaines?"

"The ring was inscribed to Ana; then there was a little heart, and the name Dave followed by the symbol for infinity. I looked at the ring; it must have cost him an arm and a leg. While I was counting out what I agreed to give him for it I said, 'Well, Dave, it looks like love didn't last as long as you thought.' Then he said, 'Things happen; cut the chatter and give me the money.' The funny thing is he didn't look anything like David Fontaine's picture in today's paper."

"Dave and Ana are common names. I doubt that there's a connection."

"I know, but how many of those women spell their name A-n-a, the way Anastasia would?"

"Can you describe the man?"

"I can do better than that; I have him on surveillance tape."

"I'm going to be in Birmingham tomorrow. I'd like to see the tape."

Howard gave directions to his business and Thad told him about what time he would be there. When he hung up, he turned to Fran and said, "It's not much of a lead. I guess it's better than nothing. That is about all we have at this time, nothing."

The phone rang again. This time Fran picked it up. "Eastabuchie County Sheriff's office, how can I help you?"

"This is Sheriff Ed Ford from Hamilton County, Tennessee. Let me talk to Thad Brownlee."

"Thad, that sheriff from Tennessee wants to talk to you," Fran said as he transferred the call to the phone on Thad's desk.

"Thad Brownlee here, what can I do for you, Sheriff Ford?"

"Thad, I'm going to be passing through your area later today. I thought I would drop off a copy of the surveillance tape from David Fontaine's hotel. There's footage from the front desk and the outside cameras. I could send it to you, but I'd like to meet you since it seems we're both going to be working on this case. Didn't you tell me you found some tire prints at the scene of the accident where the woman disappeared?"

"Yes, and I have some from the cabin where Fontaine called my office. They look like a match to the first set."

"Can you bring both sets along? I want to compare them to a set of prints found near an unidentified body."

"Sure, that would be a good idea. You can come by the office, or I will meet you, if you'd like."

"That would be better, I think. Is there someplace close to the interstate we could have a private talk? I'm driving down to pick up a prisoner, and I'm going to be pressed for time."

"I'm sure you have your GPS. Look under points of interest near here. There is a little burger place that used to be a Sonic. It's called Toot and Tell It."

"That has to be the most unfortunately named business I've heard of in years. The only one I remember that even comes close is a funeral home with a drive-through viewing window down in south Mississippi. Some original thinker down there called his business Moan and Drive On."

The two men laughed, grateful for a little levity in a profession that uncovered so many unthinkable things human beings are capable of doing to each other.

"I'll call you when I'm about ten miles from the place. See you then."

"That will be fine. Come hungry; they really have good burgers there."

"Will do."

Thad hung up his phone and said to his deputy, "This must be our lucky day. In less than twenty minutes we've had two phone calls with information that might help with our investigation."

Thad compiled the copies of the information he had gathered. When Ed Ford called, he drove to the hamburger joint. When he got there, the other sheriff was already there.

Sheriff Ford walked to the cruiser carrying the folder of information he'd collected. "Thad, I thought you were pulling my leg until I found this place on the GPS. If you don't mind, I'll get in and we can get down to business."

While Ed got in the passenger's seat Thad said, "Before we do, let's order some burgers and a couple of their belly washers."

"I can tell we're going to get along fine. That sounds like a good idea."

Thad hit his horn and a car-hop on skates came out and rolled up to his window.

"Tell it," the aging server said.

"Missy, I'll have a fully dressed burger and the biggest, coldest root beer you have. What about you, Sheriff?"

"That sounds good; make it two."

Missy skated back and disappeared into the building. "Is that a snake tattoo or a varicose vein bulging above the tops of her skates?"

"It has to be a varicose vein. Somehow, I can't picture her as a tattooed biker babe," Thad said.

"She has to be the oldest car-hop on record. Who does she think she's fooling with that blonde wig? I saw a sprig of grey poking out from under it," Ed said with a laugh.

"Yea, Missy's no spring chicken, but she's a good worker. She and her husband are trying to revive this place. It's a two-person operation just this side of being bankrupt. I try to give them as much business as I can."

Missy rounded the corner carrying a tray with their burgers and two large paper cups balanced on it.

"Thanks, Missy," Thad said as he handed her several folded bills. "Keep the change."

"That was a pretty big tip," Sheriff Ford said.

"Well, you don't always get a skating granny as a free floorshow. Let's get down to business while we polish off our food," Thad said.

After a few bites of burger, Ford began to share the information that tied their cases together. "I have several things I think will interest you. First and most important, three kids were riding on four-wheelers on their grandfather's hunting land in the southern part of our county. The trails were overgrown because no one had been out there since the last deer season. The kids were puzzled by the tracks in the tall grass. They were car or truck tracks, not four-wheeler tracks.

"The kids decided to follow the trail to find out what was going on. The deeper into the woods they went, the more they began to notice an obnoxious odor. The odor became so strong the youngest kid went back to the hunting camp where his father and grandfather were getting the cabin ready for the upcoming season. When the other youngsters turned the final curve, a bunch of vultures took to the air.

"Bobby, the oldest boy, got off his ATV and walked into the tall grass where he saw what was left of a human being. He ran back to his brother; they high-tailed it to the main road. Their father and grandfather had arrived by the time they reached it. After the boys told what they had found, their father called our office.

"We believe the body is Tony Berry's. Sheriff Goldsmith, down on the Gulf Coast, got some hair from Berry's brush and sent it up to us. We are hoping for a match when it gets to our office; but the lab is so backed up, I don't know when we'll have results.

"The deputies found where the vehicle turned around. There were tracks in the mud bank of the little creek at the end of the trail. They must have dumped the body at night. They probably weren't local and didn't know where the trail ended. In the dark the vehicle almost ran into the creek hidden by the tall grass. Anyone who lived close by would have known that creek was there." The sheriff took another swig of this root beer. "Did you bring those pictures of the prints your boys found? I'd like to see if we are looking for the same people."

"Sure, they're in here," Thad said as he pulled two photos of tire prints out of his folder. The two men compared them to the picture of the print taken near the body found in Tennessee. "At first glance all three look alike. Have you identified the make of tire?" Thad asked.

"Yes, it was made by Nexen. We lucked up there. Nexen is a Korean company that makes about 2% of the replacement tires in this country. The lucky part is it wasn't one of the big boys like Goodyear or Michelin. They have a combined 22.5% of the market of replacement tires. Still there are millions of Nexens out there. It's still a needle in a haystack, but not a hay barn."

Thad looked closer at the three pictures, and then he smiled. "Well, I think these are the same. Look in the top corner of your picture where grass is matted over part of the print. See that little jagged spot in the tread? I wouldn't have noticed it if I hadn't seen it before. Look at these pictures I took at the scene of the accident, at the old man's cabin, and another I made of a Nexen tire print by the gas pump at a local convenience store. Different parts of the cut are shown on all the pictures, but I'll bet they will fit like jigsaw puzzle pieces if we overlay all of the prints. I know this is circumstantial until we get an ID on both bodies, but I think there'll be two openings in the history department."

"I agree with you completely, Thad. Now let me tell you about the video on this disk. You'll need to see it yourself of course, but I think we may have pictures of the killers."

"That would be a break. Tell me what you have."

"The first part is at the hotel when the three of them were checking out. You can see Berry hand Fontaine a small package while the desk clerk is talking to Mrs. Fontaine. There's nothing unusual about that except all three of them are missing and probably dead. Now when you look at the second clip, you will see two men hanging around the shuttle loading area. When Berry comes out, they start walking toward him. Then one of them goes on each side of him, and all of them walk out of camera range together."

"Do you know who they are?"

"No, the faces are not all that clear, but I believe there is enough on the tape to determine this was probably a kidnapping. Tony Berry never reached the shuttle and didn't make his flight home. This is the last time he was seen as far as we know. When you get back to your office, you can study the tapes and picture in depth. I'll do the same with your pictures. Maybe two heads are better than one, as they say," Ed Ford said.

"Thanks for bringing these down," Thad said as he added the photos and CDs to his file. "I'm looking forward to working on this case with you."

"Yeah, we both need all the help we can get."

"I better go get my prisoner. I don't want him complaining to the ACLU that I rudely kept him waiting. Tell Missy I'll never forget her, roller-skates, varicose veins, and all!"

Both men laughed and shook hands as Ed started to get out of Thad's patrol car. Then Thad asked, "I was just wondering why you didn't send a deputy to deliver these and pick up the prisoner?"

"I ordinarily would have, but I thought this would be a good chance to meet you and get your take on what we have, first hand. Thank you for meeting me." He got in his own cruiser, and drove south.

The Ring

Thad had been called as a witness in a court case in Birmingham. He finished his testimony shortly before the noon recess, went to his car, and entered the address of Opportunity Knox Pawn into his GPS. He had never been in the seedy part of the city where the store was located.

When Thad walked into the pawn shop, Howard Knox, the owner, spotted him on the security monitor in his office and came out to meet him. "Sheriff Brownlee?" Knox asked the obvious. Thad wasn't hard to identify in his uniform. "I'm glad you made it. I wasn't sure you took me seriously when we talked on the phone. Come on back to my office. I have some things to show you."

The sheriff followed the short, balding man down the narrow hall to his office. "I appreciate all the help I can get, Mr. Knox. I'd like to see what you have." Thad would have bet his prize bluetic hound all he had was a good imagination and an Olympic medal for jumping to conclusions.

The store owner pulled out two photographs and a CD from his desk drawer. "This is a picture of the ring, and the other one is an enlargement of the inscription," he said as he handed them to Thad.

Thad took the photos and looked at them with mild interest. They might have nothing to do with the case; but you never know, so he would take these back with him. Maybe someone at the college where Anastasia taught art would be able to identify it as her wedding ring.

Knox continued as he put the CD into his computer. "This is from one of our security cameras; sorry it's so grainy."

This image caught Thad's attention. The man Knox had called Dave when he made his little joke about love not always lasting definitely was not David Fontaine. Still, he did look familiar. When he turned his head, Thad knew where he had seen that profile before. The same stocky build, the same dark curly hair, there was no doubt in his mind that this was the same man who was on the hotel surveillance footage Ed had given him yesterday. He was the one who had waited outside for Tony Berry, one of the men who had escorted him out of camera range, and maybe the one who left the body in the Tennessee woods.

He could hardly contain his excitement as he said to the owner of the pawn shop, "Mr. Knox, thank you for calling me. You are an observant man. I believe this might help with my investigation."

"I hope so. Have you got any leads on that missing lady? I mean a woman doesn't willingly hand over a rock like that. Do you think the man on the disk took her?"

"Well, we have no way of knowing if the ring belongs to Mrs. Fontaine, but if it does, I'd have to say finding it in your pawn shop isn't a good sign. He slipped the information into his pocket. "Thanks for your help, Mr. Knox. Do you have a business card? I'd like to keep your contact information on file just in case I need to get back in touch."

"Sure thing, let me write my cell number on it so you can get me if you can't reach me here." He pulled a card out of his wallet, scribbled his number on the back, and handed it to Thad. The two men shook hands.

Thad walked to his car and got in. Before he cranked it, he called his office.

"Eastabuchie County Sheriff's Office," Fran Shaw answered.

"Fran, I think we're on to something. The man who pawned a ring that could be Anastasia Fontaine's is a dead ringer for the man on the hotel security footage Ed Ford gave me yesterday. I think the same two men found her while Dave was making his call. They may be holding her hostage, or there might be a third staff opening at the college."

When he returned to his office, he faxed the pictures to Goldsmith. Moments later the other sheriff notified him that he was taking them to Berry's house.

Thad put the incoming fax on Fran's desk. "Bob received the fax. He is going to take the picture of the ring over to see if Jane Berry can identify it.

"The poor woman is out of her mind waiting for the lab result on the hair she sent from her husband's brush." Just then the phone rang, and Fran took the message.

"Thad, the lab in Tennessee got a match on the hair. The body is definitely Tony Berry. They have notified Goldsmith. I wouldn't want to be in Bob's shoes; he'll have to tell Mrs. Berry the news after he shows her the pictures."

"Speaking of pictures, did you see the additional pictures from the place we found Bubba's Baby?"

"No, what pictures? I thought I had seen all of them."

"I made a few with my own camera while you were talking to The Handmaiden. I printed mine out and put them on your desk. They are probably still under that pile of reports you put on the back burner to concentrate on this case," Fran said as he shuffled through the stacks of files on Thad's desk. "Here they are. I made a few I thought you missed."

"Hand them over to me. Let's see what you took," Thad said as he flipped through the stack of photos. Most were duplicates of the ones he had taken. Then he stopped and took a closer look at the familiar picture of the tire print with a jagged cut across the tread. "Fran, it looks like you mixed in a picture from the accident scene."

"No, this print was several feet behind Bubba's limo."

"Get the picture Ed Ford brought down and those I made."

When all four pictures of the tire print were placed next to each other, one thing was clear–the same car had been in four places: where the Fontaine's car had been rammed, at the cabin, where Tony Berry's body was found, and where the unidentified body was found. That fact, along with the fact that the same man who'd been seen with Berry shortly before he was killed had pawned a ring with the names Ana and Dave, made Thad almost certain it belonged to Anastasia Fontaine. In his mind this proved Berry's death and the Fontaines' disappearance were connected somehow, but how? That was the link he had to find.

☙

Bob Goldsmith paused briefly before he rang the doorbell. The sheriff was here to tell a woman her husband was dead. He ran his fingers through what was left of his white hair, postponing the act one more second. The muted sound of the bell started the chain of actions that would forever change this woman's life. Her rapid footsteps were bringing her to the end of hope. How he hated this part of his job! Before he could tell her the terrible truth, he had to get some information.

Jane Berry opened the door. Her eyes telegraphed the fear seeing him at her door sent surging through every molecule of her body. "Sheriff Goldsmith…" She could barely get the words out. There was only one reason the sheriff would be at her door, and it was unthinkable.

"May I come in Mrs. Berry? I have some pictures I'd like for you to look at for me."

"Not Tony…"

"No, they're just some pictures of a ring. Can we go into the living room and sit down?" he asked as gently as he could.

"Oh, I'm sorry. Of course, come in. I'm just not myself," she said as she led him to the living room.

As he sat down next to her on the couch, he pulled the pictures of the ring and inscription out of a folder. "Can you identify this ring?"

"That's Ana's wedding ring. Where did you get it?"

"The owner of a pawn shop in Birmingham had been following the missing persons story in the newspaper. When he read the names, he thought of the Fontaines and called in a tip to Sheriff Brownlee."

"A pawn shop! Ana never would have pawned it. Not that she really liked it; she thought it was ostentatious, but Dave took such pride in showing her off. When anyone would comment on it, he would say, 'My treasures, Ana and her ring!' and then kiss her hand just above the ring. That embarrassed her and made her uncomfortable. Then Dave would laugh and give her a big hug."

"It sounds like you saw them socially and not just at college functions."

"Oh, yes. Tony and Dave were at LSU together. In fact, Tony dated Ana a few times in her freshman year. Then Dave swept her off her feet when they met at a Christmas party. Tony actually introduced them. They got married that summer."

"Thank you, Mrs. Berry. You've been a lot of help. Now I have to confess that the pictures are not the only reason for my visit."

"No! Not Tony! Don't tell me that!"

"I'm afraid the DNA from your husband's hair was a perfect match to the victim's DNA."

The woman dissolved into soundless tears. Her body was shaking; her arms wrapped in a tight embrace across her chest as if she were physically holding herself together. Bob Goldsmith moved closer and put his arms around her, holding her as he would have held his granddaughter. She leaned into his chest and released the dreadful sound she had suppressed. It was raw grief, unfiltered and undiluted by inadequate words. He rocked back and forth as if comforting a child. They sat like that until she regained some composure, pulled away, and wiped her eyes.

"I'm so sorry, ma'am," he said knowing how worthless those trite words must sound to someone whose world had suddenly been destroyed. She nodded and wiped her reddened face with the back of her hand. "Is there someone I can call to stay with you a while?" She shook her head and lay face down on the couch. He quietly left the room and let himself out. He had never felt so useless, so… guilty.

THIRTEEN

Following

"Hello," Joe paled as the question he dreaded was delivered with more contempt than he had expected. "No, I don't have the package yet. The presenter who replaced our contact no longer had it when we took him. We had to use extreme means to convince him to tell us where it was. He gave it to the other professor who helped with the power point."

Joe was interrupted by a stream of obscenities and threats. When there was a break in the torrent, Joe continued. "I understand your concern. I will recover it. However, that's proving to be complicated. We had Fontaine, but the package and his wife have disappeared. Mitch took Fontaine to a wooded area to extract the information we needed. When I arrived, I found Mitch's body. Fontaine had killed him. I'm trying to find him and get the package, but I don't think he has it anymore."

The caller pointed out, between obscenities, he wasn't being paid to think, and finding one man on foot couldn't be that hard.

"He isn't on foot. He stole our car." Another irate interruption had to be endured before he could continue. "I do understand the importance of this mission, and I will not fail you." He felt like he was walking a tightrope over a pit of vipers. One slip and his life would be over.

The caller disconnected; Joe put the phone in his pocket, and punched the steering wheel. He hadn't completely lost Fontaine. The fool had stopped for gas before leaving town. The sheriff spotted the car about the same time he had and was making a picture of the tag with his phone. It was pure luck that he'd seen Dave come out of the convenience store and slip into the alley when he saw the sheriff. Joe made the block and saw Dave come out on a cross street and steal a beat-up Chevy. He followed at a safe distance for several hours until Dave drove down a dead-end road. Joe knew that, with patience, it was only a matter of time until his prey felt he was safe and would come back down the dead-end road where he'd vanished. Of course, he could search every house and barn along the road that led from the highway to a dead-end on the river. His map showed there was no bridge, so why risk getting caught in the process. He could wait.

Fontaine had convinced him his wife was the one with the package. David told him the package was between the passenger seat and the console, but when the police found the car, there apparently had been nothing. At least there was nothing in the news about a suspicious package. Anastasia Fontaine was still missing. She must have taken it with her. If the cops had it, there would be some buzz, wouldn't there? He had to find her.

She was so much more valuable than the ring Mitch had taken from her hand when he searched the car. Mitch had felt they needed more operating cash quickly, so he had stolen the ring and had given it to him to pawn. He felt like the pawn shop owner had low-balled him, but Mitch had been right to have him pawn it. At least he had enough cash to buy a beater to replace the car Dave stole. When Joe paid in cash for the car for sale in his yard, the old man didn't ask any questions.

Mitch had stolen that car in Tennessee. Joe was glad he was able to buy this one. This assignment has turned into a complete mess. It would be foolish to steal a car and get the cops involved.

That would just complicate things even more. He could wait out Dave at a distance in a car no one was looking for. When Dave surfaced, he would be ready to follow him.

ↄ

As Dave drove through Phillipsburg, his thoughts tumbled over each other as they raced in an endless circle. He couldn't believe he was still alive. When Mitch had made him drive to that secluded place at gunpoint and had marched him into the woods, he was sure he was going to die.

But he had kept his wits about him and recognized his opportunity when it came. The limb that hung down and blocked the path became his weapon. He had pushed forward far enough that the limb snapped back with enough power to knock Mitch off balance. After that it had been easy.

His cycle of thought continued as he headed to the one place he thought he'd be safe. After an hour he turned down a dirt road that soon became nothing more than a faint, overgrown trail. At the end of the trail, all that was left of the farm was the desecration of a boyhood memory. The barn had slumped to the right, ready to collapse; however, the farm house looked somewhat better.

His mother's Uncle Rob and Aunt Martha had entertained him with their grandchildren every summer on this farm. It was clear the old place has been neglected for many years. The only signs of activity around were the cows grazing near the pond.

Dave parked the car behind the barn. If, for some reason, someone should come down the trail to check on his livestock, he might get suspicious if he saw it in the yard. He went to the front porch and tried the door. It was just as he had expected—locked. The back door was also locked. He took a brick from the border that used to edge the flowerbeds and broke the door's glass panel. What false security, having a deadbolt on a door that was half glass. He unlocked the door and walked in.

The unmistakable odor of an old house that had been closed
for years washed over him. Dave looked around the house. It
looked like nothing had changed since he was there. He hated
to vandalize the relatives, but he had to disappear as long as
Joe thought that he was in the area. Joe knew he didn't have
the package but thought Ana did —he was probably right. He
couldn't stay there long. It was only a matter of time before Joe
found her. He had to find her first.

He began to think about funds. Aunt Martha had always
kept an old churn filled with silk flowers in their bedroom. Uncle
Rob would drop his pocket change in it. He wondered if the
family remembered the coin stash when Uncle Rob had died.

He went into the master bedroom and found nothing had
changed. The silk arrangement was still next to the fireplace. He
lifted the mass of dusty flowers and looked in the churn. "Thank
you, Uncle Rob," he said to the memory of his great uncle as he
reached in and grabbed a handful of coins. He emptied the churn
one fistful at a time. Dave began to separate the quarters, half
dollars and the occasional silver dollars from the small change he
dumped back into its hiding place.

There was enough money to buy gas for the trip, but
paying with a handful of coins would draw too much attention
to him. He couldn't afford to do anything that would make him
memorable.

He went to the closet to see if anything had been left in
there. He saw what he hoped he would—a collection of purses.
He smiled and thought how Ana always got so excited when she
pulled out a purse she hadn't used for a while and found money
she'd forgotten she had.

One by one he emptied the purses. At first the only
treasures he found were neatly folded tissues, hard candy, and
one pack of Juicy Fruit gum. He was about to give up when he
found a twenty folded in fourths and tucked between two store

credit cards. "Bingo! That's better!" he said as he stuffed the bill in his pocket.

The next two bags had nothing. He returned them to their places—no reason to advertise what he'd done. As he was closing the closet door, a fanny pack hanging on a belt rack caught his eye. This doesn't look like anything my aunt or great aunt would have used; but who knows, he thought as he took it to the bed and opened one zippered pocket at a time. He found two more twenties stuffed in an otherwise empty pill case.

He continued to search the old house looking under couch cushions, in the medicine cabinets, and in the pantry. Nothing! He was about to close the pantry door when he noticed an old-fashioned percolator in the back, behind a can of out-of-date coffee. He took the old coffee pot out and lifted the lid. His wonderful old miserly uncle! There was at least a hundred dollars. He remembered that Uncle Rob hid money.

He decided to look around a little and see if he could find any more. There was no way he would be using his credit cards with people looking for him. If there was anything he was sure of, it was that he couldn't trust or underestimate Joe.

He had bought plenty of fruit at a produce stand, so he would have enough to eat if he stayed another day. Maybe he could find some more money Uncle Rob stashed away to bankroll his trip to find Ana. He knew where she'd go to feel safe. If that wasn't where she went, then he had no idea where she was.

The Phone Call

Ana had felt guilty since she drove away on Beth's motorbike. She had every reason to feel that way for she had taken everything the woman had valued except her husband and her faith. But tonight, safe in Brosia's house on the bayou, she couldn't sleep for the guilt and regret that haunted her. After all he had done for her, she not only stole from Bax, even worse, she'd betrayed his trust. She got out of bed and walked back to the kitchen. Brosia's cell phone was on the charger on the counter.

The ringing phone woke Bax. He looked at the clock on the bedside table, two o'clock. Nothing good happens after twelve o'clock might be cliché, but it was true, Bax thought, remembering the saying that was his parents' mantra when he was a teen. I hope that it wasn't Ms. Brossard calling to tell him that her husband has fallen off the wagon and beaten her up again. He picked the phone up on the third ring. "Hello, Brother Bax speaking."

There was a long pause before he heard her familiar voice. "Please don't hang up. I need to explain what I did."

"Go on, I'm listening."

"I started remembering things. I panicked. Not all of the pieces fit, but I knew I had to leave…go somewhere those men would never associate with my husband or me," Ana paused.

"Lovie said you go to New Orleans pretty often. Is that so?"

"Yes, I'm working on my Doctor of Divinity at the seminary there, but what does that have to do with what you did?" Bax asked.

"If I tell you where you can find your wife's jewelry, will you promise not to look for me? I'll get the bike back to you as soon as I can. When my life gets back to normal, I'll pay back all the Christmas money I took."

"You're not in the state anymore, are you?"

"No," she said.

"So, are you in New Orleans?"

"Bax, all I'm saying is the jewelry will be buried in the cemetery beside St. John the Baptist Church. It's on River Road in Edgard, Louisiana. It will be behind the last of the original brick graves that are farthest from the church. They're caving in and the inscriptions are in Spanish."

"I'll find the place. I won't look for you, Ana-Grace, but I'm going to give you my cell number. If you need help, don't hesitate to call. Don't worry; I won't let anyone know you called."

He rattled off the number. When he finished, she hung up without saying good-bye.

જી

Bax left his house with a weekend bag and his briefcase. He arrived at the church office just as Mr. Peters, the custodian, was unlocking the building.

"I don't believe I've seen you here this early since you were getting ready for a visit from your daddy. I guess it is quite a strain trying to follow in the footsteps of a famous evangelist. Is he coming for another visit?" he asked as he opened the door and followed the pastor in.

"I'm afraid I'll have to disappoint you, Mr. Peters. Daddy is preaching a revival in Michigan this week. It really isn't a case of competition with my father. We have two different callings. His is to a much wider audience of people he doesn't know, and mine is to a small group of friends. We have the same message, but we have different strengths. God blesses both of our ministries. Remember in Matthew the Lord himself said, 'For where two or three are gathered in my name, I am there in the midst of them.'"

"I guess I never thought about it that way. I tend to think the more the better, Brother Bax."

"Sir, you are not alone in that. But I am content to be a small part of a great movement," the preacher said. "I came in early today because something unforeseen came up, and I will have to go to New Orleans this afternoon. I might have to be there a few days, so I want to get everything ready for Sunday before I go." He nodded to the custodian. "Mr. Peters, I'll be in my office if anyone wants to see me."

Bax went to his desk and started working on his Sunday sermon. When he finished the outline, he called his old friend and mentor. Sam Moore had been the pastor of the church when Bax came for his trial sermon. The old man had postponed his retirement until the congregation could find a suitable replacement instead of turning his flock over to an interim pastor. After Bax became the pastor, Sam moved his membership to a church in a neighboring town so there would be no divided loyalty. Still, he was only a phone call away when Bax needed advice. It was only natural that Bax would call him to fill in for the prayer meeting service.

"Hello."

"Sam, it's Bax. I've got to go to New Orleans, and I need someone to cover for me on Wednesday. Can you do it?"

"Sure, I'll be glad to. Are you going to be gone all week?" the old preacher asked.

"No, Sam, I plan to be back before Sunday. I'm taking my outline with me so I can practice my message while I'm there."

"That's good. You don't want to let life get in the way of preparation. I'll come in this afternoon and get a copy of your prayer list."

"You know if you would just get a computer, I could e-mail it to you."

"Yes, I know, but then I wouldn't have a good excuse to come over and visit with the staff."

After they finished their conversation, Bax left the church and walked to Kathy's Kountry Kitchen to get pie and coffee. She was busy with the pseudo home cooking she made for her lunch crowd. He had always suspected the only creativity involved after the canned vegetables were opened was the liberal use of bacon grease. Still, the banana pudding was pretty good, if you liked Jell-O Instant Pudding and overripe bananas.

When Bax walked in, he saw Thad and Fran sitting in a booth in the back. He hadn't planned to join them, but Fran waved him over. "Bax, come join us. Kathy's food is always better with company."

Bax slid into the booth next to the deputy. "Any leads on the Fontaines?" he asked.

"No, and I reckon you haven't heard from the woman you knew as Grace," Thad said as he pushed the paper down his straw making an accordioned inch-long tube. Removing the compacted straw cover, he dripped droplets of tea on it and watched it expand into a soggy paper snake.

Bax repeated the same juvenile activity with the straw the waitress left with his water. He kept his eyes on the straw-paper serpent and said, "I haven't 'seen hide nor hair' of her since she left." There, he had told the truth...sort of. He didn't say he hadn't heard from her or that he didn't have any idea where she was. Still, he kept his head down intently watching the wet paper expand, afraid his friends could read the half-truth in his eyes.

"I guess you know Lovie came in to the office the other day with the wild theory that her latest social work subject, Grace, aka Anastasia Fontaine, killed her husband and ran off with some man." Fran continued, "Lovie is a wonderful woman who has a way of finding facts that aren't there. Her heart is in the right place. Her intentions are kind and well meant, but sometimes they don't match reality."

Thad laughed as Bax smiled and reflected on some of the conversation he'd had with her lately. If you only knew how right you are, he thought.

Buried Treasure

na gathered everything she had taken from the cabin. She packed all of it in a plastic container along with a note saying she would reimburse him and return the motorbike as soon as she could. As she closed the butter carton she had taken from Brosia's collection of makeshift storage containers, she knew she'd made the right choice. It was large enough to hold everything but not too big; most important it was water proof. The plastic container should keep the jewelry safe until Bax could retrieve it from its own little grave in the old cemetery.

She slipped the carton into an old plastic shopping bag Brosia had carried even before being green was fashionable. Ana thought how many times she had heard the words "reuse," and "make do." As ever, Brosia was right when she said, "You never know what you may need this for." She certainly didn't have a hiding place for stolen jewelry in mind when the old lady packed the butter container away.

The drive to the cemetery took longer than she remembered. She didn't want to give Bax too many clues to her location, so Ana picked Edgard. It wasn't that close to Bayou Gauche.

She decided to stop at Grumpy's for a cup of coffee and a piece of coffee cake before going on. One of the first things she learned about herself, was if she didn't eat a little between meals, her blood sugar would drop and she'd break out in a sweat, become nervous, and not be able to think as clearly as she should.

Grumpy's hadn't changed from the way it was when she lived in Louisiana. She remembered it, just as she was beginning to remember everything else. Ana sat down, and a perky young waitress came over.

"Morning Boo, what can I get for you?" she asked as she as she handed Ana a plastic-coated menu.

"Young lady, you'll give this place a bad name! You're not grumpy at all." She surprised herself when she actually said what she was thinking. Quickly regaining her composure, she ordered in a more reserved manner.

While she waited for her food, she thought about the girl she had been before her world changed...carefree, funny, and as likely as the waitress was to call a stranger 'Boo' or 'Baby.' The terror of that night had destroyed her emotionally before Brosia took her in. The love and understanding Brosia had shown did much to heal her the year between the fire and when she left for LSU.

Somehow Brosia had come up with enough money to send her to college. She suspected Raymond had supplied most of it out of guilt. But so many things had happened since then to end that brief period that it was almost like it never existed.

Her thoughts were interrupted by the unconventional conversation of the women at the next table. She couldn't help but listen.

The plump grandmotherly looking woman said, "The party went on too long. We just slipped out and Igor went on the honeymoon with us."

Her friend said, "That must have been some Charivari. I just don't understand why Igor went on your honeymoon."

"You know Igor; he just does what he wants to, and nobody has the nerve to stop him. Besides, it was his car."

The friend shrugged. "Oh, but that's all history now. It was over forty years ago. Now I just don't know what to do with my husband."

"What did he do; cheat on you?"

"No, he died. I had him cremated. They were supposed to mix his ashes with some polymer and mold him into an attractive abstract sculpture like the advertisement said."

"That's an interesting way to deal with the ashes. Didn't they do a good job?" the grandmotherly one asked.

"Oh, no, it's just beautiful. I have it on my dining table so I can still have my meals with him. That's not the problem. They didn't use all that much of him and I don't know what to do with the leftovers."

The strange conversation had continued, and Ana stifled a laugh when she heard the widow say it would be disrespectful to sprinkle the leftovers at his hunting camp, as her friend suggested, because animals might trample them and no telling what else.

She stopped listening and bowed her head when she saw David come in the side door. He went up to the bar, his back to her. He hadn't seen her, but a wave of uneasiness, no, fear washed over her. She waited until he was engaged in conversation with the bartender then left enough of the preacher's cash to pay her bill and give Miss Perky a nice tip. Ana lowered her head as if looking for something in her tote and quickly walked out.

She almost ran to the bike, pulled out into traffic, and rode toward the church she'd told Bax about. She didn't see the dark sedan pull out of the parking lot and follow two cars behind.

☙

Joe began to smile with satisfaction. Following Dave had paid off more than he had hoped. He had recognized her the moment she came out. The hair was different, but there was no mistaking that face. The papers and newscasts never tired of putting the beautiful missing professor's face front and center. He was grateful to the news media because he hadn't gotten a good look at her when they hit the car.

He would bet it was in the bag she had stuffed in the helmet storage when she got her helmet out. It was big enough. He wondered if Dave had given her the package, or if she had had it in that tote bag all the time.

He believed that Dave was faking the worried husband bit, which he knew all the time where she had gone and had just waited until he could throw him off the trail before making his move. Dave should have known he was not easily thrown off.

He had thought Dave had gotten away when he came back and his car was gone. He had walked to the main road and hitched a ride back to town, bought this clunker, then saw Dave leave the convenience store. Dave was easier to trail than she was with that stolen car.

Looking ahead, he realized that he had a problem. Since they had gotten into a rural area, traffic had dropped off to nothing; she was sure to notice his car had been behind her for a long time. He decided to drop back a little more. The only other traffic he saw was the cargo ships on the other side of the levee.

Finally, Joe saw her turn into the parking lot of a church. He drove past the church for about a quarter mile before making a U-turn and pulling into the parking lot. He parked to the left of the church, hidden by the building. Joe walked to her parked motorcycle. From there he could see she'd gone into the cemetery.

Joe followed, moving quietly down the paths, hidden by the house-like tombs until he saw her stop behind the crumbling brick mausoleum in the far end of the cemetery. From his position he saw her pull a garden trowel from the bag. When she dropped to her knees, he couldn't see what she was doing; but he was sure she was burying the package. He smiled. He had to hand it to the lady; he would never have looked for it there.

He remained hidden until he heard her footsteps pass on the path that led to the gate and the parking lot. Then he hurried to the place she had been digging, pushed the loose dirt aside, and saw the butter carton. This sure isn't looking good, he thought as he pulled it out and frowned. Whatever it is, it isn't the package. It's too heavy, and it rattles like a lot of little things. He threw it back in the hole, raked the dirt back in place with his hand, and ran out of the cemetery. She had a head start, and he couldn't lose her.

He assumed she would go back the way she had come. That assumption proved to be right. Within a few minutes he saw the bike in the distance. This was going to be like an O. J. Simpson low-speed chase. He was not trying to catch her, just find out where she was going.

❧

As Ana turned out of the parking lot, she noticed a black sedan parked by the church on the side away from the cemetery. That wasn't there when she had arrived. It looked like the car that was behind her part of the way. She shouldn't be so silly; there were millions of black cars. They looked so much alike that she couldn't tell them apart at a distance. Even if it were the same car, there was no reason to think it had anything to do with her. It was just someone with business at the church.

Ana had forgotten about the car in the parking lot by the time Joe spotted her in the distance. Then she caught sight of a dark sedan coming up behind her. She was being followed by that car from the parking lot. She panicked and almost ran off the road, but when she looked in her mirror again, she smiled at what she saw. The sedan had slowed down and dropped out of sight, hidden from view by the tree-lined curve that was now between them; and a dark blue SUV had pulled from a driveway and taken its place behind her. She must be paranoid! She could have sworn it was the same car. If she couldn't tell a black sedan from a blue SUV, she needed help! Then she laughed with relief, happy to have played the fool.

She was getting near Boutte, and traffic was picking up. She forgot her scare by the time she pulled in to Brosia's yard. There was a different car parked in her driveway. Standing beside it was David. She got off her bike and stared at him in disbelief. He had a smile as wide as the Mississippi when he ran to take her in his arms.

Joe

Joe read the sign, Bayou Gauche. What kind of a place was this? Was it such a crude place that they put out a sign to warn people? No, he remembered; gauche was French for left. He laughed at his first impression as he turned down the road he had seen her take. He continued to follow just close enough to keep the pink bike in sight. She was headed toward a narrow peninsula. There was no way he could follow any longer without being spotted. He turned around and drove back to a convenience store he had passed shortly after he followed her to the village.

Joe parked the car and walked in. As he roamed around in the store, he picked up a copy of the *Times-Picayune*, an LSU cap, and a six-pack of Abita beer. He paid for the three items and walked out. He fumbled with his cap as he took it out of the sack and dropped it in the dirt. Bending down to pick it up gave him the opportunity to rub it in the dirt to disguise its newness. He put it on his head, stuck the *Picayune* under his arm, and started walking toward the peninsula, just a good old boy taking home a few necessities.

When he reached the narrow spit of land, he knew he was in the heart of the village. Unlike some of the attractive modern homes he had passed on his walk, this was a collection of weathered houses that, like the people who lived in them, had over the years been at the mercy of wind, water, and the occasional hurricane. Like their inhabitants, though, they hadn't been destroyed by this dangerously unpredictable existence; they had been forever changed.

Shrimp boats, house boats, and other smaller vessels were moored along both sides of the finger of land that reached out into the bayou. Soon they would be joined by others returning with live wells filled to the brim. This could be a hard life but a very good one, he thought almost wistfully as he compared it to his own.

He strolled at a leisurely pace, stopping to tie his shoe when one of the residents seemed to be looking at him suspiciously. When he finished the pantomime, he picked up his paper and beer and then nodded to the onlooker. This acknowledgement defused her curiosity. She smiled back at him, and he continued on his walk.

The back tire of a pink motorcycle was visible peeking from behind one of the houses. He continued walking as a satisfied smile grew and just as quickly disappeared. Yes, he had found her, but that was no reason to walk around looking like the village idiot. He hadn't gotten what he came for yet. There were two cars at the house. She wasn't alone; the mission would have to wait. This wasn't the time to celebrate.

Joe kept walking along the road that divided the peninsula into two slivers of land on each side. He had no choice; it was the only road there was. The monotony of the straight pavement seemed to end at the water's edge at the tip of the land. When he got closer, he saw that the pavement ended; but the road, now dirt, potholes, and patchwork, curved and continued. The houses were fewer and farther apart with trees and undergrowth covering most of the left edge and the water only a few feet from the right. He passed what looked like the remains of an oil drilling site. Finally, he reached the dead end. There he saw a derelict fishing pier and a boat launch. Perfect! If he sat on the pier, read the paper, and drank a beer, he would just look like a fellow relaxing before he went home to face the music.

At sunset Joe started to slowly walk back toward the paved part of the road. The rest of the fishing boats were coming in, their wakes leaving the water choppy. He stopped and looked out at the reflected sunset on the moving water, a golden kaleidoscope. Its beauty was lost on him. He was only waiting for total darkness to continue his walk back to the place he had seen the motorcycle. When he felt the time was right, he started walking back toward the house, avoiding any light, keeping to the shadows.

He saw immediately that the two cars were still there. A light was on in the back of the house. He had to know how many people were in the house. The only way to find out required the risk of being seen. Joe walked to the source of the light, a kitchen window. There framed in the light were Ana, Dave, and an old lady. He wasn't sure who she was, but it looked like a family reunion to him. Dave had led him to Anastasia, and now she had led him back to Dave. Thank you, Mrs. Fontaine!

He would have to plan his next move more carefully. Clearly this close-knit community wasn't the best place to take them. Then there's the old lady; a witness was one thing he didn't need. Later tonight he would be back with a boat. That wouldn't attract attention, and it would be a good way to get them off the peninsula. Yes, he would be back ready to handle the situation.

ⲉⳁ

Brosia finished washing the dishes and joined Dave and Ana in the front room. Pictures of Sully and Ana were everywhere. The exception was a faded copy of The Lord's Supper that hung over the couch where the couple sat. She usually felt peaceful being surrounded by these mementos, but tonight the tension between Ana and Dave was all she could feel. Their body language was not that of a loving couple who had just been reunited. What could be wrong?

"It's wonderful having y'all back here. It's just like old times," she said trying to break the icy silence in the room.

"Brosia, your gumbo was delicious, just as hot and spicy as I remembered. Speaking of spicy, you haven't changed a bit," Dave said as he winked at the old lady.

"Well, I wouldn't say that. I'm a good bit older, but I'm still just as sassy. That is one thing age doesn't change." She smiled at him but thought Ana had been surprisingly quiet. Something was wrong, but they'd been through so much with the kidnapping and all the other things that went on. Maybe when they had time to talk things out without an extra pair of ears in the room, they could relax. "Speaking of being older, these days I have to go to bed with the chickens! Dave, do you still like sausage and biscuits for breakfast?" Brosia asked.

"That would be wonderful with some of your good, strong coffee. Don't you think, Ana?"

"Anything Brosia fixes will be good. Thank you for supper, Thea," Ana said.

"Good-night, dears." Brosia said, as she kissed the top of their heads and went to her room.

As soon as Brosia was out of earshot, Ana began trying to get to the nugget of truth that was hidden in the story he told Brosia. "Dave, it must have been terrible being held by those men. You were a little vague when you told Brosia you escaped when you found one of those 'rams' she is always saying God hides 'in a bush.' She loves the story about Abraham sparing Isaac's life when God showed him a sacrificial ram caught in a bush. Your answer satisfied her, but I'd like more details."

"It's like I told Brosia, Mitch was holding me at gun point, walking me deep into the woods to shoot me. I pushed a low limb out of the way so we could get through a thickly wooded area. As soon as I got on the other side, I let it go. When it sprang back it hit him in the head with enough force to stun him long enough for me to get away. He recovered and chased me, shooting at me until he ran out of ammo. When he stopped to get his extra clip, I grabbed a fallen limb and swung at his head. While he was knocked out, I got the clip, loaded the gun and shot him in the face until his own mother wouldn't recognize him. Then I took his car and got out of there.

"You see, it was a little like the Bible story, but my 'ram in the bush' was a gun."

"You killed him? What about the other one?"

"I don't know where he is, but he is still after me. I should say he's after both of us."

Their conversation was interrupted by the resonant sound of snoring coming from the next room.

Dave turned back impatiently. "That's why I have to work fast. Where is that package, Ana?"

The edge on his voice sent a chill through her. "I don't know what you're talking about."

"Don't give me that! I put a small package between your seat and the console before we left the hotel. You drove the car away after we were hit, and those guys grabbed me. I don't have it; they don't have it; that leaves you. Where is it?"

"I have no idea! I drove until I ran out of gas; then I abandoned the car. I didn't know anything special was in the car. Who knows how many people scavenged it looking for anything of value before it got towed. Maybe the towing company has it, or found it and threw it out. Dave, I had amnesia after the crash. I didn't even remember who I was for days. I still have big gaps in my memory." Ana turned and started walking back toward the kitchen.

Dave jerked her around and said through gritted teeth, "Don't walk away from me, Ana! And don't try that amnesia stuff on me. Even if you chose not to remember everything in your past, I remember. As they say, 'I know where all the bodies are buried.' You do remember my cousin, Lisa, don't you?" To add emphasis, he shoved her against the wall.

"How dare you say that, Dave," she said as she wiped away tears. "Yes, I remember the whole nightmare. I wish I didn't, but there are still parts of my recent past that are still a blank. I don't know if I'll ever remember it all."

"Then you're lucky I'm here to help you fill in the blanks. We have to find the package, so you have to remember. Perhaps it will help you remember to know that they killed Tony because they thought he had it. Yes, your dear Tony's dead… You never got over him, did you?"

"Dave, I think you've lost your mind. I'm sleeping on the couch."

"Suit yourself." He slammed the door to her girlhood bedroom so hard she was sure Brosia heard it.

Ana turned again and walked into the kitchen and splashed water on her red eyes. No, she had never really gotten over Tony. Why couldn't he have been the one who escaped? While she was drying her face, she saw Brosia's phone on its charger sitting on the counter. Without a second thought she slipped them both into the pocket of the apron she had put on while she helped with supper. As she reviewed her options, it became apparent how limited they were. Subconsciously she had already chosen the best one when she took the phone.

SEVENTEEN

Trust

Bax had started the drive to Louisiana as soon as he finished his coffee. He had told Thad and Fran that something had come up and that he had to make an unexpected trip to the seminary. That was true, but the two facts were related in a strange way. It was Ana's call, not his doctoral work, which was the unexpected impetus for the trip. The stop at the seminary was just an excuse. What he planned to do there could easily have been done on his next scheduled trip for classes. He didn't like the way he was falling into the habit of deceiving his friends with twisted truths. Surely that was still a "false witness," if not technically a lie.

A promise was meant to be kept, and he would keep it and pray she was not lying to him about burying Beth's jewelry in the graveyard. She had sent him on a fool's errand before.

He had covered all the bases; the sermon was ready for Sunday, and Brother Martin was covering prayer meeting. He shouldn't be away more than a few days and wouldn't be missed unless someone had a tragedy.

By five-thirty he was driving down River Road to the village of Edgard. Bax was surprised at the architectural jewel that was coming into sight. When the beautiful twin spires and rose window came into view, he was pleasantly surprised. Who

would have thought such a church would be hidden away in a tiny
rural community like this?

Bax drove into the parking lot and parked near the golden
statue of Jesus. He got out and walked over to get a better look.
While he was absorbed in studying the details of the statue, a
voice behind startled him. "Admiring our Savior, pastor?"

Bax turned around and saw a priest coming from the
cemetery. He broke into a smile. "Good afternoon, Father. Tell
me how you knew I was a preacher?"

"That was easy, the clergy emblem on your bumper. What
brings you to our little church? You're not wearing a Roman
collar, so I assume you must be a history buff."

"Not really, I heard there was an old cemetery here, and I
find them interesting. Your church is beautiful. It's hardly what I
expected of a rural church."

"It is a bit of an anomaly, I'll admit. Saint John the Baptist is
the oldest congregation in the parish. The Spanish dedicated this
land for a church in 1770. The first building burned, and this one
was built in 1918. The cemetery has graves of members of the
first families to settle here up to those who've been members in
modern times. The Slidell family mausoleum is one you'll want
to visit if you are interested in Civil War history. General P. G. T.
Beaugard's wife was buried here with her sister's family."

"I'll be sure to check it out."

"I'd be glad to give you a tour with a little history, but I
have to get back to my office to finish a few things before I go. If
you'll come back earlier in the day, I'd love to show the building
to you."

"I'd love to see it. Thanks for the background. It'll make my
visit more meaningful. By the way, my name is Bax Alford."

"Good to meet you; I'm Peter Castile. I hope you enjoy your
walk through our 'city of the dead.'"

The two men shook hands and went about their own
late afternoon tasks. Peter went to his office to close it for the

day, while Bax walked into the ancient graveyard to dig in the consecrated ground. Just in case Peter should see him from his office, Bax took his time following Ana's directions. He made a point to stop at the Slidell tomb, then followed the paths weaving between mausoleums until he was in the earliest section. There he found the crumbling burial chamber Ana had described. Behind it he found evidence of fresh digging.

Bax pulled away the loose soil and found the butter container. When he lifted it out, the weight of it caused him to smile. At least it's not empty, he thought. When he lifted the lid, there were all of the things he had given Beth to mark special times in their lives. Seeing each trinket brought back a flood of memories. The emotional impact of recovering the things that represented events in a marriage that ended far too soon surprised him. Dirt that clung to his fingers smudged his face when he wiped his eyes.

Bax carried the dirty butter container back to his car. He didn't know what to make of Ana-Grace. First, she stole from him; then she asked him to drive for hours to dig his wife's jewelry up from a historic cemetery. He only had her word that he would get the money and the motorcycle back. How could he know the wild story she told him in confidence was even true?

The trip had been grueling. That combined with the feeling that he was being pulled deeper into something he never should have been involved in, led to a sleepless night. The battle between conflicting feelings and exhaustion finally ended in a restless truce that allowed him to sleep.

The piercing sound of his cell phone ended a dream in which Beth was telling him to fear the okra, a warning that was printed on her Delta State tee shirt. My alarm can't be going off yet, he thought as he fumbled in the dark. Finally, he recognized it was ringing, not alarming. Bax looked at the readout; it was a Louisiana number he didn't recognize. "Hello," he mumbled.

"Bax, I didn't think I would ever use this number, but he's here, and I'm afraid."

"You need to slow down, Ana-Grace. Who's there; one of those men you heard at the gas pump?"

"No, it's Dave; he was there when I got back from the cemetery. He wants the package, and he thinks I know where it is. He got ugly and hit me when I wouldn't tell him where it is. I wasn't about to tell him you took it to the police."

"It wasn't me. Lovie found it and turned it in to Thad before I got there, but that's not important. You need to get out of there now!"

"I can't leave Brosia with him. If you could have seen the look in his eyes, you would understand."

"Who is Brosia?"

"My aunt..."

"Bring her with you. Do you have any transportation beside the motorcycle?"

"There's Brosia's car, but Dave knows what it looks like. If he misses us before we get out of the parish, it would be as easy as finding a bowling ball in the crab boil to spot the car. It's old, ugly and everyone around here knows it belongs to her."

"You may have to take that risk. I'll try to think of something. Keep me posted," he said before he hung up.

Ana slipped into her Aunt Brosia's room and gently shook her. "Don't talk. Just dress; get your purse, and come with me. I'll explain outside."

Brosia quickly dressed and met Ana in the dimly-lit hall. The younger woman put her finger to her lips as she silently took the keys from the peg board next to the pantry door. The two women walked as quietly as they could across the creaking floor. Ana had never noticed how noisy the old house was. When she opened the door, she shuddered as its hinges cried out for lubrication. The sounds must have been magnified by her anxiety, for they didn't disturb David's loud snoring.

လာ

Joe had silently rowed a stolen boat to the bank behind Brosia's house when he saw the women moving toward a car. The old woman got into the driver's side to steer as Ana started pushing the old VW toward the road.

Joe jumped out of the boat and ran toward the women. Ana saw him coming and got in the car as quickly as she could. "Hit the gas, Brosia! That's one of the men!"

Joe jerked open the driver's door, but Brosia was ready for him. She had a strange looking metal object in her hand. The old lady used all of her strength to hit him on the head repeatedly. He was stunned just long enough for her to slam the door and drive away as fast as the old bug would go.

Joe ran back to the boat to get the chloroform and the cloth he had left there. As he assumed, the commotion woke Fontaine. Dave came running out the door just in time to see the taillights of Brosia's old car disappear in the distance. He didn't have time to understand what had happened before Joe came up behind him and put the chloroform-soaked cloth over his face.

He dragged Dave back to the water's edge and loaded him into the boat. He had caught the big fish, but the little one got away. Maybe he had it wrong. She could be the big fish. He pushed off from the bank. The little boat with the two men melted into the darkness as Joe used the oars to guide it to the cove where his car was parked.

Run

As the two women turned onto the main road Ana said, "We need to get in heavy traffic as soon as we can. Out here we are too easily spotted in this car. Head to the city."

"What was that all about, Ana?"

"He was one of the men who kidnapped Dave. He is still after us. I tell you I'm in danger, not just from him but from Dave."

"What do you mean? Dave loves you; he always has."

"That's not true. He never loved me. He wanted to have me, to control me, but love, no. Brosia, he's here looking for a package he left in the car. I don't have it, but he won't believe me. After you went to bed, he accused me of lying. He slapped and shook me when I couldn't give him what he wanted. He told me a little more about how he got away. He killed the other man. It was self-defense, or so he says. But instead of going to the police, he came looking for me to retrieve the package that's behind everything that has happened, even Tony's death."

"Tony's dead! Ana, if you have the thing, why don't you just give it to him?"

"I don't have it. Someone found it, and turned it in to the police. I can't tell him that. He'd blame me and go into a rage."

"What's in it?"

"That's the strange part, I have no idea. But I know people have died because of it. Brosia, I'm afraid, and now I have dragged you into danger. I really didn't believe they would follow me here. I covered my tracks; at least I thought I did. Now not only does he know I'm in the area, he knows what car we're driving. He'll find us in this. There are not many VWs of this vintage still around, especially one with flowers and peace signs. We'll be sitting ducks."

"If you think that's a problem, we'll just switch cars."

"You don't have another car, Brosia."

"No, but I'm part-owner of a hearse."

"What did you say?"

"Do you remember Sully's cousin Rab's boy, Bird? He had a hair-brained idea a few years ago. He wanted to start a murder tour business in New Orleans. There was no shortage of murders to pick from. But the competition was already well established. The ghost tours in the city have been in business for years. And people who visit in this part of the world like the supernatural, voodoo, ghosts, and the like more than seeing where some thug was killed. But nobody could talk him out of it. "You Stab 'Em-We'll Slab 'Em didn't have a ghost of a chance, if you'll pardon the pun."

"Brosia, what are you talking about? Who got stabbed?"

"Nobody did; that was the name of the business. He rented this historic funeral home for his base of operations and bought an old hearse to use instead of a van or one of those horse- drawn carriages tourists like to ride around in.

"That's where I came into the story. He needed investors to get his 'sure thing' off the ground. He came by sweet talking me, telling all kinds of sentimental stories about Sully. The next thing I knew I had co-signed for a hearse." She moved smoothly around a car going slower.

"Ana, it's not such a crazy idea when you think about it. That man would think you would want to be unnoticed, not driving around in a hearse."

"Will he let you use it?"

"I'm the one making payments. I just didn't want the neighbors to know what a fool I was, so it's parked at his girlfriend's house on one of those narrow streets of Leach; but I have all of the keys." Brosia said.

"Let's get it tonight. By the way, what was that thing you used to hit the man in the head?" Ana asked.

"This," she said, as she raised her weapon, "is my Handybar. I have a hard time getting out of car seats when my arthritis is acting up. I just put this little pointy part down in the door latch to make a handle out of the long part, so I can pry up and get out of the car. It did make a good head knocker, didn't it?"

The two women broke into laughter as they drove to New Orleans. For a moment they forgot how afraid they were.

Brosia closed her eyes as they got closer to the city. She had known something was wrong tonight at supper. Still, she was having a hard time understanding what Ana told her about Dave. The missing package, shaking and hitting her, and not loving her; none of that sounded like the David Fontaine she had known for years.

She had cooked the dinner for their wedding reception. The only guests beside her had been a few friends of theirs from college and Raymond. Tony and that girl he married a few years later had been their only attendants.

Neither of them had much family. Dave was an only child, whose parents were dead. He had an aunt and uncle who moved up North to live near relatives after their daughter died. Except for them and some cousins in Alabama, Ana was all the family he had. He was a sweet, lonely boy. He couldn't have changed that much.

As they got near the girlfriend's house, Brosia said, "Just leave my car at Cooter Brown's. There are always a bunch of cars at that bar. We can walk to that girl's house. It's not far from here, and the street is so narrow I'd be afraid to leave my car parked there.

They left the car at the bar and walked a few short blocks to a small shotgun house with the hearse parked in the yard. Magnetic signs on the doors had You Stab 'Em-We'll Slab 'Em Tours in Gothic letters.

Brosia said, "Pull those things off the doors. I keep telling him this thing will never catch on, no matter how much he advertises."

Ana removed the signs and put them in the back of the vehicle as Brosia got behind the wheel. "Where do we go now, Ana?"

"I don't know, but I have a friend who might be able to help us." She pulled out Brosia's phone from the pocket of the apron she was still wearing and punched redial.

"Hello," a sleepy voice mumbled.

"Bax, it's Ana-Grace. I did it. Brosia and I are driving an old hearse down St. Charles Avenue."

"A hearse?" He paused. "Never mind. Tell me later. Where are you going?"

"I don't know right now. I'm just driving around the Garden District trying to plan my next move. A man tried to stop us when we left. He jerked the door open so he could get to us; but Brosia hit him in the head with her Handybar, and we got away."

"You said 'a man.' It wasn't Dave?"

"No, I'm pretty sure he was one of those men I heard at the pump. Dave told me they kidnapped him a second time, and he had to kill the one he called Mitch in self-defense."

"It looks like you ladies left just in time. So why are you in a hearse?"

"Brosia's car is too recognizable; and both Dave and the man, I think Dave said his name is Joe, know how it looks. It's hard to go unnoticed in a 1963 Bug with faded flowers and peace signs all over it."

"But a hearse is noticeable, too."

"Yes, but it's the only other vehicle Brosia has keys for. Besides, no one would think we would be in something like that."

"You're right about that. Now we need to make sure you are in a safe place. I think you should go back to the cabin. Try to time your arrival after dark. I would hate to panic any of the folks around there if they saw a hearse headed up the road to my cabin. You could move around a few things in the garage and park it in there out of sight. You know where the keys are. You need to get started tonight, if you can. I'll feel better when you're out of New Orleans. Did you bring enough money to stay in a hotel along the way if you get too tired to keep driving?"

"I still have some of Beth's Christmas money, but I don't want to use it if I don't have to. Brosia and I will split the driving; and if we get too tired, there is plenty of room to stretch out in the back."

"I'm meeting with one of my professors in the morning. I'll start back as soon as I can."

"Thanks, Bax. We'll see you at the cabin. Good-bye."

"Don't hang up yet, Ana. I have to know how Brosia's hitting that man with a candy bar helped you get away."

"It wasn't a candy bar; it's a Handybar. It's a device that fits in a car door's latch. It is metal with a point at a right angle to the handle. It locks in securely enough that a person with knee problems can use it as a handle to push up to get out of the car. It can also be used to equalize pressure when a car goes under water. Just hit the window with that metal point and the water rushes in so the doors can be opened."

"Ouch! Brosia packs some weapon. I won't worry so much with her as your bodyguard. Seriously, be careful. Whoever is after you isn't going to give up."

After they disconnected, Bax held his phone for a moment. Maybe it was time to give Thad a call.

NINETEEN

Gossip

Lovie had finished her business in town. Before she went home, she'd better stop and see what they'd found out about that package she'd found. Heaven only knew why Thad wanted that torn wrapper. There wasn't anything on it to tell where it came from.

When she walked in, she could hear Thad and Fran talking in the back room. Well, at least she could hear most of what they said. It would be easy to fill in the parts they mumbled.

"Bax called me this morning before he left New Orleans. He wants us to start a regular patrol down at his cabin. He said someone has moved in, and he's pretty sure she would feel better if we resumed the security runs we did when Beth was out there by herself," Thad said.

"It's about time he put that place to use again. You know how fast an empty house gets run down," Fran said.

Lovie stopped listening as soon as the words pretty and she soaked in. Of all things! Brother Bax was moving a pretty woman into his dead wife's lake house. She had better check on their good pastor and find out what was going on before she went home.

He had been out of town for a couple of days and was sure to be out of a few things. Anyone could always use a fresh loaf of bread and a can of Community Coffee. What else could she bring that wouldn't spoil before he got home? She had some homemade jelly. She had been going to drop it off at Junior's on the way home; but he really didn't need the extra calories.

She slipped out of the office as quietly as she could and hurried to her truck. As she drove, she tried to think of ways she could get Bax to open up about his love life. It wasn't like he was still married to Beth. Maybe he would welcome a motherly ear and some good advice.

After a quick stop at Groceries and Gas to pick up the things she needed, Lovie drove to the church, parked, and hurried down the hall toward the pastor's office. She wasn't sure how she would bring up the subject, but felt sure she would recognize an appropriate opening in their conversation.

On her way to the office Lovie passed Linda, Bax's secretary, going the opposite direction. "How are you today, Linda?"

"I'm just fine, Miss Lovie, but I can't say the same for Bax. Old Man Wilson is in the office giving him a hard time. If you are heading that way, you might want to come back later. I decided this was the best time to check the supply closet. Who knows, we might be running short of staples."

"You know exactly how many staples, paper clips, and push pins are in there. You just don't want to hear the ruckus."

The women laughed, and Lovie continued down the hall. As soon as she opened the door to the outer office where Linda had her desk, she knew why the secretary had left. The old curmudgeon's voice was muffled enough that she couldn't understand the words, but the volume was unmistakable. He opened the door and stormed out slamming the outer office door behind him.

An incredulous Bax came out of the office shaking his head. When he saw Lovie, he quickly smiled and said, "Miss Lovie, how are you today? Come on in and tell me what I can do for you."

Lovie followed the preacher back to his office and sat down on the small sofa across from his desk. She put the bag of groceries on his desk without an explanation and said, "Well, I guess you know how those Philistines in the book of Judges felt."

"I'm sorry; I don't understand what you mean by that, Miss Lovie."

"Remember in the story about how Sampson attacked the Philistines with the jawbone of an ass? After the uproar I overheard, I'd say you have that much in common with those old Philistines! Wilson is a jackass, if I ever heard one. He doesn't like anybody and thinks just because he has more money than the rest of us all put together, he should run everything, even the church. What did he want anyway?"

"What happened to that plan of yours to pray for people you don't approve of? You know I can't divulge anything that is told to me in private." He indicated a seat across from him. "Let's just change the subject. What brings you to my office today? I hope Billy Ray and you aren't having any problems."

"Oh, no, everyone is just fine. It's just that while I was at the Sheriff's office, I overheard Thad talking about someone living at your lake house. You haven't sold it have you? I used to clean it for Beth's parents before they came down for their summer vacation, rest their poor souls. I'd hate to see it sold to strangers. It just wouldn't be the same if the place was out of the family."

"No, Miss Lovie, I haven't sold it, but an older widow is staying there for a while. You know I don't have time to get out there very much. My work at the church and my class work don't leave much time for fishing, and this lady needed a place to stay for a while."

"Is it someone I know?" Lovie asked.

"Mrs. Leblanc is from Louisiana. I doubt that you know her."

Not one to give up, Lovie tried another tactic. "Well, maybe I could go out there and welcome her to the neighborhood."

"That might not be the best idea. She is going through a family crisis. I don't think making new friends is high on her list. Just let her have a little time to herself."

"If you say so, but sometimes people need friends to bring them out of those depressing times. If anyone can pep her up, it's me. My friend Jody Harris over in Hahnville said, 'Lovie, you could charm the devil right out of hell and make the Sphinx laugh so hard he'd wet his pants.'"

"I'm sure your friend is right, but remember Ecclesiastes, chapter three, verses one through eight. 'For everything there is a season... a time to weep and a time to laugh, a time to mourn and a time to dance...' even 'a time to keep silence and a time to speak...' I don't think this is the time to use your charm on this lady. She has gone through a lot lately and needs time alone."

"I guess you know best; I'll do what you say. It's later than I thought; Billy Ray will be worried about me. I'll see you Sunday."

As she got to the door, Lovie turned, pointed to the bags she'd left on Linda's desk and said, "The groceries are for you. I thought your bread might have gotten stale while you were out of town." Lovie left the church office before Bax had time to thank her. She was unsatisfied with the scant amount of information she had been able to gather from her tight-lipped preacher.

An old widow? She doubted it. She was sure Thad said something about a pretty young woman. It sounded to her like Brother Bax was trying to hide something, or maybe she should say somebody. She was going to drive over there and look around. It was not that far out of her way.

Bax picked up the phone and called Brosia.

"Hello, Bax, are you checking on us already? We haven't been here twenty-four hours yet."

"No, I not checking on you ladies, I'm warning you. Ana's benefactor, Lovie, came by my office asking about the lady who was living in my cabin. I told her you were staying there, but I didn't mention Ana-Grace. She said she wants to welcome you to the neighborhood. It's more likely she wants to be the first in the church to see what the lady living in my house looks like."

Brosia said, "I understand. You would rather she sees a plump septuagenarian than a slender, sexy missing art teacher."

"That is one way to put it. I tried to discourage her, but talking her out of doing something she wants to do is almost impossible. Don't be surprised if she shows up with a plate of cookies," Bax said.

"From what Ana told me she's a wonderfully kind woman and a good cook."

"She is, but she has the tendency to jump to conclusions. She thought Ana-Grace might have killed Dave. I don't know what Lovie would do if she saw Ana-Grace. It would be best if she stayed out of sight if Lovie shows up. Frankly, I wouldn't put it past her."

"I'll keep that in mind and warn Ana to stay in the back. Just in case you're right, I'll put on a fresh pot of coffee to go with those cookies."

"Good bye, Brosia."

"Good bye."

Ana walked into the kitchen and asked, "Was that your business partner wanting to know where you took the hearse?"

"No, he called while you were taking your bath. He and his girlfriend just got back in town and wanted to know if I knew the hearse was missing. I told him not to call the police. I needed a little vacation and my old car wasn't up to the trip so I took my other vehicle. He's not happy, but there isn't anything he can do about it." She started measuring coffee into the pot. "The last call was from your friend, Bax. He called to tell us that Lovie might be on the way over to check out the person he let move in. She heard a woman was living here."

"How did she find out?" Ana asked.

"He didn't say. He just asked that you keep out of sight if she comes."

"That was the one thing that Bax wanted to avoid—gossip. Maybe she won't come," Ana said.

❧

She couldn't go out there empty-handed. But she didn't have time to go home and fix something to welcome the woman. She guessed one of Kathy's so-called homemade pies would do. Lovie pulled into a parking place so she could go in and buy her excuse for dropping in on the newcomer.

Lovie was back in her car armed with a pie in a few minutes. She wished she had checked the bottom of the aluminum pan to see if there was a Bible verse on the bottom so she would know for sure if Mrs. Edwards, not Kathy, baked the pie. Her crust was much flakier than Kathy's.

Lovie continued driving toward the lake rehearsing what she would say so she wouldn't come off like the snoop she was. It's not like she was getting into that woman's business; she was just looking out for Brother Bax. If the wrong person got hold of this bit of news, not that she was saying he had done anything wrong yet, he could find himself out of a pulpit. Like the Bible said, you have to avoid the appearance of evil, as well as evil itself, or something like that anyway.

The old truck rounded the final curve and came to a stop in front of the cabin she had cleaned for years. It hadn't changed much, Bax had kept it up better than she would have thought. Oh, well, she'd better get on with it. Lovie finger-combed her hair, pushed it behind her ears, and got out of the car with the pie. For the first time she felt a little foolish. What if Bax had been telling the truth about the old widow? Before she lost her nerve, she knocked on the door.

After a second knock, a woman said, "Yes, can I help you?"

"I'm Lovie Millburn, a friend of Brother Alford. Can I come in?"

The door slowly opened just a crack and a piercing dark eye peeked out at her. Then the door opened and a short, plump woman stepped aside to let her in. "By all means. I didn't intend to be rude, but I'm just a little uneasy out here by myself. How can I help you?"

"I don't want you to do anything for me; I just wanted to welcome you. Do you like lemon pie? I brought one." Lovie shoved the pie toward Brosia.

"Thank you, Mrs. Millburn. That was really sweet of you, and lemon is a favorite of mine. Have a seat; I just made a pot of coffee. Would you like some with your pie?"

"Yes, that would be nice. I'd like my coffee black."

Brosia went back to the kitchen to cut the pie and pour two mugs of her steaming hot coffee. While she was gone, Lovie sat on the couch feeling both ashamed of her suspicions and relieved to be wrong.

The older woman came back with the pie and coffee on a tray. She put it on an old trunk that served as a coffee table and joined Lovie on the couch. "I completely forgot my manners; I'm Ambrosia Leblanc, but everyone calls me Brosia."

"Ambrosia, that's a lovely name."

"My mama must have liked it. But my husband, God rest his soul, hated it; so, I've been Brosia since I met him when we were in our teens."

"I'm sorry, has he been gone long?"

"Yes and no, I don't mean to talk in circles, but you see even though he passed away twenty-five years ago, there isn't a day I don't feel his presence. I don't mean that he is a ghost who whispers in my ear, but the memories… just what he would say, how he would handle a problem. You see, when you love someone as much as I loved him, they never really leave you." Brosia took a sip of her coffee. "You'll have to forgive me; I'm talking like a foolish old woman. You'll tell your friend he has a mad woman living in his house. Tell me about your family, Mrs. Millburn," Brosia said, changing the subject.

There was no subject Lovie enjoyed more. She rattled on about Billy Ray and the children for half an hour, completely forgetting to find out more about her new friend. That suited Brosia to a tee. As she walked Lovie to the door and waved as the red truck drove away, she knew Sully would have approved of the way she handled her nosy visitor.

Brosia closed the door and said, "You can come out now; she's gone."

As Lovie drove away, she was unaware that two women were watching as she drove out of sight. She must have misunderstood, or Thad was losing his vision. Brosia was a lovely lady, but she looked like she was pushing seventy on a good day. Brother Bax wasn't hiding a girlfriend out there. It looked like she had wasted a perfectly good pie.

Message

Thad reexamined the brown paper Lovie had removed from the mysterious package. There didn't seem to be anything unusual about it. As he had expected, there had been numerous fingerprints on it. David's and Tony's prints were there, as well as several others including one that matched a print found at Wilson's cabin. Then he noticed a slight difference in the texture of the paper. It looked smoother, slightly thinner, than the paper around it. When he held the paper against his computer screen, he was puzzled by what he saw. "Fran, come look at this."

Fran joined him at his desk. "What do you want to show me?"

"Look at the wrapping paper when I hold it against the computer screen. Do you notice anything?" Thad asked.

"Not really, it looks like any paper on a light table. Wait, I think I see what you're talking about. There seem to be spots where more light comes through, not a big difference but enough to be noticed if you are looking for something," Fran said.

Thad said, "There is an irregular pattern of those lighter spots all over the paper. It makes me think of the grading key my wife puts over multiple-choice questions when she's grading papers. What if this was put over the text Tony Berry said didn't make any sense. Would the words that matched the lightened spots be a message?"

"You might be right, Thad. I don't see any other reason for someone to take the time to thin-out a series of spots on the paper. But we don't have anyone around here who can read that language."

"But we know who does have access to people with that capability. Get the FBI on the line again. Maybe they'll send out an expert who can figure out which side goes face down on the text, and where the paper has to be placed to match the words it is meant to identify. If they don't have someone who can do it, they can get in touch with someone who can. Fran, all I know for sure is this business is above our pay level. It's time to call in the big boys," Thad picked up his phone.

The day after Thad called the Birmingham office, a black sedan rolled down the street and parked in front of the sheriff's office. A small Oriental man got out and came in. "Good morning, I'm Jeff Abe from the FBI," he said as he handed Fran his card. "I'm here to see Sheriff Brownlee."

"Yes, sir, I'll get him. He forgot his phone when he went next door to have lunch. I'll be back with him in a few minutes. What Thad wants to talk to you about isn't something to discuss in a small-town café. Fran walked to the café as fast as he could without attracting too much attention. He looked around and found Thad seated in the back. Taking his seat across from the sheriff, he handed the agent's card to his boss. "The FBI agent is sitting in your office waiting for you."

"Thanks, I'm finished; take care of the check so I don't have to keep him waiting any longer. I'll pay you back later."

Thad glanced at the agent's card as he went back to his office. Before entering the office, he paused only long enough to run his fingers through his unruly hair and tuck in his shirt. "Thanks for coming so soon, Agent Abe. I'm Thad Brownlee."

"It's nice to meet you Sheriff Brownlee; but despite the spelling of my name, it's not short for Abraham. In Japanese Abe is pronounced Ahbee."

"Sorry, I guess it's too late for me to get off on the right foot."

"It's a frequent and understandable mistake. Let's get down to business. Can I examine the papers you contacted us about?"

Thad got out the file and handed it to the agent. "Here's the file. If you hold the brown paper up to my monitor screen, you can see the thinned-out places. Last night I experimented filing a brown paper bag with my wife's emery board, a metal nail file, and her favorite crystal file. I got almost the same results with the crystal file. The others took off too much and rubbed holes in the paper."

"That's interesting." Abe said as he took the paper and examined it more carefully. "It does look like the thin spots were filed on the paper. I'll need to take all of this back with me. Your idea about a grading key is right on track. They make a new template for each message they send. There is no code to break, so there is little chance that the wrong person would stumble on the way to decipher it."

"Then there is no danger to the person who found the package?" Thad asked.

"I wouldn't go so far as to say that. There is always the chance that people, like Dr. Berry and you, who together had enough knowledge of the language and detective skills, will see this as a potential threat to their security. When it was discovered that the document was delivered to the wrong person, I can assure you they launched a full-scale recovery operation. They won't rest until they have it back. Who beside yourself and your deputy knows about this?" Abe asked.

"There are just the two of us and an older couple who found it in their junked washing machine. Take it from me; they don't have foreign language or detective skills."

"You are forgetting one person. The person who put the package in the washing machine must have had some knowledge that caused him or her to hide it. That person may know too much," Abe said.

The men concluded their business, being sure the chain of custody was properly maintained. They shook hands, and agent Abe drove off with the document with a secret message hidden in it along with the brown paper key.

Thad stuck his hands in his pockets and watched the agent drive out of town. Who would believe there was a bigger mystery in this one-horse town than who put the junked appliances and a toilet in the soccer coach's front yard?

When he went back into the office, Fran was just finishing a phone call and motioned Thad over. He handed a page of scribbled notes to the sheriff when he disconnected.

"Fran, you know I can't read your hen scratch; tell me what whoever called had to say."

"It was state crime lab. The fingerprints we were able to get from the body by Bubba's car not only match some of those at Wilson's cabin, but also match a known anarchist. Hubert Mitchell was arrested twenty years ago for resisting arrest after a fight broke out at a student protest. He attacked another student who challenged the information on the propaganda he was distributing. It was his first offense, so he got off. Later his name was linked to several subversive movements. He was never any more than a lower-level recruit. Still his political activity has been monitored over the years. He graduated from an academically fourth tier school with a degree in political science."

Thad asked, "What exactly do you define as an academically fourth-tier school, any school that doesn't have an elephant as a mascot?"

Fran laughed. "I'm loyal, not stupid. I do recognize that there may be a few schools as good and maybe one or two better than 'Bama.' This one isn't one of those. It's nothing but a scam school, a mail-order degree mill. I guarantee none of the graduates got their money's worth from Thoth University of the South." Fran looked at his notes. "Oh, and Abe called his people and told them we needed to be briefed." Fran hit redial.

After a short pause Fran said, "This is Deputy Francisco Shaw from Eastabuchie County, Alabama. I just got off the phone with… Yes, of course, you know. The sheriff has returned to the office. Could Mr. Logan repeat what he told me to Sheriff Brownlee? I'm afraid I'll get the story so twisted the sheriff won't get the full story." Another short pause then Fran said, "Thank you, I'll put on the speaker, and we'll wait for him to come on the line"

After what seemed a decade, the gravelly voice of an older man came on the line. "Sheriff Brownlee, I understand your deputy wants you to hear this from the horse's mouth."

"Well, he took notes, but this is so important I want to be sure I understand everything," Thad said.

"I don't blame you; I'd do the same thing. There is a problem; I'm not sure I have it all figured out yet. Mitchell was never more than a lower-level worker bee. He fell off the radar for a long time. Lately he has been seen with individuals with ties to a subversive group that uses a courier for all important communications. They're a bunch of paranoids who don't trust electronic communication, like e-mail and Skype. They don't think the Post Office, FedEx and the like are secure enough. If Hubert Mitchell lost the package, it's likely he was eliminated for his carelessness," Logan said.

"What does that have to do with Tony Berry and the Fontaines?" Thad asked.

Logan said, "According to the information I was given, this group has managed to get some of their members on college and university faculties. Most of these professors are in the History and Political Science departments.

"Apparently Dr. Simpson was their key person on the Willow Wood College campus. Tony Berry surmised this when he read the first line of the message. He knew it was meant for Simpson, the one originally scheduled to read the paper he presented." Logan continued, "Berry was no fool; he knew they had to recover the document and kept it secret. Even though he planned to get rid of the paper by passing it on to his friend, Berry knew he would be eliminated because he might have read it.

"Now, the Fontaines are in the same danger. If they have seen the news, and put the pieces together; they realize they must disappear. Apparently, they tried to get rid of the document by throwing it in a junked washing machine. That, unfortunately, doesn't remove the danger. Mitchell is gone, but there will be others who will hunt them down. The group will do anything to remain undetected. They have no idea we have an informant imbedded in the group already."

TWENTY-ONE

Ending

D ave woke up. Where was he? In a dark room? No, it wasn't a room unless rooms could move. It must be the cabin of a small houseboat. The muddy smell of the water along with the gentle movement left no doubt in his mind. How did he get there? The last thing he remembered was Brosia's car driving down the road like a bat out of hell. Then everything went black. He knew Mitch was dead; it must have been Joe who had found him. How could he, when he had been so careful?

He tried to sit up but couldn't. Ropes, no the restraints were too smooth to be rope; some type of smooth cord bound his hands and feet to a small bed. Again, he struggled against his bindings; he found the task impossible.

A voice came from across the cabin. "I see you're awake. There is no reason to try to escape this time. I've taken precautions to be sure you don't slip through my fingers again. My boss wasn't too happy last time when I couldn't produce the package or you. "I'm curious, how did you find out I was out there ready to take you both and get the truth out of you?"

"I don't know what you're talking about," David said.

"Then it must have been your wife who saw me row to the back of the house. That was why she took off with the old lady and the package. Didn't she tip you off? It doesn't really matter; I would have eventually caught you even if you had run."

He flipped on the light and walked toward his captive. Dave saw the syringe in Joe's hand just before he realized what was about to happen. First, the sting of the needle, next the feel of the drug entering his body. Then, when his inhibitions were lowered, he began to answer the innocent questions Joe asked to determine when the drug had taken full effect. Dave answered all Joe's questions, giving truthful information. The only exception was the one thing he was supposed to know, the location of the document he had to recover.

"Well, I guess you were telling the truth all along. You're no use to me; it's your wife who knows what I need." He cut the cords and pulled Dave to his feet. "You're going for a little swim."

Dave stumbled as Joe walked him to the boat and pushed him in. The two men sat in the boat, one slumped forward, head hanging down, the other rowing the boat deeper into the swamp. The boat slowed to a stop; an oar came out of the water and knocked the victim unconscious before pushing him into the water. The sound of the oars moving through the water resumed. He rowed back and laughed at how easy it had been. There wasn't even a struggle. He was taken care of, now to find her.

He rowed back the way they had come. The car was parked next to the houseboat waiting with the keys still in the ignition. He got in and drove down the overgrown dirt road until he came to the highway. It might take a while to find her, but he wouldn't stop until he did.

When he was safely away from the place where he had disposed of the body, finding Anastasia and the package dominated his thoughts.

I really know so little about her. Did she have a friend who would believe her wild story and take her in? Maybe he should go to the college and ask a few questions. No, that would draw much too much attention; besides, that would be too obvious a place to hide.

Someone hid her after the wreck. That was the logical place for her to go. She would go back to that hick town and the people who hid her before. He must be careful about how he went about finding her. He didn't want to be noticed.

Before he did anything else, there was a stop he had to make in New Orleans. He worked his way into the exit lane and left the interstate.

TWENTY-TWO

Guilty

That night Brosia was awakened by a sound she had hoped she would never hear again; Ana was screaming. The old lady rushed to Ana's room and gently stroked her forehead. "Anastasia, wake up; it's all over. You're safe now."

"Oh, Thea," she sobbed as she sat up, and Brosia put her arms around her as she had done so many times when Ana woke up terrified.

"You had the dream again, didn't you?"

Ana nodded, "It was like I was living it again. I drove home, but before I got there, I could see the smoke and flames in the distance. The closer I got, the more horrible it became. I could hear them screaming for me to save them, and I couldn't. I felt so guilty."

"Guilty of what? Living? Of trading places with Lisa so your parents would see what they thought was you when they checked on you in the night? You had nothing to do with the rest of it. The fire department had put most of the fire out before you got there. No one called for you to save them; they were already dead by the time you got there."

"This time in my dream the loudest voice was David's. 'You killed them all, your parents and my cousin. Now you must be punished.'"

"Is that what you meant when you said he never loved you?"

"Yes."

"Ana, you must be wrong. Dave has loved you for as long as I've known him. He doesn't blame you. How could he? You had nothing to do with it. When your father testified against those men, he became a marked man. Don't confuse your nightmare with reality."

"Dave's punished me for Lisa's death for years, threatening to contact her parents and tell them I killed her, threatening to let the burners know that one member of the family they had vowed to kill got away. I couldn't let you know why I broke up with Tony and married David so soon after. That was the price I paid for his silence," Ana said between sobs.

"Ana, no matter what you think about David, remember we left him at my house with a killer in the front yard. I have worried about him ever since. What if he went after Dave when he couldn't get you? I have prayed Dave slept through the noise, and whoever tried to stop us didn't know he was asleep in the house. Ana, have you thought of getting in touch with Raymond? He protected you after your family died. Maybe he could help you now."

"He wasn't able to protect them. Besides, he retired from the Marshal Service years ago."

Brosia said, "It was just a thought. You know you shouldn't blame him. If your father hadn't gone back when your grandmother died…"

"Don't blame my daddy. He needed to be there, and he was disguised."

"But they still recognized him. They knew he would come back."

"Brosia, you know I love you, but there are some thoughts you need to keep to yourself. My memory of him as a brave man who brought down the key players in a crime family is the only one I choose to remember."

"You're right. Why bring up 'what if' and 'if only'? What happened in the past is beyond our control. We need to stay focused on what is happening now." She smiled at Ana. Yes, they needed to focus on the present and the future. She would be calling Raymond herself. You didn't write off a potential resource just because he happened to be an old man.

The next morning Brosia got up and took her cell phone with her on her morning walk. She hadn't walked far when Fran passed her in the patrol car. He waved as he drove past. At least they were keeping an eye out, but that wasn't enough. They needed someone who could protect them all the time, not just drive-by security.

She pulled her phone out and punched in the number she had memorized when he first brought the trembling teenage girl to her. He could have changed it in the intervening years. As she counted the rings, hope diminished. Then the familiar voice came on the line.

"Raymond Patton here," he said.

"Raymond, its Ambrosia."

"Brosia, how are you? You're the last person I would have guessed was calling. After all these years I'm surprised you remembered my number."

"We need your help again, Raymond."

He recognized the fear in her voice. "By we, I take it you mean you and Anastasia."

"Yes, she's in trouble. A man tried to kidnap us the other night. She says he wants to kill her over some package he thinks she has."

"Does she have it?"

"No, I believe her when she says she doesn't. She also thinks Dave is after the package and has threatened her."

"Her husband? That's hard to believe. What has she gotten herself into?"

"I know; I'm having a hard time believing that, too. But she is terrified of him. Last night she had a nightmare about the burning, and in it Dave was accusing her of murder. A preacher who befriended her has arranged for the sheriff to make rounds on a regular basis by the cabin where we're staying. Still, I don't feel that it's enough. She needs more protection than that. I racked my brain to think of a solution. I decided it is you. Could you come to Alabama and stay with us?"

"Hold on just a minute, Brosia, I'm just a retired, old man, no longer a U.S. Marshal. Furthermore, you'd have to be a fool not to know Ana has never forgiven me for not being able to protect her family, and I know you're no fool. This idea of yours isn't a very good one."

"I know everything you said is true, but you are my only hope. I know that man meant business. I saw the look in his eyes before I hit him in the head and dazed him. He is a killer. Tony Berry, that young man Ana dated before she met Dave, has already been killed over that package."

"You hit a man hard enough to daze him? Maybe you don't need help."

"It's a long story; I'll tell you all about it when you get here. You will come, won't you, Raymond?"

"Of course, just give me a minute to find something so I can write the address."

She gave him the address and disconnected, feeling a sense of relief.

☙

Brosia poured her second cup of coffee and joined Ana at the breakfast table. She took a sip to delay, at least for a second, broaching the subject she knew Ana wouldn't easily accept. "Ana, darling, I did something yesterday I know you won't like. I called Raymond."

"You didn't! You know how I feel about that man. I told you not to call him."

"I do know how you feel, but I know it's the right thing to do. He'll be here tonight or in the morning. You don't want him here because of what happened to your family, but who else can we call? What happened with the burners years ago may have something to do with what is going on now. He is the only other person who knows your background and is willing to help."

"My background, is that what you call the murder of my family and best friend because he didn't protect Daddy the way he was supposed to?"

"Ana, be reasonable. You know he did everything he could to keep your family safe. I'm not blaming your father for what happened. People, obsessed with revenge, will find a way to extract it. But you can't continue to blame Raymond after all these years."

"I know you think, as a mature woman, I should be reasonable and accept that the things that happened that night were unavoidable, but I just can't. Part of me is still a frightened, devastated teenage girl who can't trust that man."

"Ana, that doesn't matter. The only thing that does is the fact we need protection, and Raymond is on his way here and willing to help us. I would appreciate it if you would try to disguise your hostility to him. You don't have to gush and pretend you're thrilled he's here, but at least be pleasant."

"I don't have a choice, do I? You know I won't be rude to him; I have outgrown that at least, and I'll try to graciously accept whatever protection he can provide. That's the most I can promise, Brosia."

"That's all I ask, Ana. I'm sorry I did this behind your back, but I knew you would never agree."

❧

Why had he let Brosia talk him into this? He realized that he still felt responsible for both of them. He finished packing his bag; then he took a lockbox from the top shelf of his closet and retrieved the gun he hadn't carried since the day he retired. He strapped on his shoulder holster, put on his jacket, and looked at himself in the mirror. He smiled at his reflection. Once again, he was Marshal Patton, ready for duty. An older version, it was true, but his body was still toned from the exercise routine he'd never abandoned. He was prepared to meet any resistance he might encounter, any except Ana's steadfast loathing of him.

He had been retired for several years and was happy enough for the first few months. But soon he found the day-to-day sameness of his retirement to be a boring, mind-dulling sentence. He missed the responsibility of the job. That was one more reason he had said yes when Brosia called.

The drive from New Orleans to the small Alabama town was uneventful. Familiar Louisiana wetlands gave way to the piney woods of Mississippi. As he neared Eastabuchie County, the Smoky Mountain foothills were a pleasant change of scenery. Soon he would see the family he created the night he took the frightened girl to the lonely widow of his old friend, Sully Leblanc.

He last saw her, not a fiery teenager who hated him, but a frightened bride, on her wedding day. He had thought she was just nervous about getting married as the justice of the peace made the brief remarks that bound the two together. Thinking back on what Brosia had told him, perhaps Ana really was afraid.

He and Brosia hosted the small wedding. Now the best man, Tony Berry, was dead; and the sweet little maid of honor was a widow. Ana was having nightmares about her groom, running for her life and accepting help once more from the man she detested. Had she had a premonition of all of these things on her wedding day? The little group that watched knew her life was changing but didn't realize her life ceased to be her own that day.

Raymond wondered about her feelings toward him. Did she still hate him with the same intensity, or had maturity opened her eyes to the truth?

T W E N T Y - T H R E E

Normal

Ana was at her easel working on a painting for Bax's office. It was to be a gift to thank him for all he'd done for her since the afternoon she'd first visited his office. Brosia had picked up Ana's art supplies when she and Lovie went on a shopping trip. Lovie was happy her friend had a new hobby to keep her mind off her troubles.

Strangely the two women had developed a friendship even though Brosia couldn't be totally honest with her new friend. They had planned several outings since Lovie showed up with curiosity and pie. Today Brosia had gone with Lovie to the garden center to pick out plants for an herb garden. She wanted to buy some potted herbs so she would have a renewable supply for her signature dishes.

Ana smiled. Somehow Brosia could use her charm to win people over and get what she wanted. She had been dead set against bringing Raymond back into her life, but Brosia had won that battle with a mixture of charm and underhanded trickery. Yet, now that he was here, she did feel safer.

She was lost in thought when a noise surprised her and she involuntarily gasped.

"Sorry, I didn't mean to startle you. I'm just going out to see if Bax got any mail today," Raymond said.

She watched as the remarkably fit white-haired man went out the side door. She was just on edge today. She shouldn't have been surprised; it was time for the mail to run. Raymond never varied from his routine, and he'd taken on the task of checking the mail every afternoon. Nothing but catalogues and sale papers ever came; still it gave him something to do.

Ana went into the kitchen and poured a cup of coffee. She returned to the easel, sipping her coffee as she reviewed her canvas for a few minutes. Before she resumed painting, she checked her watch. Raymond had been out there a long time. Either the mail was late, or he was talking to the carrier, making the man late getting to the rest of the houses on the route. She would call him and see what was holding him up.

She called Raymond's cell phone and got a busy signal. Well, that explained it; he was as big of a phone addict as any man she had ever met. *Whoever said women were the biggest talkers hadn't spent much time with a retired man who was used to being in charge of a large number of people. Those retired workaholics thought unless they were in contact with someone, they were not doing their job.*

She went back to her canvas and lost herself in her work. When she finally heard the side door open again, she said, "It's about time you came back. I was getting worried. Did Bax get any mail?"

"Hello, Ana."

She spun around and saw Dave standing in the doorway. He started walking toward her.

"How did you find me?"

"What? No 'Thank goodness you're safe, Dave?' But to answer your question, I checked out all of Brosia's relatives. There was no way she would leave without making some contact. Finally, I remembered that nephew of her husband's. He told me she had taken a hearse and left him her VW."

He was so close to her; she could feel his breath.

"I had an idea you might come back to this area. It's obvious someone in the area helped hide you. Every time I stopped for gas, I asked if a hearse had gassed up there lately. It was a long shot, but finally a guy said, 'Yeah, and a pretty blonde was driving it.' That confirmed my guess."

He reached up and stroked her short, blonde hair and whispered, "I liked it better the way it was." She cringed as he slowly slid his hand from her hair to her shoulders and then down her arm before sliding it into his jacket pocket.

"It took a while but I kept my eyes open and played my hunches. One afternoon I followed the Sheriff's car out this way. Of course, I kept my distance. There in the yard was Brosia talking to some woman in a red truck. Bingo!"

"Why did you follow me? I told you I don't know what happened to that package. I can't help you find it."

"I came because you're my wife, and you belong with me, to me...till death us do part as the preacher said. Oh, but we didn't have a church wedding, did we? Just a justice of the peace. Just the same, you'll never be free until one of us dies."

She felt the muzzle of a gun press against her side. "They say killing gets easier with practice; you should know," he said as he pushed the muzzle of his great uncle's gun against her ribs. He knew he would need it when he retrieved it from Brosia's house before he started his search for Ana.

"Dave, you know I didn't kill Lisa!"

"No, you didn't light the fire, but you caused her death just the same. My aunt and uncle have been tormented with uncertainty all these years not knowing if their daughter is alive are dead. You jumped out of the car and ran toward the house when they rolled out those three gurneys with the bodies. They pushed you back before you could get near. You just stood there with your hands over your face, screaming. Finally, you ran to Lisa's car and drove away. You were the one that should have died!"

"You were there that night!"

"Of course, I was; I set the fire. My grandfather, the man your father destroyed, got in touch with me through one of his men. He said all of my educational expenses would be taken care of if I'd do a little favor for him, destroy your family. But you got away, so I had to let Lisa's mother and father believe their little angel had run away so that the old man would be satisfied and live up to our agreement. When I recognized you with Tony at that party, I realized there was a different way to take care of you. I could have you and destroy you at the same time, but you've ruined that.

"Now, I have no choice. You know too much about me and nothing about the one thing I must recover. Start walking; there's no reason to mess up your friend's cabin."

He walked her out of the cabin toward the black sedan parked just out of sight from the house. As they got closer, Ana noticed she could see him behind her reflected in the car's tinted windows. She watched carefully hoping to see an opportunity to escape. Just before they reached the car, he turned his head and looked over his shoulder as if he had heard something. In that split second of distraction, she bolted and ran toward the woods.

He raised his gun and squeezed off three well-aimed shots. The bullets tore into her leg, shoulder, and chest. She fell face down, unmoving as a fourth shot split the air.

Deputy Eugene Shoemaker lowered his gun, ran to Dave's crumpled body, and checked for a pulse; then he ran to Ana. Raymond was checking her pulse. "How is she?" Eugene asked.

"Her pulse is weak, but she's still alive. I'd call an ambulance, but I'm afraid if we wait for it to get her, she'll be gone. Do you have any plastic wrap or sheeting in your car? We need to cover that chest wound to keep it from sucking air before we do anything else?"

"No."

"I'll go back to the cabin. I'm sure Bax has something we can use."

"I'll call the ambulance for Fontaine and load her in my car; and you can drive her to the hospital while I wait here with him," Eugene said.

"We wouldn't be able to stretch her out in the back seat. There is a hearse in the garage. There would be plenty of room in the aisle between the seats on each side for her to stretch out. I can put pillow and blankets down and be at the hospital before they can get here with the ambulance."

Eugene said, "You're right. I'm not even going to ask why there's a hearse with seats in Bax's garage. While you're there, have your head injury checked out."

While Raymond got the hearse, Eugene made the necessary calls. When Raymond returned, they covered the wound with plastic and loaded her in the makeshift ambulance. He drove like a maniac down the curvy country roads. When he arrived at the hospital, the staff was waiting. They took her away; then it was his turn to wait.

He had known her before her name was Anastasia. Anna-Marie Michon, the name she was given along with a new identity, had come to him the night her parents died. The dress she had worn to the party reeked of smoke. He never saw such a pathetic sight, a girl who had lost everything, who had no one to go to except the man she held responsible.

She called him "Uncle Marshal" back then before he had failed her, broken his promise to protect her family. He had failed her again. Brosia had wanted him to protect Ana, and now she was fighting for her life.

A tall sandy-haired man approached him. "Pardon me, are you the man who brought in Mrs. Fontaine?"

"Yes, how is she doing, doctor?"

"I'm not her doctor; I'm Bax Alford, a friend who let her stay in my cabin. Thad Brownlee called and told me what happened.

First, he chewed me out for not being up front with him when I asked for a security patrol because a lady was staying at the cabin. I just told him Brosia was frightened, staying out there alone, after so many break-ins had been reported. They didn't even know Ana-Grace was there."

"Is that why the deputy got to the cabin so soon after I called the sheriff's office and reported Dave had attacked me at the cabin where Ana was staying?"

"Yes, he was probably on his way before you called. When Thad or one of the deputies was out toward my cabin, they would drive by. In addition, every two hours, one of them made a scheduled security run. They took my request seriously, even though I didn't tell them all I should have. Ana-Grace made me promise not to tell anyone she was here."

"I'm Raymond Patton; I'm glad Ana found a friend who tried to protect her. This time I'm afraid we both failed her, pastor. He shot her three times. She was so weak from loss of blood when I got her here, I don't know if she'll make it."

"All we can do for her now is pray," Bax said as he bowed his head.

eɔ

Lovie and Brosia finished their shopping at the garden center. The truck was loaded with one of every herb the store stocked. The women were pleased with their success and spent the trip back to Bax's cabin in companionable gossip.

"Did you hear about the ruckus over at Brother Burns's church in Westover?" Lovie asked knowing full well that Brosia didn't know anything about Rev. Burns or the community of Westover, but the story was too interesting not to share. "The congregation is about ready to run the preacher off."

"No, goodness. What did he do to bring about such a thing?" Brosia asked with real interest. When it comes to good gossip, it's not necessary to know any of the principals to enjoy the rumors.

"He told the congregation that certain foods would no longer be allowed at church suppers. No more green beans with cream of mushroom soup and canned fried onions or desserts that have Cool Whip as the main ingredient can be brought to any covered dish meal at the church. Can you imagine that? Folks might have been able to live with that, but when he put a ban on fried chicken, it was more than they could take."

Brosia laughed and said, "Some folks say fried chicken is the sacrificial bird of all Southern Christian churches."

"It's no joke, Brosia. One of the elders asked Brother Burns what dietary law he was following. He pointed out that as strict as the rules in Leviticus and Deuteronomy are, the banning of fried chicken and Cool Whip weren't mentioned one way or another.

"Then the preacher said he was worried about their hearts what with all that extra fat clogging up their blood vessels, not to mention expanding their waistlines."

"I can see how that could be a problem for some people, but I'm not sure that falls under the pastoral duties of the preacher," Brosia said, as she fought to stifle a laugh.

"That is just what I'm getting to. The same elder stood up and said, 'Your business is to help us get our hearts in the right relationship with the Lord. Leave the conditions of our circulatory systems to our cardiologists.'"

Lovie and Brosia were still exploring the problems at the church in Westover when they turned down the road to the cabin. Brosia said, "What's going on down there? There's a police car down close to the cabin. Something's wrong; the deputies drive by but never stop." They drove around a curve, and an ambulance parked across from the cabin came into view. "Dear Lord, please don't let anything have happened to my Ana."

Lovie was puzzled. "I thought you lived alone. Who's Ana?"

Brosia didn't hear her; she was mesmerized by the scene playing out before her. Someone was being loaded into the ambulance. "He followed us here and found her! She was so afraid he would. What has he done to my sweet girl?"

Lovie pulled the truck over and stopped. Both women scrambled out and ran toward the ambulance just as the doors shut, and it sped away. Then Thad walked from the edge of the woods where yellow tape cordoned off a bloody area. Brosia ran toward him, wailing.

"No! It can't be! He killed her; he killed my Anastasia."

Thad took her in his arms and began to reassure her. "Calm down, Miss Brosia, that isn't Anastasia; it's David Fontaine. Raymond Patton called me after he regained consciousness and told me what was happening.

"Eugene was on his way for a routine security check when I got the call. I radioed him and told him what Raymond said. By the time he got here she was running into the woods and David was shooting her. That's when Eugene shot him."

"He shot her? Tell me is my Ana dead?" Brosia asked incredulously.

"She was still alive when your friend, Mr. Patton, took her to the hospital. They are working on her now. I won't lie to you; he shot her three times, and she's lost a lot of blood. But Patton assured me that she is a fighter.

Thad turned to Lovie and asked "Will you drive Miss Brosia to the hospital?"

"Yes, please take me as quickly as you can, Lovie. I can't let her be there all alone."

"She's not alone. Raymond Patton is with her, and I've called Brother Bax. He should be there by now," Thad said as he walked Brosia back to Lovie's truck. "Drive carefully; don't speed. We don't need an accident. The emergency room is overloaded as it is."

Even though she was totally confused, Lovie took Brosia's arm and helped the dazed woman to the truck, jumped in herself, and pushed her old truck to its limit, catching up with the ambulance and passing it.

She couldn't believe what she had just heard. Bax had been hiding a woman in his cabin. Brosia wasn't a widow living alone, and David Fontaine tried to kill his wife. Who was Brosia's friend, Raymond? There are no Pattons around here. Was she the only one who wasn't going crazy? To top it all, Brosia was talking about Grace like the little liar was her daughter. Who could a person trust when their best friend and preacher turn out to be liars?

෴

When the women reached the hospital, they rushed to the waiting room. A tall, older man rose, met Brosia, and took her into his arms. He held her as she sobbed loudly. "She's hanging on, Brosia. You know how strong-willed she can be. This time that may be a blessing."

"Raymond, we tried so hard to protect her all these years. Now she may die because the man we thought she would be safe with tried to kill her. She tried to tell me he hated her and was dangerous, but I was completely fooled by him."

Bax walked over to Lovie and said, "I'm sorry I wasn't honest with you. Ana-Grace came to me and asked for protection. The three of us have been protecting her in one way or another ever since she came to me not long after you picked her up on the road. We didn't tell you everything because we thought the fewer people who knew, the safer she would be. It looks like we were wrong."

"You mean her husband really did abuse her?" Lovie asked.

"Yes, not as much physically where the marks would draw attention, but psychologically where the scars don't show. I didn't know at first because when she originally came to me for help, she hadn't regained her memory. She opened up as we talked over the phone when she began to remember and put a face to the fear that haunted her, even when she believed she was out of danger."

❧

Thad left Fran in charge at the crime scene soon after the ambulance pulled away and arrived at the hospital shortly after Lovie and Brosia got there. Raymond, Bax, and the two ladies were in deep conversation as he entered the waiting area.

"How is she doing?" Thad asked as he joined the group.

"We haven't heard anything yet," Raymond said as he took Brosia's hand. "At least they haven't had anything bad to report. As long as they are working on her, there is hope."

"I didn't expect to see you here so soon. Don't you have paper work to do?" Bax asked.

"Yes, that is one of the reasons I'm here. Raymond, you were the only witness to the shooting. I need to ask you some questions. I know you understand I have to investigate to determine if Eugene was justified in shooting David Fontaine. Eugene is on desk duty until I finish my investigation."

"Sure, I'll be glad to help. I was coming back from checking the mail when I saw movement out of the corner of my eye. Brosia and Ana have been running from one of the men Ana believes kidnapped Dave. The man tried to stop them when they were getting away after Dave hit Ana, but that's another story.

"I became suspicious when I saw a man in the edge of the woods moving close to the cabin. I thought the kidnapper might have followed them here. I veered into the woods with the intention of slipping up behind him and stopping him. When I got closer, I saw it was Dave. He saw me about the same time. He ran at me and knocked me down, and then hit me on the head with the grip of his gun. I tried to get up and stop him, but I found out I couldn't move the way I used to. I'm too old for that now. I called your office when I got to my feet and limped after him."

Raymond continued. "The Deputy must have been patrolling near there because he got there in time to see Dave shoot Ana three times. Thank God, he was able to shoot Dave before he emptied his gun into Ana. If she pulls through, it will be due to that young man's marksmanship. I'll come to your office to make an official statement and answer any questions you have, but now I belong here."

∽

Ryan Moore was the EMT who responded to the shooting. He had been so proud when he finished his training and got his first job. The day-to-day stress had not lessened his love of his work. He was making a difference, sometimes a life-or-death difference, in his patients' lives.

"We've loaded the patient in the ambulance and are rolling. He lost a good bit of blood, but I don't believe the bullet hit any organs. We were able to stop most of the bleeding," he reported to the on-duty ER physician.

"Start the Ringer's lactate. We'll be ready for him," Dr. Jonathan Harper gave the order and disconnected.

Ryan noticed Fontaine was moaning, fully conscious now and feeling the full effects of the bullet in his hip. "I can give you something for the pain. We'll be at the hospital in just a few minutes," he said, as he prepared to give Dave the Ringer's infusion.

"I don't want any pain meds. I want to be clear-headed. I see the bandages on my hip; why is my head splitting?"

"When you fell, you hit your head on a rock. You'll have to be checked for a concussion."

"Is she dead?" Fontaine asked.

"I really don't know, but I think so. Someone said something about a hearse, and you were the only one who needed transport."

The satisfied smile on Dave's face made cold chills run down Ryan's spine. At times like this, when he had the feeling that a patient was emotionally unstable or just plain wicked, he wished he were the one driving, not confined in the compartment with a confused or demented person. Yeah, today he would gladly trade places with Pete.

Dave began to get agitated and struggled against the restraints that held him to the gurney. "You have to get me out of this thing!" Dave begged Ryan. "You know with the blood I've lost, I'm so weak I'm no threat. I have cleithrophobia; you know, the fear of being trapped. If you don't take these things off, I don't know if I can stand the stress. Please, if you have an ounce of mercy in you, get them off me."

Ryan could see that Dave's panic was real. The patient was right; he posed no threat to Ryan. The escalating panic could make his patient harder to deal with when they reached the hospital and had to remove the restraints. An EMT could never tell what behavior could result from extreme phobic panic. He had seen such panic cause patients to injure themselves and others.

"All right, Mr. Fontaine, calm down. I'll take them off if you will just lie still the rest of the way to the hospital." There shouldn't be a problem; the road wasn't rough, and Pete was a good driver, he reasoned.

The ambulance raced around the snaky curves at top speed. Pete O'Hara loved this part of his job. It involved the two things he loved the most, helping people and driving fast. He took just a second to check the text his girl had sent him. How could one man be so lucky? It was hard to believe that a girl like her was in love with him. When he looked up, he was on a collision course with a log truck. He jerked the wheel to avoid driving headlong into the oncoming truck and lost control of the ambulance. It careened down the sloping shoulder of the road.

Ryan had just removed the restraints from Dave's upper body when the ambulance began to tumble. Dave's feet were secured to the gurney which was locked in place. He grabbed the sides of the gurney and held on for dear life until the vehicle came to rest.

He understood the odds of surviving depended on how quickly he could get out of the restraint that held him on the gurney. It had saved his life earlier. He had watched as Ryan's body was thrown about the patient compartment along with loose equipment.

Dave said to himself, "I have to get out of here before this thing explodes!" He tugged and wiggled until his feet were free. As he pulled the IV from his arm, he had an idea, a way he could disappear.

He could smell the leaking gas coming from outside. That along with the tank of oxygen stored under the floorboards made the ambulance a bomb ready to be ignited. He could help along the potential of an explosion, make it a reality, and disappear in the chaos.

He found some alcohol and doused the body of the EMT with the contents. Then he stuffed gauze into the almost empty bottle leaving a gauze wick trailing out. Turning the oxygen on, he left the patient compartment. Once outside, he lit the wick with the cigarette lighter he always carried, tossed it in, and slammed the door.

Dave dropped to the ground and rolled as fast as he could to the little creek that ran at the bottom of the slope. Just as he reached the shallow water, the ambulance exploded. The pressurized oxygen tank under the floorboard enriched the gas-fueled fire that in turn set the dry pine needles on fire.

The drought had turned the countryside into a tinderbox. A wild fire would be a wonderful distraction. All attention would be misdirected, and it would be assumed that he was burned beyond recognition, cremated in this funeral pyre of his own making.

The log truck had lost its load when the driver took measures to avoid hitting the ambulance. Dave could see him slumped in the driver's seat. Dead, unconscious, or just overwhelmed by the problems caused by the wreck, it really didn't matter. Rescuers would have an insurmountable task getting past the spilled logs that completely blocked the road. The flames would get to the log truck long before they would. He couldn't have planned it better.

He followed the creek bed, ignoring the pain and seepage of blood. Determination to survive and adrenalin became his pain blockers. He had to get back to the Wilson place. He thought this was the same stream that ran behind the property. If he followed it, he should come out close to the old man's storm shelter. He never would have thought that the concrete bunker of a storm shelter in Wilson's back yard would be so important to his survival. He almost felt like it was home now. If he could get back there, he would be safe.

Dave was far from being safe. The wild fire lapped at the edge of the stream bed. Only a trickle of water still flowed where once a creek meandered toward the Callahatchie River. He lost his footing and fell in the mud that remained in the creek bed. This might keep his clothes from catching on fire if the flames got too close, so he rolled around in the mud, coating his skin and clothing.

Staggering up, he pushed on, ignoring the pain that increased with every step. When the mud dried to a caked crust, he got down and rolled in the dwindling stream again and continued to his hide-out.

From the creek bed, through the trees, Dave caught sight of the three-foot-high concrete pad that covered the underground safe room. He had gotten through the area where trees were burning and falling. That danger had passed; the wind was blowing the flames up the mountain side, away from Wilson's cabin.

He went to the outdoor water hydrant and washed the mud off his body as best he could. After removing the soggy bandage, he examined the raw open places on his hip and side. Blood was pouring from both entry and exit wounds. He cleaned them with the water hose. Now he needed something to bandage his wounds.

Dave opened the shelter door and climbed down into the place that had been his home from the time he got back to Alabama. Nightly raids on unlocked cars and outbuildings had provided the eclectic mix that furnished his new home. Using a flashlight, he searched for something that could serve as a bandage.

A laundry basket full of clothes yielded clean white socks and a pair of tights. Dave layered socks over his injuries and secured them with the tights. He had thought he might need extra clothes, but he never would have thought he would use them this way. "Thanks, lady." He muttered. He didn't know if she was too forgetful, too busy, or just too lazy to bring them in when she got back from the Laundromat. She just might have saved his life.

Exhausted, Dave spread out his wet clothes, pulled on a pair of much-too-large pajamas, and stretched out on the stolen pool lounge chair that served as his bed. Within minutes he was asleep. As hours passed, he became hot and restless. The throbbing pain in his hip brought him out of his fitful sleep.

He was burning up. He had to get the fever to come down. He rummaged through the piles of supplies he had brought in and found an aspirin bottle. There were only two left. He swallowed them with water from a thermos and poured more of the water on his head.

He stumbled to his makeshift bed and drifted in and out of sleep. When he woke, he had no idea of time, not even if it was day or night. He had taken the last of the aspirin, and the water had run out. There was nothing left to help lower his temperature. I have to have more water. If he didn't cool off, fever this high could cause brain damage.

Dave crawled to the steps and tried to climb them so he could get to the surface and the hydrant with the cool water he had to have. He grabbed the edge of the second tread and tried to pull himself up, but he was too weak. He fell back and slipped into delirium.

He was back in New Orleans watching the flames eat away the house. Ana ran out screaming for help, but no one listened to her. He aimed his uncle's gun and shot her over and over. When she finally dropped, he dragged her to his boat and paddled deep in the swamp where he dumped her lifeless body. As soon her body hit the water, the swamp exploded in flames. The heat was unbearable.

Dave finally woke up. His clothes were soaked with perspiration. The pain in his hip had become so intense he began to cry. He was dying; there was no one or nothing to help him. His safe place would be his tomb. It was all Ana's fault. He should have killed her when he recognized her at LSU. Instead, he wanted her for himself. He had played with her like a cat does a mouse before the final kill.

He had buried himself in this mausoleum. What a surprise that old man would have the next time he came here for shelter. Those were his last thoughts before darkness washed over him.

Waiting

"Mrs. LeBlanc, your niece's condition has been stabilized enough to fly her to UAB. The University of Alabama at Birmingham Hospital is a level-one trauma center. Her condition is too serious for our small local hospital. I'm sure the doctor talked to you about that when you agreed to have her sent there as soon as possible."

"Yes, I know that UAB is her only chance. Mr. Patton is going to drive me there so I can be there when she regains consciousness. Thank you for all you and the rest of the staff have done for her."

The nurse patted the old lady on the shoulder and said, "I'll be praying for her."

When the nurse left the little group, Lovie and Bax came over to Brosia. Lovie hugged her friend and asked, "Is there anything I can do to help you?"

"There is no telling how long we will be there. Would you go to the cabin and pack a bag for me? My medication is in a little black make-up bag in the top drawer of the dresser. Just bring a few changes of clothes and my house shoes. My toothbrush and hair brush are in the bathroom."

"I'll be glad to. I will be coming back every day unless there is a family emergency that Billy Ray can't handle. Raymond, I'll pack for you, if you want."

Bax said, "I'll handle that. I need to do something to feel useful, besides keeping you company here in the waiting room. Is there anything special you want me to bring?"

"I've been living out of my suitcase. It's behind the sleeper sofa. My shaving kit is in the drawer in the side table next to the sofa.

"Brosia, I'll pull the car around. We need to start driving."

"Lovie and I will head to UAB as soon as we get your things together. We shouldn't be more than a half hour behind you."

The trip to the hospital was uneventful. Raymond and Brosia were both silent most of the trip, lost in their own thoughts as they drove. When they finally got to the surgery waiting room, Ana had already arrived, and the operation was well underway.

Brosia recognized Lovie's voice as she came down the hall talking to Bax. She looked up and saw her friend with a suitcase in one hand and a tangle of ribbons connected to a collection of balloons that bobbed over her head in the other. She couldn't help but smile at the sight of the two of them. Bax and Lovie were so different, yet they both shared the same sincere, caring way. Friends like Bax and Lovie were what she needed to get through this ordeal.

"Have you heard anything yet?" Bax asked as he sat down next to Brosia.

"No, and she's been in the operating room for hours," Brosia answered.

"I've told Brosia that surgery on the wound like Ana has takes a long time to heal. She was shot in the arm as well as the chest. I know from experience there is nothing simple about any gunshot wound. It isn't the way it looks on television when MacGyver gets shot in the arm, rigs a tourniquet using his shoestrings, makes a bandage from a handkerchief, and then continues to pursue the shooter, firing his gun with his other hand. We want them to take all the time they need," Raymond said.

"I'm sure you two haven't eaten. Can I get you anything?" Bax asked.

"I don't have an appetite," Brosia said, "but Raymond might want something."

The old man shook his head.

The little group waited for news, alternately pacing, praying, and making meaningless conversation to calm nervousness.

After what seemed an eternity, the doctor finally came out. "Which of you is Mrs. Fontaine's next of kin?"

Brosia stood up and said, "She's my niece. I took her in after her parents died, when she was seventeen. How is she, doctor?"

"The shoulder was only grazed. She was lucky there. She could have lost the use of her arm, if it had shattered the clavicle. The chest wound is more complicated because there is hemothorax…"

"I've never heard of that; what is it?" Brosia asked.

"Blood has collected in the pleural cavity, the space between the chest wall and the lung. I did a tube thoracotomy. In layman's terms, I inserted a drain to remove the blood. Problems with the drain are not uncommon. There can be infection, as well as blood clots. It requires intensive maintenance to keep the line open and prevent clotting.

"The nurses will tap and milk the tubes to keep them flowing. In the event this doesn't work, the tubes would have to be replaced. There is the possibility I might have to open her up and remove the clots, if the tubes don't work as they should.

"She is in the recovery room now and will go from there to ICU. You will be advised of her condition if there is any change."

He walked away, leaving them relieved that she had survived the surgery and stunned at the prospect of the complications he outlined.

After nervously waiting for what seemed endless hours, the nurse came into the ICU waiting room and approached the little group of Ana's friends. "You may see her now, but only two at a time and keep the visit to five minutes or less."

As next of kin, Brosia would go in first. "Raymond, come with me. I don't think I can face seeing her alone." The nurse ushered Brosia and Raymond to the cubical in ICU where Ana was sleeping. The sight of her connected to so many monitors and IVs, with tubes for oxygen, and tubes to drain the blood trapped in her chest brought back Brosia's memories of Sully's last trip to the hospital. He never regained consciousness.

"Oh, Raymond, she looks so frail. She looks the way Sully looked just before…"

"Remember, hearing is the first sense to return when someone is unconscious. We only need positive talk when we are with her," he whispered as he slipped his arm around Brosia's heaving shoulders. She nodded, unable to speak as the tears poured down her cheeks.

"Ana, we love you. You have to do what the doctors tell you so you can come home. Brosia will make some of her special dishes, and with her care, you'll be back to your old self soon.

"Don't worry about David. He will never bother you or anyone else again," Raymond said.

Finally, Brosia gained control of her emotions. "My darling girl, you are so dear to me. I need my Anastasia back home. I love you so much." The tears started again. She buried her face on Raymond's chest to sniffle her sobs.

"We will be back later. They won't let us stay but a few minutes," Raymond said and led Brosia out of the ICU.

When they returned to the ICU waiting room, they saw Thad had joined Lovie and Bax.

"How was she?" he asked.

"When we were with her, she was sleeping, but they say she's stable," Raymond said.

"She looks awful. It broke my heart to see her that way," Brosia added.

"I didn't come by just to check on Mrs. Fontaine. While she was being transported here, the ambulance that was carrying her husband was involved in a wreck. There was an explosion and fire that spread to the woods next to Craig Creek. That fire is still not under control. We haven't been able to recover any of the bodies, but it is pretty clear that no one could have survived."

"That's terrible! Dave deserved to die after what he tried to do to Ana, but not the EMTs. Those poor boys were just doing their jobs," Brosia said.

"At least, Ana won't have to worry about Dave any more. Now, we just have to worry about the man who tried to take Ana and Brosia in Louisiana."

છ

Ana's recovery was slow and often uncertain. The nurses were constantly tapping and milking her chest tubes to prevent clotting. Brosia prayed their constant attention would be enough to keep the drains working as they should. Dr. Boone came out to the waiting room and approached her.

"Mrs. Leblanc, I was hoping to avoid this, but I'm afraid I'm going to have to open Mrs. Fontaine's chest to remove the clots and reset the drains. This was a possibility from the beginning. I have ordered that she be prepped for surgery first thing in the morning. If you have any questions, I'll answer them if I can."

"Is she going to be all right after this operation?"

"I'm sorry, that is one of the questions I can't answer. I'll do my best, and you and that pastor friend of yours keep up your praying." With that, he walked out.

The next morning the same group of friends waited to hear the outcome to the surgery. Bax and Raymond sat on either side of Brosia. "I understand how worried you are. Just remember,

Dr. Boone may be curt, but he is the best thoracic surgeon in the state," Bax said.

"I know, but it's like she's been cursed. Just think of all the bad things that have happened to her."

Before either of the men could say anything, Lovie came in with a picnic basket. "I thought you might like some coffee and cookies. I packed a thermos of coffee and some snicker doodles. This may be a long wait, and we'll need the energy. I know none of us want to leave here to grab a bite in the cafeteria because there might some news on her condition while we're out."

"One thing I like about you, Lovie. Others may bring cheery smiles and platitudes, but you're practical. You bring something that really helps–cookies," Raymond said as he poured coffee into one of the Styrofoam cups Lovie pulled out of the basket and handed it to Brosia.

The others laughed at Raymond's quip; tension was broken for a moment. Bax was stung by the remark. He knew Raymond thought he was a platitude peddler. But he felt if Ana-Grace survived, God would use all that had happened to her to change her life in a positive way.

The time dragged by as it always does under enforced waiting for something as important as this. Brosia tried to read a magazine while Raymond worked a crossword puzzle. Lovie had taken some of her cookies to the volunteer at the desk and was giving her the recipe. Only Bax was pacing back and forth, while he fervently prayed for Grace. Her suffering was not just physical. He prayed for a total healing but knew her emotional healing could not begin until she was able to forgive herself for what had happened to her best friend.

"Mrs. Leblanc," the doctor's voice got the attention of all four of them. "Mrs. Fontaine is in the recovery room. Everything went well. The nurse will let you know when she is back in ICU."

"Thank you, Doctor." Brosia was relieved but knew this was only one small step in a long trek that had just begun.

ℰↃ

After the successful surgery this time, Ana's recovery proceeded on schedule. Brosia no longer had to steel herself each time she went in ICU. The progress was undeniable. Brosia noticed a change in the nurse's expression. She came with a big smile on her face and said, "Mrs. Fontaine, the doctor just gave orders to move you to a private room. Transportation will be here shortly." After delivering what she thought was good news, the nurse walked out, leaving Brosia and Raymond alone with Ana.

"Don't let them move me, Brosia. They're so protective of the patients in ICU. Dave can't hurt me here." Ana looked terrified; tears were welling in her eyes.

"Ana, no one is going to hurt you again. Raymond told you the ambulance carrying him to the hospital exploded when it ran off the road and hit a tree. Dave, the EMT, and driver were all killed. I've seen the wreckage; there is no way he could have escaped. He's dead, darling; he will never be able to do anything to you."

"They haven't found his body, Brosia. There is no proof that he was killed. Everyone thought I died in the fire, but I didn't. He may still be out there planning another way to kill me. Killing is easy for him. He stood on my street and watched as the fire he set killed my parents and Lisa. He thought it was me on that stretcher, not his cousin. Then he saw me running away and planned another way to destroy me. Now that I know he set that fire, he won't stop until he kills me."

"Ana, we don't have a choice; you don't need intensive care anymore, thank God, and they need this space for someone who does. I understand why you are afraid. Raymond and I will protect you just like we did when you went to him for help back then. Someone will stay with you at all times. I know Lovie and her girls will be glad to sit with you when I have to go somewhere."

"Thea, you know how much I love you. Lovie and the girls have been wonderful, but he could slip in my room and kill all of us."

"I promise you, he will not come, but if it will ease your mind, we'll have someone guard your door. They could see him coming and call for help before he even got close. Raymond, Billy Ray, Louis, Bubba, and Junior can take turns. Even Bax might be able to relieve one of them when he is here visiting you and his hospitalized church members. Would that make you feel safer?"

"Yes, but you can't be sure they'll be willing to do that. They all have their own lives. I can't ask them to devote so much time to me."

"Ana, if they knew they could provide the security you need to relax enough to heal physically and emotionally, they would have already volunteered."

"All right, I guess your plan will work. Call them and see if they're willing to help."

"I don't have to call Raymond; he's in the waiting room now. We'll be waiting for you in your new room." Brosia said, as the orderly came in to transport Ana from her haven in ICU to the room that left her unprotected.

The transfer was uneventful. After a week, the little group fell into a routine of around the clock protection for the emotional and physically-fragile woman. They had all hoped that after the two surgeries and pneumonia she had fought in ICU, her recovery would proceed with no more problems.

Doctor Boone put those hopes to rest when he examined her Monday morning. "I'm afraid you've relapsed with pneumonia, Mrs. Fontaine. I'll start treatment immediately."

"Will you be moving her back to ICU?" Brosia asked.

"No, I think we can successfully treat her here."

"It seems like I'm the frog in the well that jumps forward three feet every night and slides down two every morning. He might get out eventually, if he doesn't run out of strength and doesn't give up, but he will be a much older, extremely tired frog," Ana said.

The doctor left the room. Brosia went to Ana's bedside and stroked her forehead. She didn't need a thermometer to know Ana was burning up with fever. She had been pumped full of antibiotics ever since she was admitted. Brosia didn't know what else the doctor could do to fight the infection. With all that crazy talk about being a frog in a well, she wondered if Ana was out of her mind from fever. Then again, it did make sense in a way.

Raymond had just returned to his post at Ana's hospital room door. Bax, who had taken his place long enough to give him a lunch break, was freed up for a quick visit with Ana before he drove back to Eastabuchie County.

A candy striper with a tray of mail approached the door to Ana's room. Bax opened the door for a young volunteer and followed her in. "Mail time," the cheerful candy striper announced. "Every morning you win the most popular patient contest. I've never seen so many get-well cards for one person." Ana smiled when the stack of cards was placed on her bedside table.

"Do you want me to read them to you, Ana?"

Ana nodded, and Brosia began to read. After she had read several cards aloud, she heard slow steady breathing. Ana had gone back to sleep. The sleep will do more good than the well wishes, she thought.

"Well, I guess I can read the rest later," Brosia said as she started to put back the envelope she had just opened. When she did, a small piece of lined paper fluttered out of the plain envelope. Brosia read the note and frowned. "Listen to this, Bax. 'He cast upon them the fierceness of his anger, wrath, and indignation, and trouble, by sending evil angels among them.' What does that mean? It surely isn't a typical get-well card."

"Let me see that, Brosia," Bax said as he took a tissue out and reached for the note. *If he didn't know better, he would suspect Lovie. She had the ridiculous suspicion that Ana-Grace was an evil angel.* The ominous tone of the quote sounded threatening, and he knew Thad would want to check it for fingerprints. "I recognize the quote; it is from Psalms 78, but they left out the last part. 'Help us, oh God of our salvation, for the glory of Thy name, and deliver us and purge away our sins, for Thy name's sake.' I think Thad might be interested in this. It probably is nothing, but you are right, it isn't the spiritually up-lifting quote you'd expect in a get-well card."

Bax carefully wrapped the card and envelope in the tissue and put them in his shirt pocket. Could the man Brosia had attacked with her HandyBar have found the two women as Dave had done? Then again how many criminals would be that well-versed in scripture? He frowned when he recalled how many people with head-knowledge of the Bible had been in the news for their criminal behavior. Their knowledge had not touched their hearts, turned them to God, or changed their lives.

TWENTY-FIVE

New Information

"It seems like the Federal investigation into the papers Lovie brought in is trying to set a new record for slowness. We turned that packet over to the Feds months ago," Thad said. He glanced at Fran and saw that this had become a mantra Fran was tired of hearing.

Thad was just as impatient to find out what, if anything, the Federal agents found out from the papers with the thinned spots on their brown-paper wrapper. He had been told by many he would never learn anything from the tight-lipped investigators. This Monday morning, he was more than a little surprised when Fran told him he was transferring a call from Abe to his desk phone.

"Agent Abe, Thad Brownlee here, what can I do for you?"

"We are following up on some of the facts that have come to light after we got the package and the key. I understand that Fontaine shot his wife and was being transported to a hospital when the ambulance carrying him exploded."

"That's right," Thad said suppressing the urge to ask questions.

"Was his body ever found?"

"No, there were heavily charred body parts found spread over a wide area, but no complete bodies were found. So far none have matched Fontaine's DNA. The fire after the explosion was fueled by dried pine needles. It took days to get it under control, so I wouldn't be surprised if we never find his body."

"How is his wife doing? I need to ask her a few questions."

"She's not doing very well at this point in time. After the first surgery they had to open her up again to remove some blood clots in her chest cavity. Just when she seemed to be recovering from that, she developed pneumonia. They thought she was over it and moved her to a private room. Just the other day I heard she had relapsed, and the doctors say it could go either way. She was so weakened by the gunshot and loss of blood, combined with the toll the two surgeries took; she doesn't have much strength left to fight pneumonia."

There was a long pause before Abe spoke again. "You stay in close contact with her friends and family, don't you?"

"Yes, I talk to Miss Brosia on the phone every day and stop by when I can."

"Because Mrs. Fontaine might not be alive, much less lucid, by the time I can get there to question her, I want you to check something out for me. The next time you talk to her aunt, ask her to call you as soon as her niece is well enough to talk to you. I'm sending a sketch of a tattoo. It is the same as the one on the foot of the man found near the white limo. I just received information that one like it was on the foot of a body that surfaced in a swamp near Bayou Gauche a while back.

"Since we know the first body was connected to Fontaine, and the second was found near where Mrs. Fontaine went when she felt threatened, we want to know if it means anything to her. I know it's a long shot, but sometimes long shots hit the bull's eye."

"I'll be glad to help."

"We have an operative who infiltrated a home-grown terrorist group called the Vipers. He was recruited only a year ago, and his information is limited. The Council only lets the individual Snakes know what little information they need in order to carry out the movement's grand plan. What he has found out is the Vipers target disenchanted college students. We believe there is a leader of a node on most campuses in the country. He or she is a trusted faculty member."

Abe continued. "That could also be a link to the Fontaines. Simmons was on the council of the Supreme Serpents. The package was apparently meant for him as Tony Berry surmised. Both David Fontaine and Tony Berry taught in the same department as Simmons at Willow Wood. He was an associate professor at LSU, before he became a full professor at Willow Wood, and did research at his old school when he wrote a history of LSU while they were undergraduates there. They could have been early recruits.

"If Berry had been a Snake in Simmons' node, he wouldn't have seen the package as something he would be willing to risk his life for to protect others. Fontaine tried to kill his wife in an attempt to find out where the package is. My money is on him being one of Simmons' followers."

Thad tried to take in the implications of all this information as Abe kept talking.

"The men who delivered the package were merely errand boys who answer to the council. The Vipers don't use any form of communication other than coded documents delivered by couriers. This time that security measure may bring about their downfall. Using the key, we have been able to identify all the council members and their plans for the near future. With that information we may be able to put them out of business for good."

"You said they were home-grown terrorists, but the message was written in a Middle Eastern language."

"That was a red herring; misdirection, just in case the message was intercepted, it would lead investigators to suspect foreign involvement. Thank you for your cooperation. Contact me as soon as you can find out what Mrs. Fontaine knows about the tattoo or the Vipers. I gave my private number to your deputy. Good bye."

"Good bye, Agent Abe."

He hung up the phone and looked up at his deputy. "What do you know; we have been tasked by a Federal Agent to get information on a possible terrorist connection to Fontaine. I better call Miss Brosia and find out if Ana has improved enough to talk."

Thad got off his phone and returned to Fran's desk. "We're going to Birmingham; Eugene will be in charge of the office while we're gone. While I was talking to Brosia, the fax from Abe came in. Look at this."

Thad handed the fax to Fran. The design looked somewhat like a Celtic knot of snakes with pit viper heads at twelve, two, four, eight, and ten o'clock positions. "What is this supposed to mean?" Fran asked.

"I have no idea, but it was on two bodies that were found where Ana, Dave, or both of them have been recently. Abe wants to know if Ana knows anything about it. There might not be any connection between the tattoos and the Fontaines, but there aren't many clues to follow. Brosia told me Ana is still very weak, but she's lucid. The doctor said she can talk to us for a few minutes."

It was times like this when Fran wished he could call Joy, his girlfriend, and brag about being included in a case that was more exciting than giving their old high school nemesis a parking ticket. That was out of the question at this point; he couldn't talk about an ongoing case involving national security.

The sheriff and deputy arrived at the hospital and went to Ana's room. Billy Ray was sitting in a folding chair just outside the door. "You can take a break Billy Ray; she'll be safe with two lawmen in her room," Thad said.

"No, sir, we promised her that someone would always be guarding her door, and I won't break my word to her."

"That's mighty loyal of you. I'm sure she feels safer with you out here, but Fran will take over while you stretch your legs or get a soft drink. That's right, isn't it, Fran?"

"It's right as rain, Boss." What else could he say as he took his seat in the chair? There went his chance for being included in getting information for Abe.

Thad waited until he saw Billy Ray turn the corner before speaking to Fran. "I know you want to be in here and hear firsthand what she has to say. I just don't want any details to get out. I'm sure Abe wouldn't like it if they did, and the Millburns have a reputation for repeating anything they overhear." Fran smiled and nodded as Thad opened the door and walked in.

"Good afternoon, ladies."

Brosia said, "Hello, Sheriff. The doctor said to keep your questions short and for you to leave if she got upset or agitated."

"Yes, ma'am, I understand," He approached the bed and opened the manila folder he'd brought with him. "Mrs. Fontaine…"

"Don't call me that. After what David tried to do to me, I'm taking back the name Brosia and Raymond gave me when I escaped his first plan to kill me. I'm Anastasia Leblanc."

"Yes, ma'am, I understand, and I don't blame you one bit for wanting to get rid of his name. I want you to look at this picture and tell me anything you know about it."

He held the fax with the picture of the knot of snakes so that Ana could see it. "Where did you get my drawing?" she asked.

"You drew this?"

"Not this drawing exactly, but David asked me to make a design for a club or fraternity he and some friends were forming. He insisted the emblem had to have a tangle of vipers with their fangs exposed showing their willingness to attack ignorance. It had to be a design that demonstrated unity. "He laughed at me when I told him snakes associated with truth and knowledge made me think of the snake in the Garden of Eden promising Eve truth and knowledge equal to God's. I thought of several designs. David liked this one best. He had it tattooed on him as part of the initiation."

"Where was the tattoo?"

"He had it put on his foot. That seemed funny to me; people usually want their tattoo to show. Why go through all that pain for something no one will see?"

"What do you know about this club he mentioned?"

"Not much. I asked him why they wanted snakes, vipers in particular. He said Vipers was an acronym for their club, Vigilant Inter-discipline Professional Educators Reclaiming Society, if I remember correctly. I told him the acronym sounded more like a motorcycle gang, than a club for professors. He laughed and said, 'You never can tell.'"

"Can you think of anything else?"

"No, after I got used to seeing it on his foot, I forgot about it. He never mentioned his club again. I thought it was a plan that fell through, maybe in part because no one else would want that ball of vipers tattooed on his body."

"Thank you, Mrs. Fontaine. If I think of anything else, I'll get back in touch with you.

Miss Brosia, is there anything we can do for you?"

"No, Lovie and her family have been wonderful. I just sent Becky to buy a paperback book and a newspaper for me. I didn't think you would want an audience when you talked to Ana. She was giving Lovie time to have an early supper. I really don't need all the extra help. It is nice to have company when Ana is asleep, and having the men at the door gives her peace of mind."

Thad nodded, "I understand. You were right to send Becky on an errand. I would appreciate it if you don't tell anyone about the tattoo or the Vipers. They may have nothing to do with our investigation, but we want to check out everything. "Fran and I better head back to the office. Thank you for letting me talk to Ana. I see how weak she is. I must have worn her out; she's already sleeping like a baby. Good-bye."

When Thad left Ana's room, he saw Becky and her daddy walking toward the room ready to return to their duty stations. They both had bags from the gift shop downstairs; reading material for Brosia and snacks for Billy Ray were his guess. He waved to the Millburns, motioned to Fran, and the two men walked toward the exit.

∾

Lovie was glad to have a little time to herself. She really did want to help Brosia. She felt it was her Christian duty to do so. Still, she missed the freedom she forfeited when she volunteered to take a turn sitting with Ana. She took out her phone and called her older daughter. Nothing relaxed her more than sharing the latest gossip.

The phone rang eight times; she was about to hang up when Sister finally answered the phone. "Hello, Mama," Sister said as she answered her mother's signature ring. "How is Ana doing today? Is she responding to the treatment for pneumonia yet?"

"Yes, it seems like she may be. It's over a month since she was admitted. She'd better get better soon if she's going to at all. "Baby Girl just relieved me from my sitting duty, so I could eat an early supper and make a few phone calls. You know how funny some hospitals are about using phones in the rooms."

"Mama, why do you still call Becky, Baby Girl? You know she hates it. She's a grown young woman."

"Sister, I know I taught you better than to correct your elders. I call her that because she was, is, and will be my baby girl until the day I die. I'm sorry she doesn't like it, but I bet your daddy's sister doesn't like the name Une Etoile, but that's what Grandmamma called her."

"Well, it is her legal name, and it wouldn't be so bad if y'all didn't pronounce it Youknee Eetoil. It is French, you know."

"There you go again, correcting your elders. I didn't call you to be re-educated, young lady. I wanted to tell you what I heard in the hospital cafeteria.

"These two young people were sitting at the table behind me. The young man said, 'My daddy came into my room yesterday and said, 'You better lock your door 'cause your mama said she was going to kill you. But don't you worry; I hid her gun and ammo in different places.' I'm probably the only kid in school who prays every night that his parents will get a divorce so I can live with Daddy and be normal."

Lovie moved her phone to a better position to talk. "I had to know who those kids were so I pulled out my compact and used it like a rearview mirror. I didn't recognize the girl, but you'll never guess who the boy was."

Before Lovie could deliver her scoop, a deep voice said, "Ladies, do you ever stop to pray?" It startled her so much Lovie dropped her cell phone. When she picked it up, she asked her daughter, "Sister, do you think that was God?"

"I doubt it, Mama."

"I don't know, Sister, in the Old Testament, He used to talk to people all the time. I've heard people say He spoke to them in an inner voice that was almost audible. But I never thought God would sound like James Earl Jones with a heavy Southern accent. Maybe he uses the voice that will get the message across. I'll ask Bax what he thinks."

"Mama, I don't think we need to talk to Brother Bax or anyone else. They'd think we were crazy. Just in case it was God using his James Earl Jones voice, we may need to pray more and gossip less. Good-bye, Mama."

"You're right; bye, Sister Girl."

Sister hung up the phone and laughed. Louis, her husband, asked, "Do you think this conversation with a higher power will break her from eavesdropping and gossiping?"

"No, but it may slow her down for a while. By the way, I loved the voice."

℘

Lovie was shaken after her strange conversation. Maybe she didn't need to run the risk of telling Bax that God had told her not to gossip, but she did need to tell him that Eugene Shoemaker's son was afraid his mother was going to kill him. If Eugene thought his family's problem was one he could handle, he was mistaken. That boy was terrified, and his mother needed professional help.

Surely telling her pastor what she overheard wouldn't count as gossip in God's eyes. She pulled her little Bible out of her purse and looked in Proverbs for advice to help her decide if what she had to say was gossip. She found it in Proverbs 25:11. "A word spoken at the right time is like gold apples on a silver tray." And in Proverbs 31:8-9 she read, "Speak up for those who have no voice, for the justice of all who are dispossessed. Speak up, judge righteously, and defend the cause of the oppressed and the needy." She smiled knowing God would approve.

TWENTY-SIX

Snakes

After they returned to his office, Thad said, "Fran, find Abe's private number for me. I need to let him know what I found out from Ana Fontaine."

Fran brought the number to him. After the third ring, the call was answered. "Abe here."

"This is Thad Brownlee, Agent Abe. I just got back from Birmingham."

"What did you find out from Mrs. Fontaine, Sheriff?"

"You were right; David Fontaine was a member of the Vipers. His wife designed the insignia. He told her it was for a club of educators who wanted to attack ignorance. It had to have a closely woven group of snakes with their fangs showing, ready to attack. He insisted the snakes had to be vipers because Vipers was the acronym for the lengthy name of the group."

"It could be an acronym, but it might just be the group wants to emulate a deadly killer that blends into its surroundings so well it's hard to detect. I assume he had the tattoo."

"Yes, according to his wife, it was on his foot as well. I've been wondering why David didn't just identify himself to the other vipers by showing the tattoo."

"That is a good question. It seems the logical thing to do. There has to be something about the group we haven't uncovered

that would make him hide his membership from the men who
kidnapped him. Maybe he didn't know they were Vipers. He
might have thought they were undercover operatives, who were
following the package to identify other Vipers. We may never
know.

"Thank you for confirming what I suspected," Abe said.

"I am glad to help." Thad hung up the phone and returned
to the paperwork that had piled up while he had been in
Birmingham.

"Fran, it looks like Eugene drew in a lot of business while
we were gone. Either 'when the cat's away the mice will play' or
people feel more comfortable reporting petty theft to him than us.

"Let's see, there was Bobby Smith's bike, which he left at
the baseball field. Joe Evans said his best hunting dog was taken
out of the pen behind his house. Then Myrtle Jones had a sack of
groceries she left in the car stolen while she was taking others in
the house. That bag contained a six pack of beer and a carton of
cigarettes. Her husband was not happy when he reported the theft.

"It looks like we have a criminal mastermind or a kid who
took a mental health day from his grueling high school schedule.
My vote goes to our hooky player."

"You nailed it, Sheriff. With instinct like yours, we should
be able to solve all our cases before noon," Fran said, laughing as
he went back to his own desk.

Thad sat at his computer entering the notes he took while
he was on the phone with Abe. His file already had the notes he
scribbled down as soon as he left Ana's room. It wasn't much,
but he was driven to try to figure out as much about David
Fontaine and the Vipers as he could. Ana had said two men took
David, apparently trying to find the package. Two men with
Viper tattoos had been found dead. Were there more Vipers out
there trying to get the package back? He hoped Abe had more
information than he had shared. What he had didn't amount to a
hill of frostbitten beans.

☙

Bax had put his visit with Ana last on his list of hospital visits. He wanted to be able to take his time. Her condition was definitely improving according to her doctors; still she seemed to sleep most of the time. When she was awake, she was troubled and restless. She had reason to be. Having the man she married while she was in college try to kill her would be more than enough to destroy her peace of mind.

"Good morning, Louis. How is she today?" he asked before knocking on the door.

"The doctor was in earlier and said the pneumonia has cleared up. They will be starting some physical therapy this week. At least, that's what my wife told me. Go on in. I'm pretty sure she is still awake."

Bax knocked and slowly opened the door. Ana was sitting up in the bed. Her hair, now two-toned and much longer, was brushed and held back with a barrette. He was no doctor but that was definitely a sign that she was on the mend.

"Good morning, Ana-Grace. You're looking much better today. How are you feeling?'

"Better. If I felt worse than I have for the past little while, you would be planning your remarks for my funeral."

"Now I know you're better. I recognize that feisty side of you that put me in my place when you first came to me for help.

"Hello, Sister. Louis told me the doctor gave her a good report this morning."

"Yes, he did. She has been in a critical condition for a long time. I believe she has turned the corner and is headed toward recovery.

"Now that you're here, I think I'll go downstairs and get a cup of coffee. I won't be long," Sister said.

As soon as Sister left the room, Ana's expression became solemn. "Everyone has been so good to me. The doctor and nursing staff have been wonderful. I can't even begin to say how much that my friends have done for me means to me. I just don't deserve all that's been done." She pulled on her blanket, settling in closer on her shoulders. "I read this Oriental proverb: 'It is better to be shattered jade than unbroken pottery.' It means it's better to die with honor than to live with shame. That sums up my life. I am the unbroken pottery; I lived when I should have died instead of my best friend. Dave reminded me of the suffering I caused Lisa's family. They don't know if she is dead or just wants nothing to do with them. I caused that pain because I wanted to go to a party my parents wouldn't allow me to attend. She slipped in my window, and we traded places so I could go. I killed her with my selfish disobedience."

Bax settled into the chair by the bed and took her hand. "I like the proverb, too. However, I interpret it differently. You're the jade. Your life shattered into a million pieces the night of the fire. The girl that you were died that night, too. Maybe it wasn't a physical death, but you had to become a different person, Anastasia Leblanc. Like the jade shards, even though you were damaged and would never be exactly the same, you retained the same qualities that you had in your original state. Don't underestimate your worth. No matter what Dave told you, remember it was he who set the fire. Although God sees all sin as equal and will forgive all sin, we humans see it differently. In our eyes disobeying your parents is not as great a sin as setting a fire that killed three people. Dave was just playing mind games with you." Hearing a noise, he withdrew his hand.

Sister walked in, and Ana felt the mood change abruptly again. When her family had gone into the witness protection program, they had to cut all ties. Now she felt Lovie's family had become her extended family. She loved all of the Millburns, but she couldn't share her deepest feelings with them.

"Did you have a good visit while I was gone?" Sister asked.

"Yes, I was just telling Brother Bax how much stronger I feel."

"It's good to hear you say that. You've come a long way toward your recovery," Sister said as she handed Ana a newspaper. "I thought you might want to read a paper now that you aren't the lead story."

"I need to get back to the church. Take good care of her, Sister," Bax said as he left the room. As he walked, Bax contemplated their conversation. What type of man would make his wife feel guilty for the death of her friend and the devastation of the girl's family? He wouldn't say he was glad Dave was dead, but he was glad to have him out of Ana's life.

His thoughts were interrupted when he saw a preacher from Rainbow City who had been in one of his classes the last semester.

"Hello, Bob, I haven't seen you at school this semester."

"I took this semester off, but I'll be back. Do you have a church member here?"

"No, I've been visiting a friend. You probably remember reading about the Fontaines; Ana Fontaine is a patient here."

As the two men continued to talk, Bax watched as a new doctor talked to Bubba before going into Ana's room.

ℰℬ

"Good morning, ladies, I'm Doctor Warren," the new doctor said.

"I haven't seen you before. Where's Dr. Boone?" Ana asked.

"Dr. Boone asked me to visit with you today. He is worried because he doesn't believe you have fully processed the horror your husband put you through. I'm an expert in treating post-traumatic stress syndrome."

Dr. Warren turned to Sister and said, "As I explained to the gentleman at the door, Mrs. Fontaine and I will need privacy in order to explore her suppressed emotions. You will have to give us some time alone. Go get a cup of coffee and relax for a while.

We should have made enough progress for our first session in about a half hour." The handsome gray-haired doctor gave Sister a reassuring smile as she obediently got up and walked to the door.

"I'll be back in a little while," she said.

Ana got a sinking feeling as she watched Sister leave.

The benevolent look disappeared from Doctor Warren's face. "Mrs. Fontaine, I'm here to get to the root of your fear. I can assure you, after you tell me where my package is, your fear will leave when I walk out the door."

"Who are you? How did you find me?"

"You don't really think I'm going to answer your first question, do you? As for your second question, I've been monitoring news out of Louisiana and Alabama. When I read your dear husband tried to kill you but ended in a fiery ambulance explosion, I knew UAB would be the only logical choice for wounds like yours." He looked at her with intense malice. "Now that I've answered your questions, answer mine. Where is my package?"

"I don't know! I found it in the car and hid it because I thought David had been killed for it. Later I sent a friend to get it and turn it over to the police, but it was already gone. I don't know what was in it, but David wouldn't believe me. That's why he tried to kill me."

"He was a good judge of character; I don't believe you either. I told you, if you told me what I wanted to know, all your fears go away, and I'm a man of my word." He put his hand over her mouth and pushed her head deeper into the pillow. With his other hand he reached into his pocket and pulled out a syringe. He pulled the needle guard off with his teeth.

Doctor Boone burst through the door, grabbed Warren by the shoulder, turned him around and delivered a right cross to Warren's chin. The imposter dropped to the floor just as hospital security personnel ran in. One flipped him over and held him down, while the other unlaced a shoestring and tied Warren's hands behind his back. The security men pulled him to his feet and walked him out of the room.

Ana was crying uncontrollably. Doctor Boone walked over to her bed, rubbing his throbbing fist. "You're going to be all right, Mrs. Fontaine, but you need to calm down. I'll order a sedative for you."

"No, Doctor, I need to stay alert. I don't want a sedative. If I did and someone else came in to finish what he started, I wouldn't stand a chance." Ana was slowly regaining self-control. She wiped her eyes and in a much calmer voice asked, "How did you know to come in when you did?"

"I met your friend coming down the hall when I got off the elevator. I asked her who was with you, and she said you were fine, Dr. Warren was with you. There is no Warren on staff here. I told her to call security and then the police. Then I broke into a run. It looks like I timed it just right."

"That was some punch," Ana said.

"Yeah, I was a "Golden Gloves" contender when I was in my teens, but I never thought I would use those skills to protect a patient. I wonder what happened to the man posted at your door to protect you. He seemed to be a reliable bodyguard," Doctor Boone said.

"I remember the fake doctor telling Bubba that in order for our therapy session to be successful, we would have to have total privacy. He asked both Sister and Bubba to go get coffee while he talked with me. They trusted him because he appeared to be a doctor."

"What's going on?" Brosia asked when she and Raymond came into the room and saw Ana's red eyes and tear-stained face.

"A man, impersonating a doctor, tried to find out where the package is now. When I couldn't tell him, he pushed my head into the pillow and tried to inject me with some drug. Doctor Boone came in and knew the man had no business in my room,

much less trying to inject me. He floored the imposter and had
someone call the police."

"I can't believe it. How did he get in?" asked Brosia.

"He was dressed as a doctor and sent Bubba and Sister away
on the pretense that we needed total privacy for his psychological
help to be effective. But don't worry, the police have him now."

"How can I keep from worrying about you? The people
Dave said were trying to kill him found you in here, even with all
the care we've taken to keep you safe. That settles it; Raymond or
I will be here with you every day from now on."

Doctor Boone said, "Mrs. Leblanc, I'll admit I thought
having a man at the door day and night was unnecessary. In view
of what happened today, I'm having security assigned to Mrs.
Fontaine's door. We should have done it from the beginning, but
since the man who shot her was killed, I didn't see the need."

"Good, I'm glad to have security posted outside, but
Raymond will be out there with them tonight just to be sure your
man stays awake. I'll be in here with Ana; she can use all the
comfort she can get."

Bubba and Sister came in. "Ana, we're both so sorry for
leaving you alone with that man. I thought you would be safe
with a doctor. I guess we didn't see past the white coat. He could
have killed you, and it would have been our fault."

"I'm fine; don't blame yourselves. He fooled me at first.
Now, I know what I have feared is true. It doesn't matter if Dave
is dead or not; there are other people out there who want that
package and would think nothing about killing me."

"No one will get near you again. One of us will always be
with you."

Ana shook her head. "If they want to find me, they will. I
appreciate what you are trying to do, but I will never be safe as
long as any of the people who want the package are alive."

As if on cue the police arrived. "Mrs. Fontaine, I'm
Detective Oscar Swilley, tell me what happened."

"This man told Sister and Bubba he was sent in by my doctors to deal with the post-traumatic stress I have since my husband shot me. He told them they had to leave the area. I didn't like that at all because they have been staying close by and making me feel safe. But he said we needed total privacy for me to benefit from the therapy.

"As soon as we were alone, he put his hand over my mouth and pushed me so hard I couldn't move. He would have killed me with whatever drug he had in the syringe, if Dr. Boone hadn't come in."

"Not really, Mrs. Fontaine, the lab technician just told me there was sodium pentothal in the syringe. He might have wanted to kill you, but not before he got the information he was after. Like most people he didn't realize that sodium pentothal isn't the 'truth serum' the movies make it out to be. It does relax people and make them answer questions, but the information is suspect. The answers may be pure fantasy or an out and out lie. What did he want to know?" the detective asked.

"The same thing my husband wanted to know before he shot me. He wanted to know what I did with the package I found after the wreck."

"Wait a minute, what wreck?"

"You need to talk to Sheriff Thad Brownlee in Eastabuchie County. He investigated the wreck, and he knows more about the package than I do. I never opened it. I do know the FBI is interested in it. I can't really tell you anymore." Ana hoped he would call Thad and leave her alone.

"I will contact Sheriff Brownlee. I can see that you are exhausted, and your doctor warned me not to tire you out. I'll be back when you have had time to rest, and then finish my questions."

Swilley left the room, and Ana started to cry. "When is this going to end? It's only a matter of time before someone succeeds in killing me. I still don't know why that package is so important. What did Dave get involved in?"

Sister walked over to the bed and took Ana's hand. "Don't cry, Ana; the police will get to the bottom of this. You just have to focus on getting well enough to go home. I'm not going to leave you alone again no matter who tells me to leave the room. I know I speak for the rest of the family. We won't be tricked again."

"I don't blame you and Bubba. I believed him, too. I want help; I need therapy, but it will be hard to trust someone after what happened," Ana said as she wiped her eyes.

Brosia's expression showed she didn't share Ana's forgiving spirit. She clearly blamed them for leaving their post and exposing Ana to such a terrible experience.

"She's safe now, Miss Brosia. That's what's important," Sister said as she kissed Ana's cheek and walked to the door. "Ana, now that Miss Brosia and Mr. Raymond are here, I'll leave you with them."

"Coward, you just said you would never leave me no matter who tried to make you. Now, you are running away when a sweet old lady gives you the evil eye," Ana said. That broke the tension, and all three women laughed.

TWENTY-SEVEN

Missing

"Thad, Raymond just called. He and Miss Brosia were both at the hospital last night. When they got to Bax's cabin this morning, he thought it looked like someone had tried to jimmy the door. Someone or something must have scared them off; they didn't get in."

"Maybe I better rethink my theory about the hooky player. This might be something more serious than a teenager's petty thefts. Let's go out and check the cabin. Call Bax and ask him to meet us there. Just because they didn't get in, it doesn't mean they didn't steal something from the yard or outbuildings."

As soon after Bax got back from the hospital, he went to the cabin. Thad and Raymond were propped against the police car talking. As soon as they saw him drive up, they went to meet him.

"Bax, it looks like somebody tried to get into your place last night when no one was here. They didn't get in, but I thought you needed to check the property to be sure nothing was taken from the garage or the storage shed," Thad said.

"There isn't anything of much value in either one," Bax said as he and the two other men walked to the garage. He raised the garage door, and they walked in. After stepping around an old mower and looking at a collection of half-empty paint cans, fishing tackle, and various types of sports equipment, he said, "It looks like everything is here. I keep the things I need most at my place in town."

"Well, just to make sure nothing was taken, let's check out your storage shed," Thad said.

Bax knew all too well what was missing, the pink motorcycle many of his congregation found inappropriate for a preacher's wife to ride. He hoped Thad wouldn't notice as he opened the unlocked door, and the three of them looked in.

"Isn't this where Beth kept her bike?" Thad asked.

"Yes, but I loaned it to a friend of mine. There is something missing from here, Thad. I had two kayaks stored in here. One is gone, and so are the lifejacket and paddle that I kept with it. I can't be sure if they were taken last night or a long time ago. I haven't used them since Beth got too weak to go out with me."

"I'm just going to assume that they were taken last night. We can check to see if anyone is trying to sell it online or in second-hand sports equipment stores. Can you describe it?" Thad asked Bax.

"The one that's missing is the twin to the one still in the shed. Beth was a little afraid of them flipping over. She wanted them to be bright orange so we could be easily spotted and equipped with built-in stabilizers. The paddle was just a standard kayak paddle, and the adult-size lifejacket was orange. There're millions just like them out there."

He walked out of the shed, then turned and said, "I just remembered something. Let me check the kayak in the shed." Bax climbed over a coiled garden hose and a wheelbarrow to get to the remaining kayak. He flipped it over and checked the seat. He smiled as he returned.

"They took Beth's kayak. She liked 'girly things' so she got out her fingernail polish and decorated the seat with pink hearts. If you find one like that, you've got your thief." He turned back to the sheriff. "Thad, were you able to get any prints from the strange note someone sent Ana?"

"No, there was nothing on it except the prints Brosia left when she handled it. It was obviously sent by some nutcase who wanted to upset a fragile woman. Who, in their right mind, would send that in a get-well card?" Thad said.

"That's what I thought. Nothing is really making sense. Even the things that are being taken in these break-ins seem random," Bax said as they walked back to the house.

Thad said, "That's just what I've been thinking. There doesn't seem to be a pattern to what's taken or to the value of what's taken."

Thad continued the same line of thought as he got in his car. Every night it seems that someone in the county had been targeted by the thief. Sometimes what was taken was of no particular value, while at other times, as with the theft reported by Burt Gibson, it was.

Burt had a permit to carry a pistol. He was a retired Birmingham policeman who had been seriously injured by a drug dealer when he tried to arrest him. After the dealer was captured by Burt's partner, he testified against the man at trial. The convicted man vowed to get even with both of them. Burt retired on disability and moved back to Eastabuchie County.

A few years later the drug dealer escaped, and Burt's partner was found shot outside of his home. That was when Burt applied for a gun permit. Last night the gun was stolen from his car.

That report brought chills to Thad. The thief had escalated from beer and cigarettes to kayaks and guns. Thad only hoped the gun wasn't going to be used by the thief to escalate again, this time to the next level-armed robbery.

TWENTY-EIGHT

Eugene

Bax sat at his desk opening his mail. There was a note from Pete Gomez's family thanking him for the tribute he paid to their husband and father at his funeral, and Mary Scott's request for the use of the sanctuary for her daughter's upcoming wedding. There was nothing unusual in the mail; at least not until he opened the hand printed envelope at the bottom of the stack. As he read the note, his expression changed.

> *I am writing this note hoping you will know what to do about a conversation I overheard. Eugene and Doris Shoemaker's son was telling a friend that his father had hidden his mother's gun and bullets to keep her from killing him, the son, not the father. Eugene told his son he'd better keep his door locked. The boy said he wished his parents would divorce so he could lead a normal life. If this is true, and from the sound of the boy's voice, I am convinced it is, the boy is in danger, and the mother needs help.*

He couldn't take a chance. This could be gossip or a hoax, but what if it was true? He didn't want to seem like a meddling minister, but he had to talk to Eugene. He rang the deputy's cell number.

"Hello," Eugene answered.

"Eugene, this is Bax Alford. I would like for you to stop by my house on your way home. It won't take long, and I need to get your help with a problem that has come up."

"Sure, Brother Bax, I'd be glad to help."

After he made the phone call, the rest of the day dragged by. Bax took care of essential church business and worked on his sermon. But, in the back of his mind, he was trying to think of the best way to handle the meeting with Eugene.

As soon as he got home, he put on a pot of coffee and took out Beth's best coffee mugs, hoping those homey touches would take the edge off what he had to say. The coffee had just finished brewing when the doorbell rang.

Bax answered the door. "Come in Gene. I'm glad you could make it. Let's get some coffee first. I know I can use a cup."

"Sure, that would be great, but I don't have long to stay. Doris gets worried if I don't get home on time. She says the fear that I won't come home is the worst part of being married to a cop. She feels my life is on the line every day. I've tried to tell her that this county has one of the lowest crime rates in the state, but that hasn't helped," he said as he took a mug of black coffee from Bax.

The two men walked to the living room and sat down across from each other. Bax took a sip of coffee and began the difficult conversation. "I wanted to meet with you at my house because I'm bringing up this subject as your friend, not your pastor. When I got this letter today, I asked myself what I would want a friend to do if the positions were reversed."

Bax handed the letter to Eugene. As he read it, tears came to his eyes.

"Gene, if Doris is saying things like that, she needs help. You have a good kid, and he needs to feel safe."

"I don't really think she means it when she says things like that, but I have to take precautions, like hiding her gun and counting her pain medicine every night after she goes to sleep. I want to be sure she isn't using it to poison the boy. I doubt I can get her to see a doctor, but I know I owe it to my son to try."

"If you are that concerned, you might need to have her involuntarily evaluated."

"I have looked into that. Threats don't constitute the imminent danger requirement to do that, Bax."

"Would you let Lee move in here with me? We could concoct an excuse that would make it seem to be a favor to me. I don't know; maybe I could say that because of the recent rash of break-ins, I need someone to house-sit while I'm in New Orleans. But, that wouldn't get him out of the house often enough." He stopped and looked at the face of the anguished father. "I know, we could expand the job to cover the calls I get to go to the home or hospital when someone is near death. I could say that because I never know when that might happen, I need someone here every night."

"I don't know; let me think about it. I will say it feels good to be able to talk to someone about what is going on at home. Your idea about having him house-sit might work." Eugene put his mug on the table and stood up. "I've got to get home. Doris will be frantic. Thank you for your concern."

Bax walked Eugene to the door and watched the worried man drive away. Having a troubled teenager in his house might pose problems, but that would be nothing compared to the problems Gene faced every day.

The next morning Bax was surprised when Eugene tapped on his office door.

"Good morning, Gene, come on in and have a seat."

Eugene took the wing chair across from Bax's desk. "Bax, I thought about your idea for getting Lee out of the house. This morning before breakfast I told him you had offered him a job. When I explained what he would have to do, he jumped at the chance.

"I told Doris at breakfast, but it was hard to read her reaction. She just stared out the window and nodded her head. No question, no emotion, she just stared out at the garage. That isn't a normal reaction, but lately nothing about Doris is normal."

"Gene, you have to get her to someone who can help her. She has a problem that is affecting your son and your marriage. You can't even do your job the way you are capable of doing because you are worrying about her erratic behavior."

"I know you're right. Even if I were to take her to a psychiatrist, she wouldn't cooperate. She sees nothing strange about her behavior."

"You have to try. You know if she has threatened to kill Lee, she is a danger to herself and others."

"I'll start looking for a doctor and try to get her to see him. In the meantime, I can't tell you how much I appreciate you taking care of Lee. I'll reimburse you for whatever you pay him."

"You will not. I do need someone to house sit. I'm in Birmingham several nights a week, and church members don't plan their emergencies around my convenience. With all the break-ins we have had the past few months, I'll feel better with someone there."

"If you say so, pastor, it must be the truth." The two men shook hands and Eugene walked out. Bax went to his desk and made a note on his computer. Lee would be moving in soon. He hoped he hadn't bitten off more than he could chew. He had never had to deal with a teenage boy before. His father had enough on his mind, without having to worry about the boy.

TWENTY-NINE

Home

"I can't believe we are actually getting to take her home today, Raymond." Brosia said as she got out of Raymond's car and they walked briskly toward the entrance of the hospital for what they hoped would be the last time.

"Good morning, Billy Ray. We're here to take over from you and Lovie. If the doctor hasn't changed his mind, we'll be taking her home today." Brosia pushed the door open, and she and Raymond walked in.

Ana looked good, but she was still weak and would have to have therapy. Despite the optimistic attitude she projected, deep in her heart Brosia had never expected Ana would leave the hospital alive.

"Brosia, I can't believe I'm going home today."

"Now, Ana, as my old neighbor used to say, 'There's many a slip betwixt the cup and the lip.' We don't need to get too excited until we hear the doctor say you are going home," Lovie said.

"It's been a long time since I've heard that," Doctor Boone said as he walked in to the room. "My grandmamma used to say the same thing. I have good news; there isn't going to be a slip this time. You are going home."

"That's wonderful! Thank you, doctor," Ana said. Brosia and Lovie hugged each other.

A nurse rolled Ana to Raymond's car for her trip back to Eastabuchie County. Before the group reached the Birmingham city limits, she had fallen asleep. Last night she had hardly slept. The prospect of going home had filled her with conflicting emotions. The anticipation of being back home was chasing the fear of being in a remote, less secure place. This circular thinking kept her awake most of the night. The soft purr of Raymond's car was all the white noise she needed to drift off.

"Wake up, Ana; we're here," Brosia said as Raymond opened the car door and helped the groggy woman to her feet. He and Brosia got on either side of her to give her support as she walked into the cabin. True, she had been walking around her room for weeks to prepare her for returning to normal life, but the path to the front door was uneven and rocky.

"Let's go over there so you can sit on the couch," Brosia said as they entered the cottage. "Bax is on his way over. I'll go make a pot of coffee and thaw out some of the cookies Becky made for us. Bax said Lovie is bringing supper for us tonight. They have all been wonderful." Brosia hugged Ana and said, "I was so afraid we'd never get to bring you home. It seems like a miracle that you are here." She hurried to the kitchen before Ana could see the tears welling up in her eyes.

"Is there anything I can do for you, Ana?" Raymond asked as he sat down by her.

"No, Raymond, I'm fine. I'll take that back, there is something both of you can do; just relax. I'm not as fragile as you think. If I were, I wouldn't have lived through all that has happened this year."

The doorbell rang. "Well, at least I can see who is at the door." Raymond walked to the door and let Bax in. "We didn't expect you so soon. Come on in."

"Ana, you look great. I'm so glad you're home." Bax walked over to the couch and sat down next to her.

"Technically, I'm not home, but I don't think I can ever go back to that house. I have nothing but bad memories of my life there. I don't even want to go back to Willow Wood. The rest of the faculty would wonder what I did to change the David Fontaine they knew into a man who tried to kill his wife. I just want to forget that part of my life."

"Let's not talk about bad memories today, Ana. This is a time to celebrate your release from the hospital and to look forward to your continuing recovery," Raymond said as he got up from his chair and walked toward the kitchen. "I'll see what is holding up our coffee. Brosia may need my help."

Bax changed the subject. "Do you remember when you told me about the Oriental proverb about the shattered jade?" Ana nodded, and Bax continued. "The next time I had to go to the seminary, I made a side trip to an artisan I know in New Orleans and had this made for you." He handed a small box to her. When Ana opened the box, she saw a silver pendant set with fragments of jade.

"Bax, it's beautiful," Ana said as she took it out of the box.

"When you told me how you felt the proverb applied to you, I had a different take on its meaning. In the Chinese culture jade symbolizes nobility, constancy, power, and beauty. It's still beautiful, even when it's broken; only its form has changed. Hal thought I was crazy when I brought in a good piece of jade and told him I wanted him to shatter it and use the pieces in this pendant. I told him it was to remind someone that even though her life would never be the same, it still has beauty. Ana, you can use the parts of your life, your strength, intelligence, and courage, to make a new life. That life will be different, but maybe it will be much better."

He took the chain from Ana and hung the pendant around her neck. She smiled as she fingered it. "Bax, the pendent is beautiful, but the thought behind it is priceless. I will treasure it forever. When I get depressed, I will remember what it symbolizes."

Brosia came in carrying a tray of cookies. Raymond followed her with a tray with cups and a pot of coffee. They put the trays on the coffee table and poured coffee for everyone.

"What a beautiful pendant! Bax, did you bring it to her?" Brosia asked.

"Yes, I wanted to give her a welcome home gift."

"You are full of surprises. I heard Eugene's son, Lee, has moved into your house. Is that true?" Brosia asked.

"Yes, I hired Lee to house-sit for me. As much as I have to be away from home at night, I thought I would feel safer if someone was in the house. Whoever is breaking into people's cars and houses may think twice if they know someone is there."

"The break-ins have increased. When I first came here to keep an eye on Ana, the only things that were taken were a few inexpensive things that had been left in unlocked cars. Now, hardly a day goes by that some house or outbuilding isn't broken into, and the value of what is taken has increased. It looks like the first thefts were just practice to improve the thieves' techniques and build their confidence," Raymond said.

"You think there is more than one person involved?" Bax asked.

"Not really, it's just that there has been such an increase lately; I wouldn't rule that out."

Bax stood up and said, "I better get going. I need to stop in and see how Earl Parker is doing. He stepped in a hole and fell in his yard while he was mowing the grass yesterday. He's eighty-two, and his daughter was sure he had broken his hip. It turns out he's just got a badly-bruised hip and a twisted ankle." He turned toward the couch. "Ana, it's good to have you back. I know Brosia will take good care of you, and Raymond will be here to keep you safe. If I don't leave soon, Brother Parker will have recovered and be up on a ladder cleaning out the gutters on his house, before I get to see him. Good bye."

Bax walked to his car, thinking. He wished he could be sure Raymond would be able to keep Ana safe. The imposter who tried to drug her might not be the only one who still thought she either knew where that mystery package was or had it herself.

When he arrived at the Parker's home, he was surprised to see Thad's patrol car parked in the driveway. Thad came out the front door just as Bax was getting out of his car.

"What's wrong, Thad? Is Brother Parker all right?"

"He's more than all right, he's mad as a hornet. Apparently while he was being checked out in the hospital yesterday, someone broke in and cleaned out his house. The diamond wedding ring he gave his wife when they got married fifty-eight years ago is missing along with an antique gold pocket watch and his wallet. He wasn't carrying it when he was working in the yard, and his daughter didn't think to get it. The most disturbing thing about the break-in is that the thief took his gun collection. That's the second time our thief has stolen firearms. He may just be fencing them, or he could be building up an arsenal," Thad said.

"That is a frightening prospect. I doubt that's the case. Think of all the things he has taken. Some have had little value, such as the six-pack and cigarettes. Others like my boat and the pocket watch have value but would be hard to sell around here. It's like he takes whatever catches his eye, when he has the opportunity to take something. I wonder if he is a kleptomaniac," Bax said.

"Another thing, we both have assumed that the thief is male. However, the women in the area can't be ruled out. Personally, I think it's a group of kids who are getting spending money for things they can't ask their parents to buy. I think they are fencing what they take to get money for drugs," Thad said.

Lee

L ee fell into a comfortable routine after he moved into Bax's house. His grades started to improve, and he seemed to be happier. Eugene came by after work often to keep involved in his son's life. When he came, Bax kept out of the way so the father and son had time to talk. He usually worked in the kitchen, cooking supper or making cookies and coffee to serve his old friend.

Bax was bringing in a tray of warm oatmeal cookies when he heard Lee and his father talking.

"Bax said you borrowed his car and took Kelly out to the movies last Friday night. She seems like a sweet girl. What did y'all see?"

"I'm trying to forget it; it was the worst movie we have ever seen. The plot was so thin a third grader could have come up with a better one."

Something in the way Lee answered his father's question made Bax suspicious. "What was the name of the movie? I may want to see it. Sometimes a person my age likes a different sort of movie."

"I doubt you would want to be seen going into the theater when a show like that is playing, Brother Bax. It was X-rated; your deacons would call you on the carpet."

Lee's nervous laugh convinced Bax his assumption was correct. "Lee, if it isn't the type of show I should watch, I doubt it is one you should be taking your girlfriend to see."

"He's got you there, Lee. Next time use better judgment," Eugene said.

Bax dropped the subject. He knew Lee was lying. There was only one movie theater in the county. If he went to a movie, it had to be the one he had heard his secretary telling the daycare director about, the show she saw last Friday. It was a tear-jerking chick-flick. The deacons might question his taste in movies if he went to it without a date, but it wasn't X-rated, or soft porn either. He was home Friday night, and Lee had told him he was taking Kelly to the show. Where had he gone, and why was he lying about it?

Bax was lost in thought and hardly heard Eugene talking. "Sorry, Gene, I didn't hear what you were saying. I have a lot on my mind lately."

"I sure understand that; I just said I'd better be going. Doris will be worried about me. Thanks for the cookies. Good night, Bax."

"Tell her I asked about her. I've missed her singing in the choir. She has a lovely alto voice that adds a lot to the music."

"I'll walk you to the car, Dad."

After Lee and Gene walked out, Bax went to his office to work on a new series of sermons. He heard Lee climb up the stairs and shut his bedroom door. The boy was turning in early tonight. He wished he could. If the folks at church knew how much research he put into a sermon, they might pay more attention. If it weren't for a few dedicated wives in the 'elbow ministry,' he could advertise his services as a sleep aid.

After several hours, he turned off the lights and went to his bedroom. He was about to doze off when he heard the sound of something crunching the gravel in the driveway. He went to his window and looked down at the driveway. Lee was pushing the preacher's sedan toward the garage.

Lee must have rolled it out while he was on the other side of the house. He wouldn't have heard a thing. What excuse would Lee come up with for taking his car without permission?

Bax walked down the hall and waited at the top of the staircase. When Lee got near the top, Bax flipped the light switch. The boy's face was a kaleidoscope of emotions, quickly changing from fear, to anger, to shame. He hung his head and said nothing.

"Lee, I think you owe me an explanation. What were you doing pushing my car up the driveway in the middle of the night with the lights turned off? You know if you had asked, I would have let you use it, providing you had a good reason. This doesn't look good."

"I'm sorry, Brother Bax. I should have asked, but I didn't think my reason was good enough. I promised Kelly that I would go over to her house after Dad left. I went to my room early and waited until I thought you were so involved in your writing you wouldn't hear me leave."

"Lee, I'm not so old that I can't understand seeing your girlfriend is a good reason to borrow a car. I'm sorry you felt you had to deceive me to keep your promise. I can't let this slide. There have to be consequences for your action. I am docking you one day's pay. Don't let this happen again."

"Yes, sir, I'm sorry I've disappointed you."

"Everyone slips up sometime; just don't let it happen again. Now, get to bed; it's after one o' clock." Lee walked to his room and shut the door. He leaned against it and sighed with relief. He would have to be more careful next time. Bax wouldn't be so easy on him if he caught him again.

Bax lay down in his bed. He would like to believe the kid, but after Lee lied about the movie, he didn't. Maybe it was a good thing Beth and he never had children. He was a poor excuse as a father figure to Lee. That was really not a fair statement; he was not a father figure at all. Gene was the only father figure. He was just his employer and pastor. He turned over on his side and went to sleep still wondering what was going on.

THIRTY-ONE

Plans

Now Brosia felt as much a part of the community as she ever had in Bayou Gauche. So many people had befriended her after Ana was shot. There were meals sent to the cabin for weeks. Because she was staying at the hospital most of the time, Bax's freezer was soon filled to capacity with casseroles of every description. She had to ask Bax to thank the ladies who had supplied the windfall of food and tell them there just wasn't any more room. Now that Ana was back and all three of them were eating the frozen meals, the supply was almost gone. For the first time since they got back to Eastabuchie County, she needed to shop.

She had been working her way down the store aisles, filling her cart with necessities when she saw Lovie headed toward her.

Lovie saw her at the same time and hurried to greet her friend. "How is Ana doing this week, Brosia?"

"She's still trying to settle in. You know, start over. Yesterday she pulled out her paints and tried to get back to her art. I hate to say it, but I think she's lost her touch. What she painted looked like the way I felt when Sully died. You know, mixed up, confused, and feeling there was nothing good left in my life."

Lovie thought for a minute and then said, "You know I don't know anything about art, but it sounds to me like she's painting her own feelings."

"Well, maybe you're right. In a small section of the top, left hand corner, she painted something that looked like the pieces of jade that are in the pendant Brother Bax gave her as a welcome home gift. That section with the bits of green was the only part of the picture that wasn't gloomy. The jade pendant did seem to lift her spirits for a while," Brosia said, as the two women pushed their carts down the canned-goods aisle.

"Brosia, you know from your own experience when your husband died, people don't get over tragedy as quickly. You can't extinguish awful pain as fast as blowing out candles on a birthday cake. It is going to take a long time and some happy experiences to push the hurt into the background," Lovie said.

"You may not know about art, but you know about life. I think you're right. She needs something to make her happy, something to take her mind off the black feelings she must still be having. I think I have just the thing to do that. She turned to Lovie. I haven't told this to a living soul, and you must promise not to breathe a word of what I'm going to tell you."

"Now you have my full attention. Okay, Brosia, I promise. Cross my heart and hope to die and look the Devil in the eye."

Brosia lowered her voice to the point that Lovie had to strain to hear what she was saying. "Raymond has asked me to marry him, and I said I would. Now don't tell a soul. We wanted Ana to be the first to know, but she has been so depressed we thought it would be better to wait until she is more herself to tell her. After what you said, I think it might do her good to get involved in the plans for our wedding."

"That's wonderful news. It is pretty obvious that he cares for you, but I thought she hated Raymond."

"She did, with a passion, but that's all changed now. He saved her life when he knew what to do for a sucking chest wound. He has been there for her and for me for months. Her feelings couldn't help but change."

"Can I at least tell my daughters? They'll be so excited. This is the most romantic thing I've heard in years."

"No, I said not a living soul, and I meant it, Lovie. It looks to me that even dying and looking the Devil in the eye isn't enough to stop you if you hear a juicy bit of gossip."

"Brosia, that's just not fair. I'll admit it won't be easy to keep your news from my family, but I can keep a secret when I have to. When are you planning to get married?"

"It's like I said, we haven't made any plans yet. Ana has been our main concern. Physically she has turned the corner; emotionally she is still a basket-case. That fake psychologist or psychiatrist, whatever he was supposed to be, has made her resistant to getting any professional help. One thing the imposter did have right is she does need help dealing with all that has happened to her," Brosia said as she looked at her watch.

"Whatever happened to him?" Lovie asked.

"He's in federal custody awaiting trial."

"How can what he tried to do to Ana be a federal case? Not that what he did wasn't awful, but I would have thought it would just be a regular trial."

"I don't really know the answer to that myself. Thad has been in contact with someone named Abe who came down and talked to the Birmingham police. I think Abe is some kind of federal agent. When he left Birmingham, he took the man back with him. There must be more to this than we know," Brosia said as she looked at her watch again.

Lovie picked up on her friend's nervous clock-watching and said, "I've got to finish up here and get home and fix supper. Billy Ray will be ready to eat the empty dishes, if I don't get something on the table soon. I promise I'll be as mum as a mummy about what you told me."

Brosia hugged Lovie and said, "We'll have to get together soon. I miss seeing you as often as I did when you were taking a shift sitting with Ana. I can never thank you and your family enough for all you have done for us."

"Oh, yes, you can; let me be the matron of honor at your wedding. Now that Dave is dead, does that make Ana eligible to be the maid of honor?"

"I'm not sure it works that way. Besides, I just want a small wedding. I'm not sure I'll even have an attendant. It may just be Raymond and me on the back porch with Bax officiating. If Ana doesn't get excited about the prospect of a wedding, we may just elope."

"Think about it. A bigger wedding would be exciting, especially if it takes Ana's mind off what has happened. You may change your mind. If you do, I already have the dress I wore when Sister got married. I think it will still fit if I get some of those Spanks I heard the girls talking about."

"Lovie, you are one in a million. Yes, I'll think about having a bigger wedding, and I'll keep you and your Spanks in mind."

Lovie hurriedly pushed her shopping cart toward the check-out line.

Brosia smiled as she finished her shopping in a much better mood. Seeing her friend in size 18 pink stretch pants as she walked away conjured up the mental picture of Lovie squeezed into her six-year-old mother-of-the-bride dress. That was an image she couldn't get out of her mind. Maybe she and Raymond should elope.

Doris

Doris waited until Eugene had time to get to work before she continued her relentless search for her gun. She had checked every room in the house repeatedly. It had to be in the garage. If it wasn't there, she didn't know what she would do. He might have taken it to work, but then she didn't think he'd want to explain if Thad saw him with a gun he hadn't been issued. She knew it was still in the house.

She walked to the garage in the misting rain and began going through boxes. There were boxes in there that hadn't been unpacked since they moved in the year before. After unloading several boxes, she saw Eugene's old drill case under the workbench. That old drill hadn't worked in years. He was such a packrat.

Doris pulled out the drill case. When she opened it, she laughed out loud. He thought he could stop her by splitting up the gun from the bullets. He might slow her down, but she would find the gun. She took the bullets from their hiding place, put them in the pocket of her jeans, and began searching with renewed determination.

She remembered that when they were dating, Eugene was delighted she'd developed an interest in shooting. He had just gotten on with the Sheriff's Department, and he was spending too much time at the shooting range improving his marksmanship. She got him to take her out to his dad's farm where he taught her to shoot cans off a fencepost. She got to be nearly as good as he was, and she really liked it. Now he was hiding her gun; it was funny to think about.

With only a short break for lunch, Doris spent most of the day searching the garage. About four o'clock she went back to the house, hid the bullets in her underwear drawer, and started supper. She couldn't let any change in her routine be obvious. He must be convinced she had forgotten what she said she was going to do. When all of it was over, everything would be the same again.

The next morning Doris got up while her husband was showering and prepared to get him out of the house as soon as possible. She didn't want him sitting at the table sipping his coffee, asking for a second cup, wasting her time. She made instant coffee and reached in the freezer for her lazy day stand-by.

"Eugene, I didn't feel like cooking this morning. I nuked a sausage biscuit and fixed a thermos of coffee for you. My head is killing me; I need to get back to bed. Have a good day at work." Doris handed the thermos and a brown bag with the microwaved biscuit to her husband and kissed him on the cheek. There was little for Eugene to do except kiss her back and leave early for work.

As soon as his car was out of sight, Doris pulled off her robe. She had dressed in shorts and a tank while Eugene was in the shower. After she put on her sneakers, Doris went back to the garage and resumed her search.

Again, she combed every inch of the garage. Time was running out. "It's not in here. There must be some place I've overlooked," she said out loud as she kicked Lee's bike and left the garage.

Thank goodness he had to work late tonight. She hadn't even thought about supper. She would tell him she stayed in bed with a headache all day. Maybe she would get lucky and find it before he got home.

She started with the kitchen, moved on to the family room and other first floor rooms, before going back upstairs. She had looked in their bedroom more than any other place. She decided to go back to Lee's room.

Doris went to Lee's room and looked around. It seemed funny to call it Lee's room now. All the clutter was gone. He even took his trophies with him when he moved in with the preacher. That was all the better for her; there would be less of his junk to dig through.

She started by taking everything out of his closet. There were only out of season clothes and some of his sports equipment he no longer used but wouldn't give up. She checked the pockets of each garment before hanging it back in the closet. Nothing... wasted time... She had to finish quickly before Eugene got home. She pulled out the box of equipment and started digging through his collection of catcher's mitts, shin guards left over from soccer, and two of his favorite bike helmets. At the bottom of the pile was the chest protector he wore the year he made the Little League All Star team. Didn't he ever get rid of any of this junk?

When she lifted the chest protector, she saw a wad of socks he had worn when he played various sports. Doris was about to dump all the equipment back in the box when she noticed that one black soccer sock had an unusual shape.

"There you are baby," Doris said as she fished out her gun from the sock. She jumped to her feet, leaving the equipment scattered on the floor, and ran to her room. She grabbed the bullets from her drawer and loaded the gun.

Doris changed into her black jeans and tucked the pistol in her waistband. She put on a stretched out black tee-shirt, pulled it down covering the gun, and went downstairs. With Eugene working late, maybe she could get this done before he got home.

She was walking toward the door when she saw headlights light up the driveway. Doris went into the living room and hid behind the couch. She heard the car door slam and Eugene walk into the house.

"Doris, I'm home, honey." He walked into the living room looking for her. She stood up and fired. He dropped to the floor.

She walked over to him and said, "I told you not to get in my way; I'm going to kill him." She ran out into the night.

Eugene pulled his cell out and hit speed dial for Thad.

Thad picked up on the second ring. "Eugene, haven't you had enough of me today? What do you want?"

"Thad, she shot me, and she's going after Lee."

"I'll call an ambulance for you, and we'll find Doris before she hurts Lee or anyone else. Hang on, help is on the way."

"Tyler, call an ambulance for Eugene; he's been shot. Then get everyone out on the street. Doris has shot Eugene and is looking for Lee to shoot him." Thad left the office and started driving toward Eugene's house, looking right and left hoping to catch sight of Doris. He punched in Bax's cell number and waited for him to answer.

"Hello, Thad, what can I do for you?"

"Is Lee home?"

"I don't know? I'm on my way to New Orleans for class tomorrow. Why do you ask?"

"Doris shot Eugene and is looking for their son to shoot him," Thad said.

"I'm turning around. I should be back in a little more than an hour. You call my house and check if he's home. I'll call his cell and get back to you. You might want to call Kelly Grant, Lynn and Susan's daughter. Lee has been seeing her. If he's not with her, she might know where he is."

Thad called Bax's house first; there was no answer. Then he called the Grants. There was no answer there, either.

His own phone rang. "Did you get him on his cell phone, Bax?"

"No, how about you; did you get an answer at my house or the Grants' house?" Bax asked.

"No. I just hope Lee is watching a good movie with Kelly, and we catch his mother before they roll the final credits. I have every man, even those who were off duty, out looking for her. Call me when you get here."

"I will; good luck," Bax said. He and Gene had been friends since Bax's family moved to Alabama when he was in his early teens. Gene's father had been the man he turned to for advice when his own father had been out of state preaching in revivals. His drive back would be a rolling prayer session for Gene and his family. It seemed that awful things were happening to all the people he cared about the most.

♥

Doris wandered through the town, keeping to the shadows, looking for her son. Eugene thought Lee was so perfect. While she was looking for her gun she had found where Lee hid some things he stole. That night she went out after Eugene was asleep, she saw Lee slip out of Bax's house. She knew he was up to something. She followed him that night and saw him take something out of the Patterson's car. If she had had her gun with her then, she wouldn't have had to hunt him tonight.

A twig snapped, and Doris slipped deeper into the shadows. Someone was coming. She could see him silhouetted in the moonlight as he crossed the yard directly in front of her. There was no mistaking his lanky frame. He was making it easy for her.

Doris followed her son, quietly closing the distance between them until she was only about two feet behind him. She lifted her gun and pushed it against his back. "You have destroyed my life. After you were born, everything changed. If I get rid of you, my life will go back to the way it was. I'll be happy again. You've cost me sixteen years. I should've done away with you when you were born."

Lee whirled around, knocked the pistol out of his mother's hand, and ran toward the nearest house screaming. "Help me! Help me; my mother is trying to kill me!" A shot was fired, and his frantic screams ended.

Several neighbors ran out. Buck Turner, a former college football player, ran toward the woman running with the gun and tackled her. He wrenched the weapon out of her hand and threw it out of her reach. Stripping the football from an opponent had never been as rewarding.

Some neighbors called 911 for help while others were trying to help Lee as best they could until the ambulance arrived.

A cacophony of sirens was punctuated with Doris' screams and curses. The fleet of police cars yielded to the ambulance that wove its way through the streets and pulled into the Turner's driveway. The Emergency Medical Technicians checked Lee before loading him for transport to the hospital.

Thad got out of his patrol car and ran to Buck. "Thanks, Buck; I'll take over now." He pulled Doris to her feet. "Doris, what in the world has gotten into you? No, don't answer that until I read you your rights. 'You have the right to remain silent. Anything you say can and will be used against you in a court of law. You have the right to an attorney. If you cannot afford an attorney, one will be provided for you. Do you understand the rights I have just read to you?'"

"Of course, I do. I've been married to your deputy for eighteen years, and he's watched every cop show that has ever been on TV. How could I fail to understand my *Miranda* rights?"

"Doris, what's going on? Why did you shoot Eugene and Lee?"

"I want a lawyer. I told you I understood my rights." Doris shouted.

ℰℐ

Bax got to the hospital to check on Eugene and Lee. Thad had called and told him what had happened. Pat Daily saw him come in; she left the nurse's station to meet him. "Brother Bax, both Eugene and his son are in room 204. They are both doing well."

"Thanks for telling me, Pat; I'll go right up."

When he got off the elevator, he overheard two other visitors talking as they walked down the hall ahead of him. "Can you believe what happened to Eugene and his kid? Doris has always been a little different, but to shoot her family…she must have been stark, raving mad."

The two women went into the rooms on either side of 204. Bax thought how he agreed with the ladies. He had thought that since he got the letter from an anonymous friend, but there wasn't anything he could do to protect her family. He did try to shield her son, but it didn't do any good.

He opened the door and saw the father and son sleeping. Bax took a seat to wait until one of them woke. Before his four-hour drive, Bax had worked all day at the church, and stopped to help Raymond move the tree that fell during a storm last week blocking the driveway to the cabin. He was exhausted; soon he too was sleeping.

THIRTY-THREE

Progress

T had brought Doris to the county jail and locked her in a cell. She turned to the sheriff and spat at him. "You're as blind as Eugene. Check our garage, and you'll find the things that have been taken from people's cars and houses. I knew he was slipping out. At first, I thought he was going to meet Kelly somewhere. Then I found where he stashed the things he took. I was right about him all of the time. He's no good; his father is a fool not to see it."

"I didn't think you wanted to talk to me, Doris. Have you changed your mind, or do you still want to call Robert Lawless, defender of those wrongly accused? My mistake, I mean Robert Lawford."

"Just be sure he's here before you try to talk to me again," Doris said.

He went back to his office and picked up his phone to call Fran; then he decided he would check out Eugene's garage himself. He owed it to Eugene to keep as few people involved as possible until he knew for sure if Lee committed the thefts. It wouldn't take long to search the garage. He would talk to Eugene if he was awake and get permission. If he refused, he would get a search warrant.

Thad went home. Bren met him at the door, put her arms around him and said, "I heard what Doris did to Eugene and their son. The phone has been ringing all night. Most of the callers knew more than I did, but I guess they thought you'd called with more details."

"I think she is off her rocker, Bren. Not only did she shoot her husband and hunt down her son, now she claims that Lee is the thief who has been working the county for the past few months. I'm going to talk to Eugene and Lee in the morning." He squeezed her tight. "Thank God, I have a loving, stable wife. I don't know how Eugene is going to deal with all of this. Lee will probably have emotional scars that will last a lifetime."

"Have you eaten?" Bren asked.

"No, I haven't even thought about it. Now that you mention it, I'm starving."

The next morning Thad went to the hospital before he went to the office. When he opened the door, he was surprised to find Bax already there. "You're up bright and early. How did you beat me here? Did you flash your clergy ID?"

Eugene said, "He did that last night. When the nurse woke me up in the middle of the night, there was Bax crashing on the couch. She didn't have the heart to send him home, so she got a blanket for him." Eugene looked from Bax to Thad. "Tell me about my wife."

"I locked her up last night, and she's asking for a lawyer. She wants that bargain-basement version of Johnnie Cochran, Richard Lawford. She also accused Lee of being our thief. That is why I'm here. I want permission to search your garage."

"I can save you the trouble, Sheriff Brownlee. I am your thief. Mom must have found the things I hid in the garage," Lee said. "Mom has been threatening to kill me. I just wanted to get away from her, but I didn't have enough money to get away."

"Bax got a letter from someone who overheard you talking about your mother," Eugene told his son. He turned to Thad and continued, "He came to me, and we worked out a way for Lee to move out of the house that wouldn't seem strange. I didn't know about the stealing, and I'm sure Bax didn't either."

Bax said, "No, I didn't know, but I had gotten suspicious. Lee, you lied to me about being at the movies with Kate. Then I saw you rolling my car into the garage with the lights out. I didn't know what you were up to, but I knew you were keeping a secret."

Eugene continued, "I checked to see if I could get Doris committed to a mental facility, but she had only threatened Lee. She hadn't done anything, and the threat could have been hormones talking. She has had a hard time in that department. The lawyer I talked to said a threat doesn't meet the criteria required to be classified as a clear and present danger. It wasn't enough to have her involuntarily committed. The plan Bax and I hatched up was the best I could do to keep Lee safe. Last night was proof that it wasn't good enough."

"Lee, do you still have all the things you took, or have you sold them?" Thad asked.

"Yes, sir, I have everything. I didn't really know how to get rid of any of them. I was afraid if I sold anything to my friends, it could be linked to me if anyone realized it had been stolen. I sure don't know a fence. Everything is either in our garage or in Brother Bax's tool shed. I'm sorry about that, Brother Bax."

"It is clear to me that Lee is not likely to become a habitual criminal. He's just a scared kid looking for a way out of an impossible situation. I am going to contact Bodette Goodman. She is the Juvenile Community Corrections Officer for the county. I think she will agree that in this case the best solution would be Informal Adjustment," Thad said.

"What's that?" Lee asked. "I've never heard of it."

"It's a way to resolve juvenile cases without going to court. If Bo agrees, you and your dad will have to meet with her. You must tell her exactly what you did and why you did it. This information will be held in confidence and will not be used against you. If she thinks this is the best way to handle your case, she will give you certain conditions you must meet. It could be as simple as restitution of the stolen property, or it may involve community service. She may want to place you in a different home for a while. She could let you continue to stay with Bax, or she might think that since your mother is no longer in the house, you can move back in with your dad. You must comply with whatever she decides. If she accepts this as an Informal Adjustment, your case may never go to court."

"Do you think she will go along with the adjustment?" Bax asked.

"I can't promise, but Bo is a reasonable, compassionate woman. Her job is to stop juveniles from getting deeper into trouble. I think she will recognize the extenuating circumstances that led Lee to do what he did and realize when the threat has been removed, he will no longer feel he must do anything he can to escape. After all the time you two spent killing tin cans at your dad's place, I thought Doris was a better shot. She just took a little flesh off your left arm and barely grazed Lee's leg. I think deep inside something stopped her from killing the two people closest to her. There was a little bit of sanity that kept her from that." He picked up his hat and moved toward the door. "I better get to the office and call Richman Lawless. Oops, did I say that? I meant Richard Lawford. I can't question her until he has had a chance to tell Doris not to tell me anything. I'll do a monologue and call it my interrogation."

Thad left the hospital. He called Lawford as soon as he got to the car. The lawyer agreed to meet him at the sheriff's office in an hour. Then he went to Eugene's and Bax's houses and searched their garage and tool shed. He found only a few miscellaneous items from the list of stolen property. There were no guns, no wallet, and certainly not the kayak with a decorated seat. Either Lee hadn't been truthful, or it was as he had suspected; there was more than one thief in the county.

After his non-interrogation of Doris, he went back to the hospital to talk with Lee. "Lee, when I searched your garage and Bro. Bax's tool shed, I didn't find the most valuable things that were reported stolen. Would you explain why?"

"I didn't take anything big, just small things I could hide under my shirt. I took a cell phone and some games. I took a lot of CDs that people left in unlocked cars, and a GPS that was so old the only road on it was the Oregon Trail."

"Don't try to be funny. This is not a laughing matter," Thad said.

"I know. I'm sorry I got smart-mouthed, as Mom calls it."

"If you didn't take the rest of the things reported missing, who did? Did you see anyone else prowling around when you were out?" Thad asked.

Lee paused for a split second before answering. "No, I didn't see anyone."

"Son, I noticed you paused before you answered. Are you keeping something back to protect someone?" Thad asked.

"No, sir, I didn't see anyone, but a friend of mine thought she saw me in her neighbor's yard. I told her I was home sick and didn't go anywhere that night."

Thad continued to question the teen. "Lee, you're not lying again, are you? Who is this friend?"

"It's Kelly; she thought I was coming over. I had to slip out to go over to her house; but like I told you, I was sick. She said she saw me next door and thought I just changed my mind about seeing her."

"I will need to talk to her. I'll ask her mother to bring her in to answer a few questions about what she saw," Thad said.

After he left the hospital, Thad began to review what he had accomplished. All in all, it had been a productive twenty-four hours. He had locked up Doris, found out who was responsible for the petty theft increase, and discovered that there was probably another more ambitious thief still at large.

When he got back to the office, there was a message indicator blinking on his phone.

He played the message. "Thad, Abe here. I just got information that there is another Viper in your area. The code name is Medusa; we believe she is a high-ranking female in the organization. I have nothing more specific at this time; but as soon as I learn more, I'll get back in touch with you."

He rubbed his neck in frustration. He guessed he could add one more thing to his list of accomplishments for the day. He found out there was a high-ranking member of a subversive organization on his doorstep. How he missed the slow pace the job used to have. Speeding tickets, kids shoplifting, and old ladies afraid there was an intruder when tree branches brushed against the window...those were the days he missed.

He finished his paperwork and drove home to Bren and the kids. At least that part of his life was still predictable and peaceful...happy. He had never defined happiness in those terms, but he was happy when he was home with them. He only wished Eugene and Lee had the same kind of home life. He was a lucky man.

THIRTY-FOUR

Thanks

Brosia had decided to have a picnic for the community to show her appreciation for all that had been done for Ana since she had been shot. She and Raymond were interlopers in a small Southern community, yet everyone had treated the three of them like family, not strangers. Lovie would help if Brosia asked her, but they were the very ones she wanted to honor the most. She was determined to keep her plan secret, so she went to town to start putting that plan in action.

Brosia pulled into a parking slot and tooted her horn. Missy skated out to her car and said what she always did when customers tooted their horn for attention. "Tell it."

"Missy, can you sit down in the car with me? I have an unusual order, and I need to talk it over with you," Brosia said.

"How unusual could an order placed here be? All we have are hot dogs, hamburgers, cheeseburgers, malts, shakes, soft drinks, and fries," she said as she plopped down beside Brosia. "My legs are killing me. I'm getting too old for this skating."

Brosia nodded in understanding. "It's not the menu that is unusual; it's the amount that I want to order. I would like for you to grill one hundred fifty hamburgers ahead of time and warm them in a microwave at my picnic. Then on the day of the party set up a burger bar with all the trimmings so my guests can make their own. You have one of those hotdog cookers that roll the wieners while they cook, don't you?" Missy nodded, and Brosia continued placing her order. "I want a hotdog bar, too. One hundred of the dogs should be enough."

"We can do that, but it will cost you."

"I know it will be expensive, but this is how I want to thank all the people who were so good to my Anastasia. Here's my phone number; when you've figured the price, call me and I'll bring the check for the deposit over to you."

Missy couldn't believe her luck. Brosia had just given her the chance of a lifetime. She smiled as she watched Brosia drive down the road on her way to the second stop to put her plan in action.

Brosia parked outside of Kathy's Kountry Kitchen and went in.

"Good afternoon, Kathy, I want to place an order."

"Sure, sit down; I'll get today's menu."

"No, I don't want to order a late lunch. I'm planning a party, a picnic, to thank all the people who helped us while Ana was in the hospital and when she first came home. You sent in some wonderful food; I'd like for you to make potato salad and baked beans for about two hundred people. The cake you sent was just wonderful. Would you make one for the dessert?"

"That would have to be a mighty big cake. Do you think making several smaller ones would work?"

"Let me think about that, and I'll get back to you when you work up your price for the party. I'll give you a check for the deposit as soon as you give me the price."

"That sounds good. Thank you for thinking of using me." She waved to Brosia as she got back into her car and drove away. That was a real blessing; business had slacked off, and she was worried that she might not be able to pay her only employee. Not only would the deposit buy a little time, but the idea of catering might just bring in the extra income she needed to cover the loss of lunch trade.

As Brosia drove home, she worried about Bax's friend, Gene. The poor man and his son were supposed to come home from the hospital today. They weren't injured as seriously as Ana had been, but she knew a person didn't just bounce back from a gunshot wound, even if it weren't life-threatening.

Since they wouldn't have anyone to take care of them, she would make a big pot of gumbo and take it over. That way she could help Gene and Lee the way so many helped her. She planned to go over once a day and check on them. Then while she was there, she would tidy up things.

Brosia made one more stop; she needed gumbo makings. She ran into Bax in the produce aisle. "Brother Bax, I'm planning a picnic to thank everyone. You have done so much for Ana and for Raymond and me as well. I want to be sure you will be able to attend. I want to have the party next month. You have so many irons in the fire, what with your classes and all of your pastoral duties. I want to schedule the party on a date you're sure you can attend."

"Miss Brosia, I am flattered. I'd love to be there. I'll check my calendar and send you the dates when I have nothing scheduled. However, if someone has an emergency or if there is a death, I will have to bow out."

"Well, I'm just going to pray for everyone in your congregation to have a healthy, uneventful month," Brosia said.

Brosia finished her shopping and went home with a feeling of accomplishment.

Raymond met Brosia in the driveway. "I just got a call from Thad. Agent Abe called him today and told him they suspect another Viper is in the vicinity. He wanted to put us on alert so we can be on the lookout for any strangers hanging around. The part I found interesting is that they think this Viper is a woman.

Just be careful about getting too friendly with strangers. The Viper could be posing as a friendly Avon lady, for all we know."

"Raymond, I won't be inviting a strange Avon lady in for tea. I'm sorry; I shouldn't have said that. This is no time for silly jokes. You, of all people, should know that women can be just as relentless and just as deadly as any man. No matter if the one they sent this time is a man or woman, these people aren't playing. There must be some way to convince them that we don't have what they want." She moved past him into the house, and then turned around. "Why do they think it's a woman anyway?"

"The code name, Medusa, was given for this person. That name is synonymous with a deadly woman."

"Raymond, do I have to remind you that my parents emigrated from Greece? I was raised on the story of the beautiful Gorgon who insulted Athena. She ended up with a head full of snakes and a face that turned people to stone. So, do you think we should be looking for an ugly girl with snakes for dreadlocks, or a beautiful Greek girl who insults goddesses? I think you're reading too much into the code name. We shouldn't rule out men. It is only a code name, not a description."

"You're right, of course, Brosia; neither of us should be making flippant remarks. Ana can't withstand another attack."

"Do you think we should warn her of the possibility?" Brosia asked.

"No, it would only worry her. We just need to be very careful and make sure no one gets near her."

"Do you think we should postpone our plans or even cancel them, Raymond?"

"By no means should we do either. We don't even know if this person exists. The agent only said that they suspected another Viper was in the area. We can't put our lives on hold for a mere suspicion. You have invested a lot of time planning a way to show the community how much we appreciate all they have done to help us while Ana was critical. I think we should continue as if we hadn't heard about what they suspect. Of course, we will be careful, and not lulled into a false sense of security."

"Why can't everything get back to normal? I'm so tired of looking for some sign that everyone I meet might hurt Ana."

"Are you forgetting that has been our normal since we worked out a way to help her when her parents were killed? We were only fooled into comfortable ignorance when she met and married Dave." He put his arm around her matronly waist and walked her back to the house. "Maybe one day all of this will be behind us, and we can discover what is normal to other people."

Picnic

Lovie pulled up in her pick-up an hour early and burst into the cabin wagging a five-gallon plastic bucket. "Brosia, I know you said not to bring anything because you had the food covered, but whoever heard of a picnic without coleslaw. I came over early to help you set up for your party, but it looks like you have already got everything ready to go. Do you have a dish big enough to hold this slaw?"

"Oh, Lovie, you shouldn't have gone to all that trouble; you really shouldn't. I don't have a bowl large enough to hold that much slaw. Maybe you can fill all of the bowls that are in the cupboard and rotate them when the ones on the serving table are empty. That bucket won't fit in the refrigerator and we will have to keep it refrigerated until it's time to serve the meal," Brosia said.

"I know what we can do; I'll empty your refrigerator crisper drawers. Then I'll empty my slaw into them. We'll just fill the bowls from the drawers, problem solved." Lovie bustled into the kitchen and began unloading and washing the crispers drawers before filling them with the abundance of shredded cabbage and mayonnaise from the oversized plastic bucket.

Brosia looked at Ana, shook her head and thought there was no stopping a force of nature once it gains enough momentum.

At this moment, hurricane Lovie was cutting a swath through her kitchen. She knew it was only a matter of time before Lovie extended her helping to the ladies she had hired to cater the party. Maybe they won't mind Lovie trying to take over.

A few other vehicles had arrived. People were pulling their folding chairs out of the trunks and establishing their claims on the best spots. Teens and school age children were surreptitiously spreading out as far from the old folks as they could, without running the risk of being called back into the family fold.

Brosia noticed that when Lee jumped out of Bodette's car, he couldn't get with the young folks quickly enough. It was too bad Gene had to work today, but someone had to be on duty. It was nice of Bo to give the young man a ride.

It was time for Brosia, Raymond, and Ana to go out and welcome their guests. They walked out on the porch and greeted the folks who were making themselves at home in the porch swing. When they saw Bax get out of his car, they waved. "This is a step in the right direction, Brosia. No one in the church had an emergency. Bax made it."

"Yes, and both Missy and Kathy have everything set up and ready to serve. It looks like everything is going to go off without a hitch."

Thad had just pulled up with his wife. Fran and a beautiful Oriental lady were with them. "I'm so glad they came. Those men are top notch in my book. They've been there for Ana for so long and have seen some of the worst parts of our lives. It's time they see us happy," Raymond said.

"I'm glad to finally see Fran's girlfriend. I was beginning to think she only existed in his imagination," Brosia said.

Ana, who had been unusually quiet, spoke up. "I'm going over and introduce myself. I know what it feels like to be the newcomer in a small town, examined by the curious eyes of strangers."

Ana walked over to the place where Thad and Fran were setting up the folding chairs. "With the county's two best lawmen here, I know we'll be protected from everything but the mosquitoes." Everyone laughed at her weak attempt at humor. She turned to the stranger and introduced herself. "I'm Ana Leblanc."

"It's nice to meet you, Ana; I'm Joy Wing. I thought your name was Fontaine."

"I decided after all that has happened to go back to my maiden name, and the judge agreed."

"I apologize. I can't believe how thoughtless that comment was."

"Don't worry about it; sometimes things just pop out of our mouths," Ana said.

"Joy is a wonderful, intelligent woman, but she has no filter. If she thinks it, she says it before she even realizes she's talking. However, whatever she says is what she truly thinks. The woman doesn't know how to lie. That's why I worry about her career choice. She going back to school to study political science, but unless she learns to spin a yarn with the best of them, she won't stand a chance to get elected to the legislature." Fran said, as he put his arm around her shoulder.

"Fran, I've told you I don't plan on being a politician any more than a person who studies animal science plans to become an animal. I just find it fascinating to study."

"Let's change the subject before she dies of embarrassment," Ana said, with a soft laugh. Men don't let well enough alone. The girl was blushing and twisting her hair. Couldn't he see that?

Joy truly did want a change of topic. She was trying to think of something to say when she saw the silver and jade pendant around Ana's neck. "What an unusual pendant you have on! It reminds me of a saying of my grandmother's. She used it to remind my sisters and me to always hold our heads up, even when something bad happened to us. We might be broken, but we were not made of common clay. We were jade; nothing could devalue us. It gave us an abiding self-confidence."

Ana smiled as she fingered the pendant and said, "Yes, I know the proverb. A friend gave this to me to remind me of that truth."

"My grandmother believed wearing jade protected us and gave us all jade bracelets. It is a common belief in our culture that the bracelet will take the harm meant for a woman. It breaks so she can escape damage. I've done it again; I talk too much," Joy said as she began to twist her long hair. "I'm sure you have had more than enough ancient Chinese wisdom for today."

"No, really. I found your grandmother's story interesting. I don't know if the jade that was broken for my pendant would fall into that category, but it would be nice to think I was protected from more harm," Ana said again fingering her gift.

Bax walked over and joined the group. Thad and Bren returned from carrying a large tray of assorted homemade candies to Brosia. Thad said, "Bax, why don't you and Ana join us. Fran, do you mind going back to the car to get two more chairs? It looks like Ana and Joy are enjoying each other's company."

Ana held up her hand in protest. "I promise I'll be back. I want to visit with all of you but, as one of the hostesses, I need to visit all of our guests. After I've made my rounds, I'll join you and have some of Bren's candy. I haven't seen Forever Ambers in years. I was always a sucker for any candy made with candy, and those sugary-orange slices were among my favorites,"

Ana walked toward Mr. Wilson. "I'm so glad you came to our picnic, Mr. Wilson. How are you doing today? Are Al and his family going to join you?"

"I can't say if they will or they won't. We don't see much of each other outside of work. I hope they come. Seeing my grandchildren would make this picnic worth my time. On the other hand, I don't see Woodrow if I can help it, but I can't avoid it today. I saw him eyeing those wieners over at Missy's cookout setup." He pointed back at the hot-dog-cooker. "I hope you're serving something besides those hot dogs I saw Missy put on that silly roller-cooker thing she brought over from the Toot. Why would a grown woman name her business such an asinine thing as Toot and Tell It? That husband of hers doesn't have any sense and even less backbone if he went along with such a fool thing."

"I know there are several other things you might enjoy on the menu. Have a good time."

As she walked away, she heard him mumble, "Fat chance, but at least it's free." She just shook her head and walked over to ask Billy Ray if he had seen where Sister had gone. Before she could ask, a huge man in cut-off scrubs joined them. It was Hank's older son. Woodrow Wilson was less than presidential in his appearance and behavior. In fact, his father was totally embarrassed by the scion of the family.

"How are you, Woody? Have you met Ana?" Billy Ray asked.

The mountain of a man, whose five-hundred-pound body looked like it had avalanched to a lumpy mass at his midsection, replied. "No, I haven't; it's nice to meet you, ma'am." With the decidedly Southern show of manners out of way, he turned his attention back to Billy Ray.

"I guess you've heard Freda Kay and I split the sheets last month. I just couldn't get along with her boyfriends. Some people say I got a raw deal. I got both of the children, but she got the house and its contents, except for my clothes. It was like that old country song, She Got the Goldmine, I Got the Shaft."

"That doesn't seem fair, Woody," Billy Ray said.

"Well, it could have had something to do with what I said to the judge," Woody said.

"Woody, even a knucklehead knows you don't talk back to a judge. What happened?" Billy Ray asked, half dreading the answer.

"You know those lawmen who hang around the courthouse? Most of the time they're nice as can be, but when push comes to shove, they'll haul your rear end out of the courthouse in a heartbeat."

Billy Ray's interest rose at this hint of fresh gossip. "Woody, who did you push?"

"Oh, I didn't push anybody. That's just an old saying. All I did was suggest, in language that might have been a little too crude to repeat in front of Miss Ana, that the judge, as well as my next-door-neighbor, might have been sleeping with my wife. He took offense and had them strong-arm me out of the building. At least I got to keep my racecar and motorcycle. My old daddy was so embarrassed by my court appearance, he nearly died." Woody laughed loudly and said, "That almost made up for losing the house."

Billy Ray failed to see the humor, so he grunted, "We are supposed to mingle and make everyone feel welcome. Come on, Ana, let's talk to Bodette." He had had enough of Woody.

In her role as a mingler, Brosia walked over to meet Joy and welcome her. "Fran, where have you been hiding this lovely young lady? I'm Brosia Leblanc; I wanted to personally welcome you. I'm delighted to see this workaholic is taking a little time away from the office with someone much better looking than Thad."

"I'm Joy Wing; I met your daughter a few minutes ago. Ana has a way of putting people at ease; I really liked her," Joy said.

"I'm so glad you got along; she does make people feel comfortable. But Ana isn't my daughter; she is my niece. I do feel like she is a daughter. I couldn't ask for a sweeter person in my life.

Brosia turned to Bax and said, "Bax, I need to steal you away from these folks for a few minutes."

Bax followed her back to the cabin. He turned on the speaker system he brought over from the church for the occasion and began to try to get the attention of the crowd. "Friends, may I have your attention for an announcement." There was little response. People were so engrossed in their conversations they didn't hear him. The guests finally turned their attention to the man on the porch after he repeated his request three times.

"We are here to celebrate Ana's recovery and to thank all of the community for the help given to her and Brosia. As special as a celebration of those things would be, that's only a part of the reason you are here. I must confess I am part of a conspiracy to gather you here under false pretenses. We are here to join Brosia and Raymond in marriage."

Bax had to interrupt the crowd's excited reaction in order to continue. "They have known each other most of their lives. Raymond and Brosia's late husband were friends. After Sully died and Ana came to live with her aunt, Raymond looked in on his friend's family from time to time to help them through rough times. When Ana's husband tried to kill her, Brosia turned to her old friend. He stood by them and did his best to protect them.

"During this terrible time, the two old friends depended on each other and grew closer. When they realized their friendship had matured to love, they came to me and asked me if I'd marry them.

"Lovie and Billy Ray, will you join us here on the porch? Raymond and Brosia want you along with Ana, to be their witnesses."

"I never thought my matron of honor outfit would be blue jeans and a Roll Tide tee-shirt. You know I have a nice dress I could have worn," Lovie whispered to the bride as she embraced her.

"It wouldn't have been proper for you to outshine me in my LSU shirt," Brosia whispered back as she tugged her purple and gold tee over her hips. "I wanted a simple wedding with the only decorations being the smiles on my friends' faces."

"The couple has asked that the ceremony be short and as informal as this picnic," Bax said. "Raymond, do you take Brosia as your wife?"

"I do."

"Brosia, do you take Raymond as your husband?"

"I do."

"You may exchange rings, if you promise to treat each other with love and respect as you live together as man and wife using the Bible's guidance."

"We promise," they answered in unison and exchanged rings.

"I now pronounce you man and wife."

Bax hardly got the words out of his mouth when movement in the woods caught his attention. He saw a rifle barrel pushing branches out of the way as David emerged from the thicket. Bax dropped his Bible and raced toward David just as a gunshot split the stunned silence of the wedding guests. All eyes followed the preacher as he hit the ground and rolled behind a large tree.

Thad and Fran ran past him toward David, who was crumpled against a tree, the gun still in his hand.

"He's dead; Fran, we need to call the Handmaiden. Then call Eugene and Red. Tell them to get over here pronto to help question the guests. Somebody must have seen who shot him."

"Bax, what did you see that made you run like you did? Did you see who shot him?"

"No, I just saw some motion in my peripheral vision in an area where no one should have been. Since Ana was shot, I have been more aware of such things. When I turned my head to get a better look, I saw Dave coming through the woods with a gun pointed toward the porch where the wedding party was standing. There was no time to tell anyone what was going on. I just took off running, planning to tackle him before he could shoot."

Thad said, "I guess the big question is who shot Dave? Everyone here is an invited guest. Besides Ana, Brosia, and Raymond, no one knew him."

Brosia ran up to Thad. "Have any of you seen Ana? She was standing beside me when Bax bolted off just before the shot. Now I can't find her!"

"Don't get so upset; I'm sure she is around. Have you checked the cabin? She might have gone in there," Thad said.

"Yes, and she wasn't there."

"We'll be questioning all of the witnesses. I'll ask if anyone has seen her. She was probably scared out of her mind and ran to hide. I'm sure she will turn up before long. There was so much confusion when the shot rang out and Bax dove for safety; no wonder no one you asked remembered seeing her," Thad said.

"Thad, I know you have a murder to solve, but I'm not so sure you can relegate Ana's disappearance to a low-priority problem. She has been a target too many times to ignore the possibility that the same person who shot Dave might have taken her," Bax said. "I'm going to check the property. There are a few places I can think of that she might have thought would be safe. If she is hiding, one of those would be the place she went. Why don't you and Raymond come with me, Brosia?"

Terror

When Bax started running toward the woods, Ana saw Dave step out of the trees with a gun pointed toward her. She turned and ran in the opposite direction. The sound of gunfire spurred her to run faster. She had to get away. She knew where she could go. She would be safe in the abandoned cabin Bax showed her when they were walking last week. That old cabin was almost completely covered with kudzu. It looked like a rustic topiary. If she could find a way in, no one would be able to find her there.

Ana zigzagged between the cars that were parked on most of the cleared land and headed toward the wooded area across the unpaved road that ran by Bax's land. The sound of crunching gravel was the only warning she had before a hand grabbed her, just a moment before a blow to her head knocked her to the ground, and enveloped her in a void of darkness with no sound, no thought, and no hope.

The sound of a motor penetrated the blackness. Slowly the rest of her senses returned. The vehicle bumped over rough terrain. She realized she was prone, tied hand and foot, on the floor of some type of van or truck. Her eyes began to adjust to the darkness; but it was so complete, and her position so limiting she could only make out a few darker spots on the floor.

Dave hadn't died in that explosion, and now he had her. He must still think she knew where that package was, or he would have killed her. How did he catch her with all those people between them? They must have seen the gun and heard the shot. This wasn't making any sense. She knew Bax was trying to stop him. Did he shoot Bax? No, if he had, Thad or some of his men who were at the wedding would have stopped him.

Her head was pounding. She couldn't think straight. There was something she was missing. It couldn't have happened that way.

The vehicle hit a deep pothole, and Ana's head slammed against the floor with enough force to knock her out again. When she came to, she was no longer tied up; but her condition was no better.

Ana was in a stuffy, totally dark place. She rubbed her wrist and ankles. Thank God for small favors. At least she wasn't tied up anymore. She began to explore the area. When she tried to stand up, she was stopped when she bumped her head on a metal screen. She dropped to her knees. When she crawled forward, she bumped into another medal screen. She was in a cage!

Ana reached out and threaded her fingers through the mesh. No wonder it was stuffy and dark; there was a blanket over the cage. She crawled to the nearest corner of the cage. She knew she could span an octave on a piano, and that the width of a key was just slightly less than an inch. So, an octave would be between seven and a half inches and eight inches long.

Ana started measuring from the corner and continued measuring the perimeter of her prison. The results were devastating, seven and a half octaves long, five octaves wide, and six and a half octaves high. She approximated the enclosure to be about 17 square feet. When she multiplied that by the height, she screamed with anger and frustration. "My world has shrunk to 74 cubic feet, a crate suitable for a large dog! I guess I should be grateful for the bottle of water and granola bar I found in the corner. Oh, yes, I must include the gallon plastic zipper bags and box of wet wipes, all the comforts of home!"

She grabbed the sides of the cage and shook it at hard as she could. All of her fear, anger, and grief poured out in a guttural cascade of wordless emotion. She collapsed into a fetal position as the terrified cry dissolved into deep sobs. At last, she succumbed to a restless sleep. Sleep was her only ally, her only escape.

The sound of a heavy door closing woke her. Footsteps were getting closer to the cage.

"Bet…" He caught himself between syllables. He had almost called her the name she used when they met years ago in college before she dropped out of sight and devoted herself to the mission.

"Don't call me that! If she heard you, we would have no choice but to get rid of her," a muffled female voice warned him.

Ana slowed her breath and feigned sleep. She could feel cooler air on her skin and knew the blanket had been lifted. They were deciding her fate. If she flinched, she died. Bet or her companion dropped the blanket and began to kick the cage and call her name.

In a sleepy voice Ana said, "What do you want with me? Why did you take me?"

"I have the only question that needs to be answered. Where is the package? I know your husband lost it, and you found it. What did you do with it?" The voice sounded different from either of the ones she had heard when they came in. It could be electronically altered, or maybe there were more than two people out there.

"I honestly don't know anything about what you want. I heard two men talking after a shot was fired, and someone screamed. Then one of the men searched my car and said 'Should I shoot the woman?' when he couldn't find what he wanted. Later I did find the package and hid it because I didn't want any part of a thing they would kill for."

The strange voice said, "Where did you hide it?"

"I passed a dump and put it in a junked washing machine. That's all I know."

"Where is the dumping place?"

"I don't know. I had a head injury, and things from that time are a blur," Ana said.

"Yet you remember hearing the men shoot someone, and that you hid my package. It seems strange to me that the only thing that is, in your words, a blur, is the location of the package. I find that hard to believe. Before long I think I can help you remember."

Ana listened carefully to the footsteps as the people left the room. She was right; only two people walked away. Not that it helped her; she was still outnumbered and caged.

After a marathon of nightmares Ana awoke to face a reality even more terrifying. She felt a piece of paper next to a solitary bottle of water and a small flashlight. When she turned it on, a dim light illuminated a note. *Perhaps a few days with no food will clear away the blur in your memory, so you will be able to tell me what I need to know.*

They thought they could starve information from her. She would not tell them any more than she had already. No one else needed to be targeted the way she had been, Ana turned off the light. She should only use it when she needed to. Even with careful use, the weak batteries didn't last.

The time dragged on with no food or contact from her captors. She had no way to judge how long she had been without food. The peppermints she kept in her pocket to keep the symptoms of her hypoglycemia under control had been used hours before. Now she had broken out in a sweat and was shaking. Those symptoms were far worse than the increasing thirst and hunger pains that punctuated brief intervals of sleep. She had rationed her water, but it had been gone for a while. Her weakness was overwhelming, and she feared she was becoming delirious.

Ana heard the heavy door groan on its hinges, then footsteps. Perhaps that was all in her mind, a figment fueled by the fervent hope they had not left her here to die. Then she heard the familiar, disembodied voice.

"Ana, you have had time to think. Has that fog lifted? Tell me what I want to know and I'll see that you get a juicy, hot hamburger and something cool and refreshing to drink. I know you must be hungry and thirsty."

Ana begin to cry softly and thought, I can smell the food. Maybe Bet, or whatever her name is, brought the burger and drink with her. She was so hungry and wanted them both so badly she was tempted to make up a story just to get the food. Who was she trying to kid? There was no food out there. She was probably having an olfactory hallucination, or maybe she had lost her mind.

Her sobs became so much louder that Ana didn't even hear the cage door open and quickly close before the footsteps grew more distant. The heavy door opened with the familiar groan. They were leaving. She barely heard the voice say, "Maybe that water and energy bar we left will keep her alive long enough for us to break her."

Ana felt her way toward the place she found the bar and water the time before. When she reached out to feel for the bottle, her hand touched the end of the cage. She drew it back for a moment then quickly pushed it. She was right; it had moved. The cage door swung open. They had forgotten to relock it.

Ana found the bar and ate half of it and drank sparingly. As much as she wanted the food and water, she knew it wouldn't be wise to eat or drink too much after being without so long. She put the rest in her jeans pocket and crawled out of the crate.

She had to go slowly. She tried to stand. Her legs ached as muscles, inactive so long in the cramped pen, tried to support her weight. Staggering, she caught herself on the cage before she fell. Maybe it would be better if she just crawled. She was more stable on all fours than on her feet, plus she thought she would be less noticeable down low.

She looked in the direction the footsteps came from when her captors came and went. There was a thin line of light near the floor. That had to be the door. She crawled toward the light. At least now she knew it was daytime. She would be more exposed and easily spotted, but she couldn't afford to wait for dark. They could come back at any time.

She pulled herself up by the doorknob and opened the door and came face to face with a person she recognized. Before she had time to react, the woman punched her in the face, knocking Ana down and then kicking her in the head and stomach with her heavy boots.

The man ran toward them screaming, "Stop it! You're going to kill her, and she won't be able to tell us where the package is. The starvation was working. If we put her back in the cage a few more days, she'll break." He dropped to his knees and felt for a pulse and shook his head. "I can't find a pulse. Help me load her into the van before someone drives up and sees her. We can dump her where we dumped that old couch."

He picked up the limp body, waited until the woman opened the door, and then threw Ana back into the van that brought her to her prison.

Woody

W oody Wilson got out of his truck. He walked to the bed and said, "Hop out you lazy things; it's time for a little exercise. It'll be hunting season before you know it, and I don't want you fat and lazy." The two labs jumped from the back of the truck and danced around his feet, ready for their morning run.

At least he could kill two birds with one stone this morning. He was going to put an end to the dumping, and who knew what else on his daddy's place. If Daddy were dead, he'd roll over in his grave if he could see the trash folks have been dumping on the land he worked too hard to buy. People just didn't respect private property anymore. When they dumped that old couch he had found yesterday, they stepped way over the line. He pulled out the tools and chains he had brought to cut off access to the logging road he had maintained after his father replanted the timberland.

The old man thought he was good for nothing. His daddy had no idea how much he did to maintain this land. Money does grow on trees, if you take good care of them.

He started by nailing a no dumping sign under the weathered posted sign on one of the ten-year-old trees. Not that anyone ever obeyed a sign, but at least he was trying to protect these trees. In five more years, this tract would be ready to thin, if he could keep these idiots out of there. He had picked up enough beer cans and cigarette butts to know kids came down there to party. They could start a fire that would ruin this whole stand.

The two dogs had been playing nearby, waiting for him to take them for their morning run. Woody looked around when he heard Nick's distinctive bark. He caught sight of Patty running into the trees about a quarter mile down the logging road.

"You scoundrels, get back here." They both had the bad habit of running away, if they thought he was distracted. Woody dropped his hammer next to the long chain and ran after the dogs. He could see where the two had left the road. Weaving his way through the saplings and underbrush, he followed Nick's excited barking. The sound seemed to be getting closer, as if the dogs had stopped running, and he was closing the gap.

He could see a clearing up ahead and recognized where he was. The dogs had found a shortcut to the dumping sight. "The game's over. You nearly gave me a heart attack. This body isn't made for running after you two outlaws. It looks like I'm going to have to use the leashes to keep you boys from running away," he said as he took two leads from his pocket and clipped one on each dog's collar. As he tried to guide the pair back to the road, they both began to pull toward the discarded couch and began to howl. "What's wrong with y'all?"

"What's that?" he asked as they pulled him closer and closer. Then he saw what had excited the dogs, a human foot. He dropped the leashes and ran toward the trashed couch. Behind it was a woman. She was gaunt and so badly beaten that she was almost unrecognizable, but he recognized her silver and jade pendant. It was Ana.

Woody knelt down and touched her cold face. "Not the cold of death yet…" He took her pulse. "It's faint and irregular, but she is still alive. You boys may have saved her life," he said as he rubbed each dog's head and then took out his cell phone and called 911. "Darn. There's no signal. I should have known there wouldn't be one this far out in such a wooded area." He positioned the dogs on either side of her, close enough that their body heat would give her a little warmth. "You boys stay here with her. I'll get help."

Woody walked back along the logging road to his truck. There should be a signal when I get to some open country on the other side of the bend. He drove and redialed several times, hoping he was out of the dead spot.

Finally, a woman came on the line. "911, what is your emergency?"

"This is Woody Wilson. I've just found Ana Fontaine just off the old logging road that runs through my dad's tree farm. She is unconscious and has a faint, slow pulse. Get an ambulance out here, and call the sheriff."

As the woman took his information, he turned the pick-up around and headed back to the spot where he'd found Ana. He didn't know how long she had been there, beaten and alone. He knew instinctively she needed to know she wasn't alone now. The dogs were just warm bodies; she needed the sound of a human voice. He edged the old truck well above the speed limit and drove back to the place someone dumped the woman the whole county had been searching for.

Woody found the dogs lying on either side of Ana. Patty was licking her arm. He brought an old jacket from the truck and covered her as best he could. In the distance he could hear the wail of the siren. "It won't be long now, Miss Ana. Help's on the way; just hold on."

The ambulance, followed by Thad, threaded through the narrow logging road. Woody was waving them forward to the littered area ahead. The paramedics jumped out and followed him to the place behind the torn brown couch where Ana lay. As they checked her vital signs, covered her with warming blankets,

and loaded her in the ambulance, Thad started questioning
Woody.

"Tell me how you found her, Woody. When you called, the
signal was poor; and I might have missed something," Thad said.

"Sure, Sheriff, it's like I said. I had my dogs with me while
I was putting up no dumping signs on my daddy's land. I was
going to put chains across the road, so cars couldn't get back
where kids had been partying, and folks had started dumping
stuff. I was paying more attention to what I was doing than I was
to the dogs. They took off through the woods. I saw them just
before they got out of sight and followed them. They led me back
here.

At first, I didn't see her, but the dogs were awfully interested
in what was behind that old couch. When I got closer, I saw her
foot. At first, I thought she was dead, but I found a weak pulse
and called you. That's all I know."

"Did you see anyone else out here?"

"No."

"Were there any tire prints or footprints in the loose soil?"
Thad asked.

"Not that I noticed. I was just following those dogs, not
tracking. If there were any prints, I guess the dogs and I messed
them up. Nick and Patty were jumping around, all excited, and
I was just trying to get a leash on them to get them back to the
truck."

"Thank you, Woody. I know you did your best. You may
have saved the woman's life. I don't want this to be public
knowledge. It will be better, if whoever did this thinks she is
dead. Call me if you remember anything else, anything at all."

"I sure will, Thad. I'm just sorry that I can't help more."

The two men walked back to their vehicles leaving Eugene
to photograph anything that seemed out of place.

As soon as Woody got out of the dead spot, he punched his
speed dial for Bax. Surely the preacher had the right to know.

The phone rang five times before Bax answered. "Hello, Bax Alford here."

"Brother Bax, this is Woody Wilson. I've just left my daddy's tree farm; I found Ana Fontaine out there."

"What! Is she all right?"

"She's alive, if that's what you mean, but she's in bad shape. I called the sheriff. He guided the ambulance out to daddy's place and then followed it to the hospital. The deputy is still looking for clues, I guess. He was photographing stuff when the sheriff and I left. Even though the sheriff said he didn't want the public to know Ana had been found, I thought I'd better call you. I know you are close friends with her and those folks she lives with out at your cabin. If the sheriff didn't think about calling them, maybe you should."

"Thank you for thinking to call. I'll call Brosia and Raymond as soon as we get off the phone."

"I'll let you go so you can get to the hospital. Good bye," Woody said.

"Good bye, Woody. Thanks again for letting me know."

Before Bax could dial her number, Brosia called him. "Bax, they found Ana. We're on our way to the hospital now. I wanted to call Lovie and Billy Ray, but Thad said she would be safer if less people knew she had been found alive."

"Woody Wilson just called me. He's the one that found her. I'm on my way; I'll see you there," Bax said.

"I'm sure the sheriff won't mind that you know. As a pastor you are used to keeping secrets. I know I'm happy to have a friend to be there with us."

When Brosia and Raymond got there, they were brought in through the service entrance and up the service elevator. Bax had arrived before and was in the room when they came in. Brosia caught her breath when she saw Ana. She walked to the bed and took the hand of the bruised and sleeping woman connected to a drip; an assortment of monitors recorded her condition. "What did they do to you, darling girl?" she whispered.

Raymond joined her at the bedside and put an arm around her shoulders. He could feel the silent sobs she struggled to suppress. "Ana, we're here to help you get through this. Bax is here, too," he said.

Bax stood near the door watching as the old couple whispered assurances to a woman whose bruised and swollen face bore no resemblance to the person they all cared about. How had she endured the deprivation and punishment she must have been through?

THIRTY-EIGHT

Hank

Hank Wilson stormed into the Sheriff's office and frowned when the only person he saw was the new addition to the staff. "Girl, where is everybody; I need help," he gruffly demanded.

"They're all working on a case. I'm Deputy Cath Jordan; can I help you?"

"Not unless you can control a mule. I borrowed that Bardwell kid's mule to move some trees that blew down on my land in that storm last week. The dang thing is so cantankerous; he gives that whole branch of the equine family a bad name."

"I'm afraid I can't do that, but I don't understand why you need the Sheriff to control a mule, Mister... I'm sorry; I didn't get your name."

"I didn't give it to you, and I didn't say I wanted the Sheriff to work that mule. I want to find out from Eugene where I can find his boy. Bardwell said Lee had worked Colitis for him a while back." Wilson muttered something about law enforcement being no job for a female as he slammed the door behind him.

Cath shook her head. "That has to be the rudest old goat in the county. He and the mule deserve each other." She took a sip from her diet drink and a bite from a half-eaten candy bar, before she went back to her paperwork.

When she heard Fran come in, she looked up and asked, "Was it Ana Fontaine?" When he nodded, she waited for more information. None was given, so she asked, "She's not dead, is she?"

"No, she's in bad shape, but she's recovered from worse. Thad went to the hospital after he finished getting information from Woody. Eugene is finishing up where we found her. There isn't much to photograph, just an oily spot near where they dumped her. Of course, that could be from a different vehicle than the one she was in."

"Some old man came in looking for Eugene. He was the most disgruntled old coot I've ever met."

Fran laughed and said, "Deputy Jordan, you have just met one of our most outstanding citizens. Believe me, Hank Wilson would not appreciate being called an old coot, not that he hasn't been called a lot worse. What did he want with Eugene?"

"He wanted Eugene to get Lee to help him move some trees. It seems he borrowed a cantankerous mule he can't control, and he heard that Lee could handle the animal," Cath said.

"I know where Lee is. I'll give him a call and tell him Wilson has a job for him. He's doing odd jobs to save for college. If Wilson will give him combat pay, he might consider it," Fran said as he punched in Lee's number.

"Combat pay. You have to be kidding," Cath said.

"It's clear to me you've never worked with a stubborn mule or Hank Wilson. I'd be hard pressed to say which of the two would be worse, but I have a feeling it would be Hank."

The phone rang; Lee answered on the fourth ring. Fran said, "Lee, Old Man Wilson has a job for you, if you think you can handle a pair of stubborn mules. I know you can handle the four legged one; it's Wilson I'd worry about."

"If he pays me well enough, I can put up with anything. When does he want me?" Lee asked.

"I think the sooner the better. Go out to his place and see what he wants done."

"I'm on my way. Thanks for calling me; I need the money."

Lee got on his bike and rode out to Wilson's place. Before he saw the old man, he could hear him yelling at the mule.

"You have no pride of ancestry or hope of posterity, you low-down, lop-eared son of a jackass!" Wilson yelled and prodded, but the mule stood his ground, refusing to move, let alone pull the downed tree away from the entrance to the storm pit.

"Mr. Wilson," Lee called to let Wilson know he was in earshot, before the old man launched into another round of insults aimed at the immovable mule.

"Lee, it's high time you got out here. Do you think you can do anything with Colitis? Old Bardwell knew what he was doing when he named this no-good mule. If there ever was a well-named animal, it's this one."

"I've worked with him before. Tell me what you want moved and where you want it put. I think I can get this old fellow to cooperate."

"I'll pay you double what you make per hour over at Kathy's bussing tables. I've removed the limbs from the tree that blocked my storm shelter door. Then I cut it in sections, but I can't get my truck back there. It's too tight; I'd damage my truck for sure. If you can get that dang mule to pull the sections away, I can get in. There's nothing like a shelter to keep you safe if a storm comes up out here."

Lee nodded but thought Wilson wouldn't have been very safe if he had taken shelter in the storm pit and been trapped inside. "Yes, sir, I'll get it done for you. If you want me to, I'll chop some fire wood for you from those sections. I'd charge the same rate."

"I'll have to think about that. You'd better get busy. That old mule isn't getting younger or more cooperative." Wilson walked back to his cabin, happy to turn the job over to Lee.

Lee went over to the mule, rubbed his ears and patted his back. Then he reached into his pocket and pulled out sugar cubes. He talked to the mule as he gently led the animal toward the blocked door. He tied ropes around each section, and he and Colitis moved them one by one until the door was cleared. Wilson came out in time to see the last section moved away from the entrance.

"Mr. Wilson, you'd better check the door to be sure it wasn't damaged. It looks like one of the hinges is loose and might be broken."

Wilson pushed the door open. Just as Lee had suspected, one of the hinges had pulled away from the doorjamb. That was the least of the old man's discoveries. In the shaft of sunlight that flooded the pit, he saw bloody clothes and piles of stolen goods.

"Lee, call the sheriff. Tell him I've solved the case that has had him stumped."

Cath answered the phone. "Sheriff's Office, Deputy Jordan speaking; how can I help you."

"Miss Jordan, this is Lee. Mr. Wilson said to tell the sheriff he had solved the rash of burglaries and for him to come out to the cabin to collect the evidence."

"Lee, the sheriff is here. I'll put him on, and you tell him what you told me."

She handed the phone to Thad. "Lee said Wilson found evidence that proved who's responsible for the burglaries that have been happening in the county."

"Lee, what is it?" Thad listened as Lee repeated Wilson's message. "What, exactly, did he find?"

"I didn't go down in the storm pit to see. The last thing I need is to have my fingerprints on anything down there. I could see some bloody clothes and a gun Mr. Wilson said was taken from his house."

"I'll be there to collect everything. Lee, you were wise not to touch anything. I hope Wilson didn't."

"No, sir, he didn't. We've both seen enough cop shows on TV to know that could destroy evidence. We'll be waiting for you."

"Cath, ride out to Wilson's place with me. You know he'll never let us forget that he, not the Sheriff's Department, solved our mini-crime wave. I'll need some moral support, plus it will gall him to see a female officer collecting evidence."

The two drove to the cabin. "Here he comes. Get ready to hear how incompetent our department is, and he alone, an observant citizen, cracked the case," Thad said.

Wilson didn't disappoint them. "Well, at least you two were able to locate my house. Your detecting skills must be improving, even if you were unable to find the stolen items I found for you. Follow me to the storm pit."

The sheriff and deputy exchanged looks, smiled, and followed Wilson to the back of his property.

"Be careful when you open the door. The tree broke the top hinge when it fell against the door," Wilson said.

As Thad and Cath started down the steps to photograph the piles of stolen goods strewn around the cramped space, Wilson followed them. Thad turned around and said, "I'm sorry, Mr. Wilson, you can't come down here while we're working. After we've finished, you and Lee can come down, fix the door and clean up the place."

Wilson mumbled an unintelligible remark and returned to watch Lee split the firewood. His disappointment at being excluded from farther investigation of the case he had personally solved was evident. "Lee, I'd feel a lot better if they had let me help. Those incompetents will probably overlook some important clues. I know your dad is a deputy, but you have to admit the sheriff doesn't have a good record in closing cases."

Lee didn't answer but continued chopping wood.

Thad and Cath went down into the storm cellar and looked at the piles of goods that had been reported stolen. "It looks like everything is here, except those things Lee confessed to taking, and the Kayak stolen from Bax's place. Cath, make pictures of everything in place before you bag them. We'll inventory them when we get back to the office," Thad told the young deputy.

While she was busy with the stolen goods, Thad photographed the bloody clothes and carefully bagged it. If it was Fontaine's blood, as he suspected, they would have proof that he was the one who had stolen from the homes and cars of the locals.

He also took pictures of empty cans. The number of them indicated Fontaine must have been hiding here ever since he escaped the fire. Some thought his body had been totally destroyed in the fire and explosion that followed. Thad had doubts at the time because there was no trace of him, while there were remains of the others in the ambulance and the log truck.

After David Fontaine was shot at the wedding, at least they knew the man who tried to kill Ana was dead. Then who would want to kidnap, beat, and starve her? It had to be tied to the package he had turned over to Abe. He would need to contact Abe and update him. Abe knew more about this case than he was willing to share. Thad finished bagging the bloodstained clothes.

Investigation

A na was dehydrated, malnourished and bruised. Her nose was broken, and one of her ribs was cracked. Considering all she had been through; she was in relatively good shape. Still Agent Abe was visibly shaken when he came into the hospital room. The swollen, discolored woman looked nothing like the picture in her file.

"Mrs. Fontaine," he began.

"I've taken back my maiden name. I'm Ana LeBlanc now."

"Of course, may I just call you Ana?" She nodded, and he continued. "I understand you saw the woman who kidnapped you and did this to you. Can you describe her?"

"She was a large woman, with grey hair, about Brosia's age I would guess. I can't tell you much more because she punched me in the face immediately after I opened the door. I know I've seen her before; I don't remember where. It was just an impression, mixed with the shock of coming face to face with her.

"The man, who was with her when she came in to question me about the package, slipped up once and called her Bet. She told him, if I heard him say that, she would have to kill me, so I pretended to be in a deep sleep when they approached the cage. That is all I remember."

"Ana, as soon as your doctors think you are well enough to leave the hospital, I want to move you to another location. These people know exactly where you live and who your friends are. I want to put you…"

"I won't go into witness protection again. I can't leave the people I love and start over for a third time," Ana said emphatically.

"I'm not talking about total, life-changing witness-protection, but you do need to be in protective custody until we eradicate the Vipers. Then you can resume your normal life, without abandoning the people who are important to you."

"Agent Abe, you must think I'm extremely naïve. The Vipers may never be eradicated, as you put it. My protective custody could be a life sentence. I will take my chances here."

"Ana, we have someone inside the Vipers. That along with the information we were able to get from that document you hid in the washing machine, has put wiping out the Vipers within reach. We just need to find Medusa. I believe she is the woman who left you for dead. Will you let a hypnotist help you remember more details? With what you recall under hypnosis, you could work with an artist to come up with a drawing that others might recognize. You said you thought you had seen her before. Maybe someone else could put a name with the face."

"I'll do both, if I don't have to leave," Ana said.

"I'll have them come to the hospital to work with you. You'll need to stay here a while to gain strength and heal. We can extend your stay until we can find a safer place in the area, but you can't stay at the cabin any longer. They know that's your home. You are in danger there, as are your aunt and her husband. I know you don't want to put them in that position. We will relocate all three of you here in the general area."

"I really don't have a choice when you put it that way. Keeping the two people who have tried to protect me most of my life safe is more important than anything else."

"I'm glad you've changed your mind," Abe said as he left the room.

A few days later a nurse Ana hadn't seen before came into her room. So far she had only seen nurses especially assigned to take care of her. Terror rose as she had a brief flashback to her experience with the imposter who had tried to kill her.

"Ms. LeBlanc, I'm Kate Thomas. Agent Abe asked me to help you remember the person who did this to you."

Ana was surprised at the speed Abe was putting his plan in action. "I didn't think you would be here so soon. Where is the artist he told me he was sending with you?"

"That would be me. I was an artist for the agency before I got interested in hypnotherapy."

"Can you really make me remember that woman? I've heard people have false memories under hypnosis," Ana said.

"That can be true if the hypnotist asks leading questions. I will put you into a relaxed state and only ask you to describe the person who beat you."

"When are you going to start? I don't see a sketch pad."

"I planned to start today, if you feel up to it. A sketch pad might be a suspicious thing for a nurse to be carrying around, so I'll use this little recorder," Kate said as she pulled the device from her pocket. "When I get back to my office, I'll use the recording to make my drawing. It will also be a record of the questions I asked if anyone thinks I suggested anything to your description."

"I'm ready, Kate; let's get started."

"Ana, when you are totally relaxed, I want you to see the face of the person who beat you. You will remember eye color, hair color, the face shape, and anything else that is unusual and might help us find this person. Are you ready to start?"

"Yes."

"Ana, have you ever been hypnotized before?"

"No."

"You will remember everything I say and do as well as everything you say or do. You won't say or do anything unwillingly. You will just be in a relaxed state that allows memories to surface," Kate said as she turned down the lights to the lowest setting.

"Ana, close your eyes. Remember a place you were safe and happy."

"I remember a place like that," Ana said.

"Imagine you are there," Kate said, timing her words to match Ana's breathing. "Where are you, Ana?"

"I'm in a boat on Bayou Gauche."

"Tell me about it. What do you see?"

"It's fall. There are red berries on the bushes on the banks. Lots of birds are flying overhead. We have just launched the boat and are going into the swamp."

"You said 'we.' Who's with you?"

"Tony."

"What do you see as you get into the swamp?"

"Calm water and shady trees."

"How do you feel?"

"Safe. The burners won't find me here. Tony won't let them. No one will find me, I'm happy."

"Ana, remember that happy, secure feeling and relax your body. Start with your toes and move on up your body until every part of you is relaxed. Do you feel yourself relaxing?"

Ana nodded.

"The more I talk to you, the more relaxed you will become, until you sink into a deep hypnotic state. Every word takes you deeper and deeper. The deeper you sink, the more you will remember. You are completely in a deep, peaceful sleep. You will stay in this state until I bring you back.

"I want you to remember the day you escaped from the cage. You crawled to the door, pulled yourself up, and opened the door. This time the person will freeze so you will not be hurt. That

person can't move, so you can see everything about her. Open
the door and tell me what you see."

"It's an older woman. She hates me. I can see it on her face.
She has blue eyes and grey hair cut really short, almost like a
man's. She is in walking shorts and a big shirt. She has on steel-
toed boots, like my daddy wore sometimes. Her socks show a
little above the boot top. There's a snake crawling out of one
of them. No, it's not a real snake; it's a tattoo. Her face looks
familiar. I've seen her before, but I don't think I know her."

"Can you tell me about the shape of her face?"

"It's round and dissolves into a fat neck. She has sun-
damaged skin with deep wrinkles. Her eyebrows are bushy and
growing together."

"Tell me about her mouth and her nose."

"She has thin lips and a small mouth. Her nose is broad."

"Can you tell how tall she is?"

"She's about my height, maybe five feet eight or nine."

"Can you estimate her weight?"

"I would guess she weighs 250 pounds or more. She is
fat, but I can tell she is muscular underneath. She is a strong,
powerful woman."

"Can you remember any other detail about this person?"
"No."

"I'm going to count from one to five. When I get to five,
you will awake. You will be alert, refreshed, and will remember
everything we have said.

"One, two, three, four, five, welcome back, Ana. I'm going
to take the recording back and do an initial drawing. When
I come back, I'll hypnotize you again. I have you look at the
drawing and tell me how I need to change it."

"Do you think I gave you enough information?" Ana asked
as she watched Kate put her recorder back into her pocket.

"You were a very good subject; however, I'm sure we can refine the image when you see what I have drawn. I'll see you again in a day or two," Kate said and started to the door,

Ana smiled and said, "Thank you for your help. I just hope we can get a drawing that will help put that monster away."

The next day Kate, again dressed as a nurse, returned carrying a clipboard. A drawing based on Ana's description was hidden under several blank sheets and topped with an official-looking form. "Good morning, Ana. Are you ready to help me revise my original drawing?"

"Yes, I want it in the hands of your agents and the sheriff's office as soon as possible."

Again, Kate hypnotized Ana, and then handed the rendering to her. She clipped a copy of the drawing under a sheet of tracing paper. "Ana, you should be able to remember the face you saw. Look at the sketch and tell me if there are any changes that need to be made."

"Her face should be a little less round and she had a deep eleven furrow between her brows."

Kate moved so that Ana could see the changes she was making to the drawing as she made them. "How is that?" she said as she slightly slenderized the round face and added the parallel wrinkles.

"That's better, but her hairline isn't right," Ana said as she closed her eyes and tried to remember what was wrong. "She has a receding hairline," she said as she opened her eyes.

They continued making small changes to the overlay of tracing paper until Ana was satisfied. Finally, Kate brought out her pastels.

"You said her hair was gray. Which of these grays is the closest to her hair color?" Kate asked as she began to add color to the drawing.

ॐ

After the final version was completed, Kate sent it to the Birmingham office. The local agent took the copy from the printer and called Abe in Washington. "We have the drawing our artist made from Mrs. Fontaine's description," Hernandez said. "I know this isn't much to work with. Information obtained while the witness is under hypnosis can be unreliable, but it is the only thing we have."

"Give it to one of the forensic artists to do age regression and see if we can get a match," Abe told the agent.

"How far back do you want to regress the drawing, Abe?"

"Go back in ten-year increments and run each regressed picture for a match to females known or suspected to be associated with subversive or seditious groups."

It took a little longer than Abe had hoped for the artist to do the four-age regressions of Kate's original drawing and complete the search for a match. Abe knew Hernandez had been successful when the Alabama agent made a video conference call to his office. The younger man had a smug smile and a manila folder on the desk in front of him.

"You got a hit." It was more of a statement than a question.

"Yes, George, our best man at age regression, had to go back forty years, but we found a match. Elizabeth "Betty" Ingram, an LSU student who was under investigation for her involvement in anti-American activity on campus," Hernandez said.

"Son, it was the seventies, and there were lots of student demonstrations. How serious was this? Was she just a young girl photographed at a sit-in against an unpopular war with some people the government considered dangerous?"

"It was a lot more than that. From what I've found out, she was about to be charged with sedition, if not treason, when she disappeared. She hasn't been seen since. Here's another thing I think will interest you; she had been dating a younger man.

She was a senior, and he was a freshman. I know that in itself isn't significant, but the man was Simmons, the man originally intended to receive the coded document.

"We dug deeper and got a copy of his interrogation, after she disappeared. When he was questioned after she disappeared, he claimed he knew nothing about her involvement with anything other than normal campus activities. The group she was involved in was more like the Symbionese Liberation Army, than a sorority or any other campus organization. The leaders modeled it after the group that kidnapped Patty Hurst. In fact, they studied Donald De Freeze's tactics. Some of the things Ana endured indicate a link to that group.

"Simmons went on to get a doctorate, and became a professor at Willow Wood College. He returned to LSU to do research for a paper he was writing on the old military school's role in the Civil war. While interviewing research assistant candidates, he met David Fontaine. Apparently, he recognized him as a disillusioned, morally-weak student, who was just the type to recruit for the Vipers. It's clear he and Betty continued their association from their student days, until his death."

"Let me see the match," Abe said. George held up the younger version of the drawing and a photograph of a wide-eyed smooth faced girl. She wasn't pretty by accepted standards, but he found the confident look of a purpose driven, high achiever engaging. He could see how others would be drawn to her.

"I've had it faxed to your office," George said.

A young woman came in as if on cue and handed Abe the copies of Kate's original drawing, the regressed picture of Betty, and her college photo. He compared the photo to the age regressed drawing of Kate's original sketch. They were not a perfect match, but the eyes, broad nose, and thin lips Ana had remembered were there. That tied to the connection Betty had to Simmons left little doubt this was the same woman.

Satisfied with what he saw, he said, "Send the original drawing to local law enforcement agencies in Alabama. Be sure they understand they are not to release it to the media at this time, but just be on the lookout for a woman matching this picture. If Betty sees herself on TV, she'll drop out of sight again. We don't want her to know we are on to her."

FORTY

Solution

Joy didn't often stop by the office to see Fran. He had told her, often enough, Thad liked his deputies to keep their personal and professional lives completely separate. Still there were times when the two overlapped out of necessity. She thought this was one of those times.

"I thought you might need this," she said as she put a big bag of doughnuts on his desk.

"There you go, stereotyping cops like a lame comedian. Why are you here? You know how Thad feels about drop-in visits from friends and family."

"These are very special doughnuts I'm sure you need today," she answered pushing the bag closer. "Just take a peek."

He opened the bag and smiled. "You're right as always. I don't think I could have made it through the day without these." He looked around the office to be sure Thad or one of the deputies hadn't come in. Then he retrieved a powdered sugar covered plastic bag holding a pair of handcuffs, trashed the bag, and pulled out a doughnut. "Where did you find these? I looked all over for them this morning," he said as he took a bite from the doughnut.

"Remember yesterday you asked me to take you to get your car out of the shop. They must have been uncomfortable because you removed them and put them on the floorboard. We forgot about them. While I was going to get groceries, I heard something rattling and thought I had car trouble.

About half way to the mechanic's shop, I caught a glimpse of them while I was at a red light. I bought the doughnuts because I knew the guys would rib you if they saw me bring them in. Anyway, doughnuts were cheaper than having the mechanic check my car."

A familiar sound announced the arrival of a document. Fran walked over to the printer and pulled off the picture of Betty that the Birmingham FBI office was circulating. As he put it on his desk to study, Joy said, "I've seen her before. Let me think where it was." She paused a moment and said, "I know; it was at the wedding, but they have it all wrong. She didn't have a receding hairline; she had bangs. The gray hair Ana saw isn't the color I saw. Maybe she was self-conscious about losing her hair and wore a wig."

"You seem pretty sure about this. It's been a while since the wedding."

"I have a better than average memory. Some would call it photographic, but I won't go that far."

She started to say more, but Fran jumped up, got a piece of paper and put it over the copy. "Trace the original and make the alterations it needs to look like the woman you saw at the wedding."

Joy lightly traced the shape of the woman's face. "Her nose was wide but not as wide as this," she said as she narrowed the nose and drew bangs over the prominent forehead. She made the eyes more dramatic by adding liner and mascara. Then she added rimless glasses. "I think she made her lips look fuller with a make-up trick most girls learn if their lips are too thin. This is more like the woman I saw," she said as she turned the drawing around for Fran to see.

She saw the expression on his face change. "Do you recognize her?" she asked.

"I surely do. I'm calling Thad. I want to be sure he sees what we see before we call Agent Abe's office."

Thad came back to the office. He had planned to eat lunch at home today, but the urgency in Fran's voice compelled him to pick up a readymade sandwich at the convenience store. He might be able to forgive Fran for calling, if the new evidence he had was as important as the deputy seemed to think it was. However, he didn't know if his taste buds could.

"Okay, show me what you have. It better be worth as much as you implied. My wife made fried chicken, butterbeans, and cornbread for my lunch."

"You'll have to be the judge of that. Here, do you recognize her?" Fran said as he handed Joy's version of the drawing to his boss.

"You have to be kidding. She's been right under my nose. Joy, why did you make the changes?" Thad asked as he looked from her version to the original.

"I remembered seeing someone who looked a lot like the original drawing. She was at Bax's place the day Ana was taken. I made the changes I remembered, and Fran recognized her."

"Fran, call in everyone. I want to surround her place as soon as we can. We need to move fast," Thad said as he dumped his half-eaten sandwich in the trashcan.

The deputies reported quickly, and Thad laid out his plan.

Thad's deputies converged from all possible directions on the location where they were sure she would be. They kept in radio contact, so they would be able to surround the building simultaneously. When they got in place, there was no sign of life, no cars, no people, just a piece of paper taped to the entrance.

"Eugene, what does that note say?" Thad asked the deputy nearest the door.

Eugene pulled the paper off the door and read it. "'We decided to take a vacation. See you soon. The management.' How did they know we were coming?"

"Maybe they didn't; maybe they just took some time off," Red said.

"Maybe they just took off because they were tipped off," Cath said.

"One thing is for sure, Agent Abe will not be pleased," Thad said as he scanned the only people who knew the raid was planned for today. Unless someone bragged to the wrong person that they were going to be involved in a raid to take down a terrorist, his most trusted deputies were the only ones who knew the raid was planned. One of his people was either a traitor or a fool. The sad thing was at this time the only people he could trust were Abe and himself.

He walked back to the squad car where Fran was waiting. "Drop me off at my house, Fran. I need some uninterrupted time to think. I'll drive my personal car back to the office in a little while." The two men drove on in silence.

Thad walked into his kitchen, poured a glass of iced tea, and sat down at the table. Bren noticed how distracted he was as he picked at his food, but she knew better than to question him when he withdrew this way.

He shook his head and rubbed the stubble on his chin as he tried to think of the best way to tell Abe their prime suspect had vanished. The hardest part would be telling the agent he believed one of his own people tipped off the suspect. Delaying wouldn't make it any easier; he pulled out his phone and pushed Abe's private number.

Abe's cell phone played the theme song to *The Andy Griffith Show*, the ring he'd assigned to the small-town Alabama sheriff as a private joke. Although it was his day off, he took Thad's call. "Hello, Sheriff, you must have something important to tell me to call on this number."

"Yes, I do, but as the old saw goes, there's good news and bad news. The good news is we recognized the woman in the drawing. The bad news is when we went out to her place to arrest her, she had packed up and gone. Someone tipped her off, and only my staff knew we had found her. One of them had to have leaked the information to her or one of her cohorts. You're the only person I can trust."

"Give me the names of everyone who saw the picture," Abe said. "I'll run a background check on all of your people to see if there is any connection between them and Betty. We can't rule out the leak being on our end. I'll look for an FBI connection as well.

"I doubt that it will be on that end. One of my deputy's girlfriends was here when the drawing came in. She was at the wedding and said she thought she had seen the woman there.

"She traced the copy you sent and changed a few things. When we saw the second drawing, we recognized the woman immediately. My people are the only ones who have seen that version."

"Just to be on the safe side, send the second drawing and pictures of the suspect, if you have them, with all the information you have on her to my home e-mail. My address is Abe_NOTas_inLincoln@yahoo.com. At this point we need to keep all further developments from our own people until we find the leak."

"I'll get on it and send it from my home computer as well. Thanks for taking my call at home on your day off," Thad said.

"Thad, you know as well as I do, we never really have days off when a case is getting hot. Goodbye."

When the agent hung up, Thad felt a little less alone. He had an ally. Abe had investigative tools available to him that the people of Eastabuchie County would never be able to afford. But even more important, Abe was a man he could trust.

Thad left his home office and walked to the kitchen where his wife, Bren, was putting away the supper dishes. "Honey, thank you for supper; I just wasn't hungry enough to do it justice. I'm going back to the office to do some work I have to finish tonight. Don't wait up for me."

"I thought you were more there than here all during our meal. Is something wrong?" she asked.

"Not really, I just hit a snag, and I need some quiet time to work it out. With most of the night staff on patrol and just a skeleton crew in the office, I shouldn't be bothered back at my desk. I'll see you in the morning." He kissed Bren and left to find the things Abe wanted and to begin searching the personnel file of the employees he had never before doubted.

He worked all night looking for the information Abe requested. The hardest thing to find was a picture of "Betty." He'd gone back over copies of the pictures of wedding guests that had been made before the shooting. There was nothing of interest, just family groups and pictures of the bride and groom before the shot that killed Fontaine was fired.

Even though he thought it was useless, Thad had brought his laptop from home so he could review all of the wedding pictures his wife had taken. Bren said she was a frustrated photographer who thought she'd missed her calling. Frustrated or not, she wasn't a good photographer, just a prolific one. He went through hundreds of her attempts to catch candid shots of the guests. There was none of Betty.

Just when he was about to give up, a picture grabbed his attention. How had he overlooked this bit of evidence when he and his wife watched the wedding slideshow one lazy Sunday afternoon? He knew how; he had only given the pictures an uninterested glance. Bren had narrated each picture except this one. It was a photographic nightmare she had skipped over with apologies. Bax was the subject; she snapped just as he dashed after Dave. But it wasn't the blur of Bax that caught his attention.

Thad cropped and enlarged the section that interested him. There in the background was Betty, holding what looked to be a rifle. Her face was out of focus, but you couldn't miss her signature outfit. No one else in town had anything like it. Betty had killed Dave, and here was the proof.

Thad needed only one more picture. He wouldn't find what he wanted in the wedding pictures. He was afraid he would have to go through all of his wife's picture files to find a picture of the camera-shy Betty with her face in focus. There was no doubt in his mind that one existed; no one escaped his Bren's Canon.

In the early morning hours, he found a close-up of an unhappy couple surrounded by happy people waving little American flags as they watched the Fourth of July parade. Look at those faces; they look like they're about to spit out watermelon seeds! She's the killer, and I'm pretty sure he's the man Ana heard call her Bet. He would never doubt his wife's talent again.

He was sending off the last of the information and photographs when the morning shift arrived.

"Thad, are you trying to show us up? One of the night shift said you'd been here all night."

"No, I felt restless and knew I wouldn't be able to sleep, so I came in and got caught up on some things that had been tabled until we found Fontaine's killer and Ana's kidnapper. That may never happen now, so I worked on other things that have to be done. You could say I killed two birds with one stone. I made some progress, and I'm so sleepy I won't have a bit of trouble falling asleep when I get home. I'll be back after lunch."

Abe

A be flew down to the Birmingham office to personally oversee the investigation of the people in that office who had access to the pictures of their suspect. He was careful not to involve any of the locals in his background check of Thad's staff. In fact, they were also being checked for any connection to Betty Ingram or whatever she called herself now. In cases where only a few people had access to information, everyone had to be a suspect, even Thad and his wife.

The results were beginning to come in. It was no surprise. Neither Thad and Bren nor Fran and Joy were connected to Betty, but he had to check. Other results were equally as reassuring. The last two people to be processed were the two women involved in the investigation, Kate, the agency's hypnotist/artist and Cath, the new deputy in Thad's office.

Abe read the reports on the women's background with interest. It seemed both of them had something in their past that raised a red flag. Kate was born in the same small Texas town listed as Betty's home town in her college record. Cath, who grew up in that town, had a juvenile record in Texas. Both girls were named Katherine. Both were the same age, Katherine Thomas and Katherine Thompson.

Cath, aka Katherine Thompson, changed the spelling of her name to Catherine when she was released from the reform school. She had her record expunged when she was twenty-one, but she neglected or didn't know to have all of the documents destroyed also. She married Daniel Jordan immediately after being released. Her high school diploma and Community College diploma were for Catherine Jordan. Katherine Thompson ceased to exist.

Katherine Thomas was born after her father was killed in a traffic accident. According to neighbors, they didn't know her mother was expecting. Her weight gain was attributed to coping with grief by emotional eating. They didn't suspect she was pregnant until shortly before Kate was born. Katherine was delivered at home without any medical attention. She weighed only five pounds. The family declared her birth and survival were a blessed gift from God. The birth certificate listed the parents as Marcus Thomas and Susan Ingram Thomas.

Further checking on Susan Thomas showed she had a twin sister, Elizabeth, who left home to go to college just before Susan and Mark married. Elizabeth never returned to Texas. The neighbors seemed to think all that schooling made her 'too big for her britches.' One woman said she'd 'outgrown her raising.' Whether that assessment was true or not, one thing is sure; Betty Ingram was Kate Thomas' aunt.

Abe phoned Thad on his personal cell phone. When the sheriff answered, Abe said, "Thad, I'm virtually certain I've found the leak. It is no one in your office. The artist that hypnotized Ana in order to get a better description of her attacker is the niece of Betty Ingram. I think she recognized her aunt and tipped her off.

"In addition, I found out your new deputy is not being totally up front with you. She has a juvenile record. You might want to ask her about it. She doesn't have to tell you; but if she doesn't, I would limit her duties to activities that aren't sensitive. That's just me. I don't believe in secrets in law enforcement," Abe said.

"Thank you. It's a load off my mind. As for Cath, whatever she did as a kid is her business, I guess. I'll think about bringing up the importance of being completely honest. She needs to understand openness and trust are essential in law enforcement. This is one job where your life can depend on being able to completely trust those you work with. I have some information for you, also. I found and sent some pictures that you will find interesting. My wife is a compulsive camera bug. She drives people crazy with her candid pictures of them in ridiculous situations. I thought maybe she snapped a picture of the woman Joy saw at the wedding. Not only did I find a close up of her at a parade, but I found a picture of her with a gun pointed toward David at the time he was shot. I sent them to your home computer because you weren't sure you could trust everyone in our office."

"Great, Thad, I'll check them out as soon as I can, and I'll contact you if I find any more information," Abe said.

When the two men disconnected, Thad was relieved that no one on his staff had tipped off the suspect.

Abe lost no time accessing the pictures Thad sent. This time he didn't hesitate to send the pictures of the two suspects wanted in Alabama for the kidnapping and murder case to all law enforcement agencies in the southeastern United States.

He put copies of the photos of Betty and Bud in a folder along with both versions of the drawing of Betty and put it on his desk. Then he called Kate into his office.

The woman looked assured and professional when she came in. "Is there any progress on the Fontaine kidnapping case?"

"As a matter of fact, there is something new. Look at the pictures in this folder," Abe said as he pushed it across his desk. "We got a name on the woman based on your drawing. Take a look."

"There's another sketch in here. Did Ana change her description?" Kate asked.

"No, someone at the sheriff's office recognized her from your drawing and changed it to look more like the lady she saw at the wedding. Do you recognize her?" he asked.

"No, I see the resemblance to the original sketch, but that's it," Kate said.

"Look at the photograph under the sketches," he said.

"She really looks like the second drawing. She must have been wearing a wig when this picture was made."

"There is another picture; look at it," Abe said.

She lifted the first picture and revealed the one of Betty pointing the rifle toward someone out of the frame. "What is this?" Kate asked.

"Don't you recognize your Aunt Betty? You know the one you tipped off when you realized whose picture you were drawing."

"I don't know what you are talking about. I don't have an Aunt Betty. I'll take a polygraph test to prove it."

"I have a copy of your birth certificate listing your mother as Susan Ingram Thomas. She has a twin sister, Betty. In addition, your paternal grandparents helped Susan as much as they could, but they didn't have the money to send you to college when she died. You didn't have grants or scholarships, yet you attended a very good university. Did Elizabeth Ingram, your only other living relative, pay your way? Was the warning a way to pay her back? You may need a lawyer before you take that polygraph test."

"I'll be glad to take the test. I don't care what you think you've found. If I have an aunt named Betty, I never knew her. The only family members I ever met were my father's parents and my mother. You have the wrong person."

Kate walked to the door, turned, and said, "I'm taking a sick day. Your accusation has literally made me sick. If you want to arrest me, you have my address on file." She didn't bother to slam the door; the cadence of her heels telegraphed her anger.

Abe shook his head. He could prove the two women were blood relatives. Kate had worked with him before and knew how much he hated her gum-chewing habit. He had seen her put the ever-present gum in its wrapper and drop it in the trashcan as she opened the office door. There it was, shining in its silver wrapper, the only thing in the container.

Betty

etty looked out across the grey lake punctuated by millions of raindrops. The pines that surrounded it swayed recklessly as if they knew, as she did, when to hold their position and when to give enough to ensure survival. Watching as the storm did its worst and then passed improved her mood. Just as the trees had survived this storm, she would survive the tempest that was ripping apart her life.

She walked away from the window and looked at her surroundings. The cabin was adequate, furnished with sturdy but worn pieces. Just the essentials, it was state park simple. This was the perfect place for someone wanting anonymity. With no nosey neighbors or hotel desk clerk noticing their comings and goings, they could be as nondescript as the weathered wood cabin itself, drawing no attention, blending into the background. She would be able to reinvent herself here.

Bud had worried about their being recognized by other park visitors, but everyone was involved in their own fun. Young teens running around in the dark playing flashlight tag and couples enjoying the peace and privacy the park offered had no interest in the old couple in the furthest cabin. Although one or two people about his age had waved at Bud when he drove past them on his way out of the park to buy supplies, his face wasn't the one the authorities were looking for.

Betty sat down on the vinyl-covered couch and assessed the events that brought her to this point. She had never considered the child she gave birth to a blessing. When he used that adorable little euphemism, love child, after she told him she was pregnant, it made her laugh. He was just a convenient indulgence, and the child would have been a burden who would have hindered her mission.

My sister was delighted to help her hide until the baby was born. No one even knew she was home, let alone that she had given birth in the house where they grew up. Susan even padded herself so no one would question the appearance of a newborn in nine months. She was able to get a birth certificate for the child, who was born at home, unattended by a doctor or midwife.

Then, years later when she had almost forgotten the pregnancy, Susan had given up their secret. Before she died, she told the kid everything. The brat found her and blackmailed her into financing college.

It was funny, but she would have to admit what she thought was a disaster turned out to work in her favor. The brat had tipped her off. Bud and she were able to get away. They were safe in this cabin before the authorities could load their guns, polish their stars, and go on their fruitless raid.

ॐ

Bud and Betty had been hiding at the cabin for several weeks. He made supply runs as much to escape the claustrophobic feeling the cozy cabin was beginning to give him and to replenish their cupboard.

Betty kept busy preparing another one of her coded epistles to be routed to her followers. Bud wasn't sure how she planned to have it delivered. So many of her trusted couriers had died or disappeared. He was the only person she had contact with now, and he was needed here. This isolation and her obsession with regaining control of her disciples were suffocating to him. The supply runs were his only outlet. "Bet, I'm going to buy some gas at the station across from the park. We're down to a quarter of a tank. I might get a bite to eat while I'm out. Would you like anything?" Bud asked.

"Yes, pick up something for me. I'm tired of those frozen dinners we stocked up on so we don't have to cook."

"What do you want?" he asked.

"Whatever you get will be fine; I don't care," she answered.

Bud filled his tank and walked into McDonald's. He had wanted a good hamburger for a while. The Big Mac combo wouldn't have been his first choice, but it would have to do.

✑

"Next," the young lady behind the counter said as her customer walked past Bud with his order.

Bud stepped forward and ordered two combos to go, received his bag, and walked back to his panel truck unaware he was being followed. When Bud turned into the park's entrance, the off-duty sheriff's deputy knew he would have no trouble finding the old panel truck. There were limited campsites and even fewer cabins in the park. Of course, there was the park hotel, but the faded black panel truck would be easy to find in any of those places. He pulled over and called the sheriff's office on his cell phone.

"Scott County Sheriff's Office," the familiar voice said.

"Hal, this is Lester; you won't believe this, but I just spotted that suspect those folks with the FBI are looking for."

"Where did you see him?"

"He was in line behind me at McDonald's. When I turned around with my lunch, I recognized him from that ridiculous picture of the two of them at the parade."

"Wait, I'm putting you on speaker. The sheriff just walked in."

"Lester, this is Jared. What's going on?"

"Sheriff, I spotted one of the suspects the FBI is looking for. I followed him to Roosevelt State Park but let him get well ahead of me. There were only a few places he could go. It didn't take long before I found his panel truck parked in front of cabin twelve on the lake. I'll be parked by the entrance. We can take them if we move quickly."

"We'll be there as fast as we can. On the way there, I'll plan out a strategy to take them by surprise. Lester, just to be sure this is the right man, I'm sending the picture of the suspects to your Smartphone. We don't want to break down the door of some innocent old man enjoying a vacation in our state park, do we?"

"Jared, I don't blame you for being cautious. Send the picture, but I'm sure he's the man."

As soon as Lester received the picture and verified it was of the man he had seen, the sheriff and several of his deputies left to meet him at the park entrance. When they arrived, Jared walked over to the off-duty deputy's car and laid out his plan.

"My first concern is for the other families in the neighboring cabins. We have to anticipate the suspects might realize we are surrounding them and open fire. We don't want any civilians hurt. I've called the park office and found out which of the other cabins are occupied. I'll send someone to the backdoor of each occupied cabin and escort the occupants out of the area. They can avoid being seen from cabin twelve by going out their backdoors and walking across the earthen dam to the park office. Lester, since you are out of uniform, I want you to be the one to warn the park visitors."

"Yes, sir, whatever you say."

"When you have them out, we'll cross the dam and go back to the cabins. They won't see us because the view from their cabin is of the other side of the lake. I want you to walk down to the lake and casually glance back to see if the drapes on the back windows are drawn. If they are, go to the front door of the cabin and knock while we surround the cabin. We hope that small distraction will allow us to break down the back door and bedroom windows so we can take them by surprise. Before we do anything else, we need to synchronize our watches. Exact timing is essential, if we are to pull this off."

The sheriff and his deputies parked their cars at the visitor's center and informed the office staff of the plans. Park personnel went to the camp grounds and hotel to make sure no one went to the cabins until the sheriff gave the okay.

Lester took a deep breath and walked across the dam and began going from cabin to cabin evacuating the visitors. At first everyone was cooperative, accepting the story he told them.

He knocked on the door of the last occupied cabin. Two teenage girls opened the door just a crack. "What do you want?" the taller redhead asked.

"I'm deputy sheriff Lester Newman. We have to evacuate all the people in the cabins. There is a suspected murderer in one of the cabins. Your cabin is the last to be evacuated. Get any other people in there with you and come with me."

"You must think we're crazy. How do we know you are a deputy? You didn't show us any identification." The redhead slammed the door.

"I'm off duty. My badge is with my uniform at home. I'll show you my driver's license. You don't need to open the door; I'll hold it up to the window."

"What would that prove, that you can drive? Just go away or I will call the sheriff's office," she yelled through the closed door.

"That's just what you should do. Tell the person who answers what I look like and ask if the sheriff and his deputies are trying to capture someone in the park."

"What did you say your name is?" she asked.

"It's Lester Newman; my wife is named Sarah, and we have three daughters."

After a short wait both girls bounded out the door. The little blonde said, "We were just doing what Mama told us."

"She will be proud of you. I hope my daughters are as cautious as you young ladies are. Now follow me."

After he saw the girls had safely crossed the dam, Lester walked across the road and down to the edge of the lake. He stopped, picked up a few stones, and skipped them across the water as he walked. That gave him an excuse to take his time. When he was behind cabin twelve, he bent down again to gather more stones. In the process of getting them, he turned to the side enough to be sure the drapes were drawn, and then stood up and continued his walk. Just in case one of them might pull the drapes, he waited to go to his assigned position until he was out of sight.

Lester called the sheriff. "Jared, everyone is out, and I'm in position. The drapes are closed, and I could hear the TV when I walked nearer the cabin."

"Good, stay there until we get in place. I'll call and tell you exactly when to knock on the door."

The sheriff and the rest of his deputies crossed the dam. Half of them quietly positioned themselves at the back next to the door and windows, while the rest waited for the sheriff's signal as they crouched under the bedroom windows.

Lester felt his phone vibrate in his pocket and answered it. "I'm ready, Jared."

"Lester, wait until five minutes after the hour, then knock on the door. We will make our move 15 seconds after you've knocked. That's when you'll come through the front bedroom window. Do you understand?"

"Yes," Lester said as he looked down at his watch. "I will start walking in that direction now. I'll be there at exactly five after."

He walked the short distance with a measured pace. The timing was almost perfect. He arrived at the door five seconds ahead of schedule. As the second hand ticked down, he raised his hand and knocked loudly. Not waiting for the sound of movement, Lester walked around the corner to the bedroom window as he counted one Mississippi, two Mississippi. By three Mississippi he had reached the window and continued his deliberate count. He heard the front door open. That was just enough distraction to slow his count. The door slammed, cutting off what Bud was saying about those kids who knock and run.

The sound of breaking glass and shouting men propelled him into action. He broke the bedroom window and hoisted himself up, carefully avoiding the glass shards. As he was climbing in, he heard more commotion.

The plan's working seamlessly, Jared thought as his men surrounded the shocked man. Then he heard a sound behind him.

"Drop your guns or the sheriff's dead." Betty pushed the gun barrel against Jared's back. "Looks like you're the ones who were surprised. All of you get over there with Bud. Bud, take their guns."

Bud busied himself collecting guns from all the men as Betty continued talking.

"Out of a force of habit I took my gun to the bathroom with me. I couldn't have remained free to carry out my mission all these years if I had been careless."

"Drop your gun, ma'am. You too, fellow, drop the weapons you took from the sheriff and his men. If you don't, I'll have to shoot both of you," Lester said as he walked from the front bedroom with his gun trained on Betty.

As she turned to shoot him, Lester kicked the gun from her hand, and Jared tackled the woman. He thought she looked more like a disheveled grandmother than the leader of a subversive group.

Bud, his hands above his head, looked as his wife who struggled while the sheriff handcuffed her. "Bet, it's over."

FORTY-THREE

News

Thad recognized Abe's personal cell number when the call came in. He was on his way to Lovie's place, responding to her report that an insane mule was "tearing up Jack and killing Jenny" in her garden. Thad didn't get overly concerned about this reported violence. His own grandmother used the same expression when someone or something was making a terrible mess. It sounded like Colitis had escaped again and was having a picnic in Lovie's garden.

He pulled over to take the call. Colitis and Lovie would just have to wait. If he took the call while driving, it would be his luck for old man Wilson to see him. Knowing him, Wilson would try to have him impeached for breaking the law and setting a bad example.

"Hello, Agent Abe. What can I do for you?"

"Nothing this time, but I do have some news for you. A Mississippi sheriff has both of our suspects in custody."

"How did he catch them?"

"An off-duty deputy recognized the man at McDonald's and followed him to a cabin in a nearby state park. The sheriff organized a raid on the cabin. The woman got the drop on them, but the same off-duty deputy came in a bedroom window and turned the tables on Betty."

"I can't wait to give this news to Miss Ana and her family. Where did you say they were captured?"

"They were at Roosevelt State Park in Morton, Mississippi," Abe said.

"I can't say I know where that is, but they evidently grow observant deputies there." Thad laughed at his lame joke and continued. "Seriously, that was good work. I hope that off-duty fellow gets a commendation for it."

"There's one more thing I want to tell you. The woman has an unusual tattoo. When she came out of the bathroom in her robe, she was barefoot. On the back of her heel was the face of a woman with snakes growing from her head, winding in all directions up her mid-calf."

"Then she is Medusa!" Thad said.

"It seems that's the case," Abe said.

"I can't believe how much I have over-tipped her. I thought she and her husband were struggling to keep Toot and Tell It afloat. Missy was a hard worker I truly admired. It is hard to understand how she, Betty, and Medusa can be the same person."

Abe said, "Missy never existed; she was part of an elaborate charade designed to give Betty a new identity. That struggling business was just a cover to serve as the base of operations for her organization. They deliberately worked to give the impression they were just hanging on. Too many customers would take time away from their main business.

"We had an informant in the Vipers, but he wasn't in her inner circle. In fact, he never saw her or knew her cover. His most important contact was Simmons, who had recruited him. With Betty's old friend as his sponsor, our man was able to get close to some of her council members. It was the information we found in the document Berry turned over to Fontaine that filled in the gaps in our information. I believe we have enough to put them away for acts of treason and terrorism. I'm sure you'll want to call Ms. Leblanc and let her know she is no longer in danger." Agent Abe disconnected.

Thad put his phone in his pocket, turned, and grinned at his chief deputy. "Some off-duty deputy over in Mississippi just captured Missy or whoever she really is. They got old Bud too. The Feds with all their equipment and highly trained people couldn't have closed the Vipers down without the help of two Southern sheriffs' departments and our own one-woman snooping force, Lovie. If she hadn't brought in that package, there is no telling if the Vipers would have ever been stopped."

"That's the best news I can imagine. Does Ana know they have captured her?"

"No, Abe gave us the job of informing Ana and Brosia. Get them on the phone."

The phone was answered on the second ring. "Ana, I have some news," Thad said. "It's over. The Scott County, Mississippi sheriff just called Agent Abe. Missy and her husband, Bud, have been arrested and will be charged with murder, kidnapping, and conspiracy to commit acts of terrorism. The FBI is closing in on the rest of the Vipers."

"That's wonderful! I can't believe this nightmare is finally over. Does Bax know yet?" Ana asked.

"No, do you want me to call him?"

"No, I'll call him, but now I've got to tell Brosia and Raymond. Thanks so much for all you have done. Good bye." She hurried to the kitchen where Brosia and Raymond were washing dishes after a late lunch.

"They've arrested Missy and her husband and are rounding up the rest of the Vipers."

"Thank goodness for that. To think I hired her to cater our wedding picnic and arranged the perfect opportunity for her to kidnap you. I feel so responsible for all you went through," Brosia said.

"Thea, I've told you over and over it was not your fault. She would have found a way eventually. I'm sure she had a plan before you approached her," Ana said as she embraced her.

"Let's call Bax and tell him the good news if Thad hasn't beaten us to it," Raymond said.

"Thad hasn't called him; I asked him to let me tell Bax," Ana said.

She called Bax and waited for him to answer. The one time she had good news, his phone informed her that he wasn't available at this time. This wasn't something she wanted to leave on voice mail. After the beep she simply said, "Call me."

Shortly after she disconnected, her phone rang. "I got your message, you sounded excited," Bax said when she answered the phone.

"I couldn't be more excited. They've arrested both of the monsters who held me in that cage and then left me for dead. I wanted to be the one who told you. You've supported me from the beginning of this nightmare; I wanted to share the joy my family and I feel."

"That's wonderful! I couldn't be happier for you. This is going to the top of my praise list."

"I have to call Lovie now. I'll talk to you later," Ana said.

Bax was thrilled when he heard Ana's news. It hadn't been the appropriate time to discuss the thing that had haunted him ever since she had told him about the fire. Perhaps today was too soon. She was so happy, so relieved she didn't have to live the rest of her life looking over her shoulder for mobsters, burners, or Vipers. She was reveling in her freedom, but he knew it was only a matter of time before she realized she wasn't free yet. She had to completely put the past behind her before there was chance for a future not tinged with guilt.

The next day Bax drove out to the cabin to talk to Ana. When she came to the door, she looked relaxed for the first time since he met her. "Isn't it wonderful! I don't have to worry about any of the people who have hurt me in the past."

"Yes, it is wonderful. I'm so happy for you. Now you can begin to rebuild your life. Before you start making plans for your future, we need to talk. Let's go for a walk," Bax said.

"There isn't a problem is there?"

"No, I just want to talk without Brosia bringing in cookies and coffee." The two walked toward the kudzu-covered cabin that Ana had been running to when she was captured. Bax knew in some ways she was still running, looking for a hiding place.

"Ana, do you remember the first time you told me the Oriental proverb? You blamed yourself for your friend's death."

She nodded, then turned to Bax and said, "I still do. Her parents don't know what happened to her. I can't imagine how they have suffered all these years."

"You know there is something you can do about that. You can find them and explain what happened."

"I can't face them; Bax, I just can't."

"Ana, until you do, you will never be totally free. If you want moral support, I'll be glad to go with you."

"I know you mean well, but I'm not ready to relive that night. Her parents aren't the only ones who have been hurt by what happened when Dave set the fire."

"I understand, and I won't bring it up again. If you ever feel differently, the offer will still be good.

"Let's start back to the cabin. I think we can both use some of Brosia's coffee and cookies now."

Ana had avoided thinking about Lisa for months. The fear for her life had pushed all other things to the back corners of her mind. Now Bax had brought Lisa and her family to the forefront; Ana could think of little else.

She had returned to painting. There was a demand for her work from two groups of people. Some wanted a souvenir of the woman who was involved in the case which revealed that their little part of the state was a hot bed of criminal activity. But more important, there was a group of art lovers who had collected her work when she was relatively unknown. The notoriety made her work even more collectable.

Her obsession with the night of the fire and Lisa's death impacted everything she painted. Surrealistic paintings of women superimposed over stylized flames, wraiths rising from smoldering ashes, faceless women whose body language told of grief more poignantly than words could ever convey; and similar themes were found in her current works.

Brosia worried as she saw Ana sinking deeper and deeper into the depression that was her inspiration. "Why can't she just paint sunsets and flowers? The ladies at the senior center may not paint as well as Ana; but they're happy, and their paintings make people smile. I think if she had more upbeat subjects, they would lift her mood," she told Raymond.

"She is an artist not a hobbyist. She has to paint from her soul, and right now her soul is troubled. Until she has resolved what's going on inside her, don't expect a change in the mood of her canvases," Raymond told his wife.

She knew he was right, but what had her so moored in those past nightmares? She should have been happy. Dave, the Vipers, and all the things that were a danger to her were out of the picture. And anyone with half a brain could tell Baxter Alford was interested in more than Ana's soul.

Oh, well, maybe if she baked one of Ana's favorites, it would brighten her mood. Brosia went to the kitchen.

Brosia was pulling the pan of baklava from the oven when a male voice startled her. "That smells mighty good. Do you mind if I have a sample?"

She looked up and saw a man who apparently tasted quite a few calorie-loaded treats. "Hello, Mr. Wilson,"

"It's Woody, ma'am. I wanted to talk to Miss Ana about giving my teenage daughter art lessons. Sheila Ann is having a hard time adjusting now that her no-good mother is celebrating becoming a grass widow by moving in with one of the men she's been running around with. My little girl needs something to throw herself into. My old Daddy makes it clear to everybody that he has nothing to do with his black sheep son, but he has a soft spot for my kids. I don't have the money for private lessons, but the old fellow will pay."

"Come with me; Ana is painting down by the creek. I don't know why she bothers to paint plein-air. What's on the canvas doesn't look anything like what's down there."

The two walked down to the creek, but Ana wasn't at her easel. "It looks like she left for a while," Brosia said.

"I don't mind waiting. I can look at what she's working on." Woody walked over to the canvas. "I see what you mean about it being a waste of time for her to paint from life. These blotches of color don't look much like the trees. What is this orange blob over here supposed to be?" Woody asked.

Before Brosia could answer, they heard Ana splashing across the shallow creek. "Call Thad; I've found out how Dave got to Bax's property without being seen. Bax's missing kayak is hidden over there. It caught my attention while I was painting. The orange looked so out of place in the shades of green and brown I was painting. It couldn't be seen except from the spot I set up my easel."

The kayak was the last piece of the stolen property to be recovered. The plein-air painting with the orange blob that represented it became the background for Ana's latest painting. Superimposed on the green and brown background was the faint, gray outline of a gunman with blood on his hands.

Search

Bax began an internet search for Lisa's family shortly after his conversation with Ana. He located them in Blackjack, a country community on the Mississippi side of the Tennessee state line. He called the pastor of the only church in the community.

The phone rang seven times before it was picked up. "Blackjack Baptist Church, this is Pastor Billings speaking." The voice seemed both young and out of breath.

"Brother Billings, this is Bax Alford. I hope I haven't called at a bad time. You seem a little out of breath."

"No, I always have time for someone who needs help. What can I do for you, Mr. Alford?"

"I'm a pastor myself; I can call back if this isn't a good time."

"I'm a one-man staff today. The secretary is in the hospital, the custodian quit, and I'm trying to do their jobs as well as my own; but I have time to talk. It will be nice to rest a minute."

"We all have days like that. I'll make it short. I have information about the daughter of a couple who live in your community. Ben and Lora Cutrer may not be in your congregation, but I imagine you know them."

"Mrs. Cutrer is in our church. Her husband died long before I came here. From what I've heard, they were a sweet older couple who retired here years ago. I didn't know they had a daughter. Miss Lora has never mentioned her."

"I can understand why she wouldn't have; Lisa disappeared the night of her high school graduation. I know someone who knows what happened that night. Before I bring this person to Blackjack, I want to be sure Mrs. Cutrer is emotionally and physically strong enough to hear the news."

"It's bad then," the young pastor said.

"Yes, but I believe she will be better off knowing than wondering what happened for the rest of her life. I wanted to talk to someone who knows Lisa's family and could give me some idea of their resilience."

"There isn't much family here, just Mrs. Cutrer and her nephew. I'm not a doctor so I can't say more than she seems to be strong enough to deal with bad news. The family must have suspected as much for years. I would want to know the truth about what happened to a child of mine, wouldn't you?" Billings said.

"Thank you for your help, Brother Billings. You have been a lot of help. Now all I have to do is convince the person who has the answers that it is time to come forward."

Bax disconnected. What he had told Billings was all wrong. He didn't need to try to convince Ana to do anything. He needed to take a step back and not put any more pressure on her. First Ana had to realize her fears would never go away unless she faced them head on. She would have to decide for herself what she needed to do. But if she asked him for help, he had information for her.

FORTY-FIVE

Decision

Ana sat on the side of the bed, her hands gripping the opposite arm, hiding behind the barrier they formed to protect herself from the fear and guilt she couldn't escape. Dave had reinforced them with his constant threats to expose her as a killer. Even though she knew on an intellectual level she was not to blame, deep within Ana couldn't forgive herself. The anguish the Cutrers went through, not knowing their daughter's fate, was a direct result of her actions.

She knew Bax was right. If she was ever going to be able to move forward, she had to find Lisa's family and tell them what had happened. Ana went to her computer and started her own search. It didn't take long to locate Lisa's mother. She packed a bag and wrote a note for Brosia and Raymond.

Ana heard Brosia walking to the kitchen and getting something out of the refrigerator. She must have made too much noise getting out her bag. Brosia was getting some milk or yogurt to help her get back to sleep.

Ana sat on the edge of her bed until she heard the predictable rhythmic duet of snores resume. "Good," she thought, "Brosia has gone back to sleep. Now if I can get the car out of the garage without waking them." As quietly as she could, Ana slipped out of the house and went to the garage. There was no turning back now. She knew this was what she had to do.

∽

Brosia and Raymond were each reading their favorite section of the newspaper and finishing their second cup of coffee. Brosia said, "It's not like Ana to miss breakfast. I didn't want to bother her earlier. I heard her moving around late last night and thought she needed to sleep in this morning. But it's really getting late; maybe I should check on her."

"Don't be such a mother hen. Ana's a grown woman; she'll get something to eat when she's ready. It's nice to have breakfast alone for a change. Don't pretend you didn't enjoy it too."

"That has nothing to do with it; I'm worried about her." Brosia got up from the table and knocked on Ana's door. When there was no answer, she knocked louder. "Ana, are you awake?" Again, there was no answer. She pushed the door open and walked in. "Raymond, come here."

When he entered the room, Brosia was holding a piece of paper. "Read this," she said as she handed the note to him. The note said, I have to take care of some unfinished business. Tell Bax I know he was right. I'm borrowing Raymond's car. The hearse would draw too much attention. I'll be back when I'm done. Love, Ana.

"What does she mean by that?" Raymond asked.

"I'm calling Bax. He must know what she means." Brosia found her phone and pushed Bax's cell number.

The phone rang several times before Bax answered. "Brosia, isn't it a little early for a call? What's the problem?"

"Ana's gone. She left a note about unfinished business and said she knew you were right. Do you know what she meant?"

"Yes, I know where she's going. It's something only she can do. Everything will work out; don't worry. She will tell you about it when she gets back. I'll call if I hear anything."

Bax smiled as he disconnected. Yes, this is something she needs to do by herself.

ფ

Ana drove for hours following the directions of the perfectly poised voice coming from the GPS. At least one of us isn't nervous, she thought. Finally, she saw a motel with a vacancy sign. Thank goodness. She didn't think she could have driven much farther. She pulled in and hoped for the best. Judging from the outward appearance of the place, it would be a misplaced hope.

When she went in, she thought she saw the clerk pass what looked like a small package of powder to a kid who looked to be under the influence of some substance. The leering desk clerk looked her up and down in a way that made her uncomfortable. She remembered the advice her father had given her when they entered witness protection. "Sweetheart, if something seems off, not quite right, trust your gut." Her gut said get out. She turned and went back to the car. Nothing that could happen in the car would be worse than what she imagined went on in that motel.

The adrenalin that shot through her system was better than a cup of strong black coffee. Ana was in survival mode, fully awake. The self-preservation instincts of fight or flight were fully engaged. She chose flight. As she put distance between the sleazy motel and its patrons, she lost the surge of hormone that kept her alert and turned to external stimuli.

Even with the radio blaring and the air-conditioner blowing full-blast, she was unable to stay alert. Ana caught herself nodding several times before she ran off the road. The jolt as she hit the shallow ditch woke her. She tried to back out, but her tire spun splattering mud all over Raymond's car. She was stuck; at least she knew where she would spend the night.

The next morning, she awoke to the sound of a car door slamming and gravel crunching under running feet. Finally, someone has come to help her out of the ditch. When she turned toward the sound, she recognized the underage kid she saw buying drugs at the motel. Ana quickly checked to be sure the door was locked and slid to the middle of the bench seat to get as far away as she could.

"I recognize you. You were at the motel last night," he said through the closed window.

"Go away; leave me alone," Ana screamed.

He reached into his pocket to get something; Ana screamed and closed her eyes.

"Calm down, ma'am; I'm not going to hurt you. Open your eyes."

Ana did as she was told. Pressed against the window was a badge. The smiling young man said, "I'm sorry I gave you a scare. You walked in on a drug bust last night. If you hadn't left when you did, we would have had to call it off."

"I thought you were a drugged-out kid."

"That's my job; I have to look and act the part to make the buy. I'll give you a ride into Blackjack. Your car is bogged in up to the axle, and I wouldn't be surprised if you damaged your front end. Don't tell me; I think you dozed off," he said as he called a wrecker on his cell.

"Hey, Paul, this is Jim. I want you to bring in a car down on Jackson Road." He continued to give directions as she got her purse and overnight bag from the passenger seat. When he disconnected, he turned to her, gave her a mischievous smile, and asked, "You weren't under the influence of anything were you?"

"Oh, no; I was just so sleepy when I stopped at the motel, I could hardly keep my eyes open. All I could think about was getting a room and sleeping. What I saw going on there made me feel so uneasy, I couldn't stay. I just drove, hoping I'd find another motel; but I was sleepier than I thought. Are you going to give me a ticket?"

"That's not my department. Get in my car; I'll drive you to Blackjack. I'm Jim Watson; what is your name?" he said as he opened the door for Ana.

"I'm Ana Leblanc." She looked at herself in the rearview mirror. "I look awful; I have to do something before I meet them."

"Are you going to an important meeting?" he asked.

"I need to find Wesley and Lora Cutrer, a couple I knew when I was a teen. I found out they live in Blackjack. You could say this might be the most important meeting of my life."

Jim said, "I can drop you off at my aunt's house. You could freshen up there."

"Your aunt might not want a disheveled stranger in her house."

"We're talking about a woman who rescues stray dogs and sponsors lost causes," Jim said.

"Well, if that's the case, I'll fit right in," Ana laughed for the first time in days.

They drove past Blackjack Baptist Church as they entered the small town. "People joke about the Catholics' Bingo games; it looks like the Baptist here have a small casino," Ana said.

"The town and the church are named for the blackjack oak that grows around here. You're not the first to think the name is inconsistent with a conservative church. A friend of mine told me playing cards show up in the offering plate as a joke, and it's not unusual to get a check for 21 dollars."

As they drove into the one-stoplight town, Jim pointed out a two-story house. "We're here; that's my aunt's house up ahead," he said as they approached a yellow Victorian.

"I don't know how to thank you. You not only picked me up and called a wrecker to bring my car to a shop, but you helped me take my mind off a meeting I dread. I'm looking forward to meeting your aunt. She sounds like a very nice person."

"She is, and I know she will be glad to see you," he said.

They entered the old house, a painted lady that had seen better days but retained her Victorian dignity. Jim showed Ana to a bathroom where she could freshen up before meeting his aunt.

The claw-foot tub and other period fixtures gave Ana the feeling she had stepped back to a simpler time. As she washed her face, combed her hair, and put on a little make up, Ana thought how lucky it was Jim who found her.

"Hello, Anna-Marie," a voice from her past said.

Ana spun around and faced her greatest fear. There in the doorway stood an old woman, Lisa's mother. Everything she had planned to say to the woman left her. No rehearsed speech could fill the silence.

The woman spoke in a soft, controlled voice. "I went to your funeral. What irony, I wept for you and your parents. You don't have to tell me. I know that it's my daughter buried with them. I lost her in life and death thanks to your deception. I recognized you on the news, and it all fell in place. We knew David had married someone he met at college, but never saw your picture. I can't imagine why you came to Blackjack after all these years. You and David made certain we didn't find out you were the one who lived."

Ana wiped away tears from her cheek. "After graduation Lisa took my place in bed so my parents wouldn't miss me if they checked on me before I got back from the party. They constantly checked on me. Threats had been made on all of our lives when dad testified against the man I later learned was David's grandfather.

"Still like so many young people, I didn't think anything could really happen to us. After all, we were under the protection of the U. S. Marshal's Office. So, Lisa and I made our plans. The party that meant so much to me didn't really matter to her. We switched places. After I got home and said goodnight to my parents, Lisa climbed in my window, and I climbed out. I took her car and went to the party.

"When I returned, I saw them being rolled out and knew the people who wanted to kill my family had succeeded. I ran to the U.S. Marshal assigned to us and told him what happened. He took me to a safe place, and arranged a new identity for me. He told me the killers found our family because my dad went home for a funeral. They were watching for him and followed him back. He said I must let Anna-Marie remain dead and take on the new identity, or I would probably be killed. "I'm so sorry. I would have done anything to bring Lisa back if I could have. There was nothing I could do, and I was so afraid the burners would find me. It was cowardly and selfish to let you believe she ran away. I should have told you the truth so you could claim her body and mourn her, instead of living in limbo all these years."

Lora paused to collect her thoughts before responding to what she'd heard. "I think I always knew she was dead. Lisa wasn't the kind of girl to run off without a word. But my husband never gave up hope she would come to her senses and come back home. We spent most of our savings hiring private investigators to look for her. He died three years after she disappeared, still hoping we would find her and bring her home. I guess there are worse things than false hope."

Ana continued her story. "I didn't know David in high school; he went to another school and was ahead of me. He saw me at a party in college. At first, he cultivated a friendship with me. Just when I had started to feel safe with him, he dropped the bomb that destroyed me. He told me he knew I was the friend of his cousin who'd killed her, just as surely as if I had set the fire.

"I tried to explain what happened and about the threat made by an old gangster to kill my family. Then he told me if I didn't do as he said, he would make sure the old man had a chance to finish the job. Dave said he had connections. I believed him."

Lora nodded and said, "He was talking about his grandfather. We all were glad when he was sent to prison. Dave's mother was afraid of him. He was a terrible man. Dave was just a child when she divorced his father. Mary found out her husband was involved in his father's nefarious business. One of her greatest fears was that David would fall into the same pattern. She later married my brother, who adopted Dave. They raised him from the time he was ten. His biological father had little contact with him after the adoption. We had no idea Dave had gotten involved."

Ana reached for the older woman's hand and said, "He was more involved than you can imagine. Before Dave shot me, he told me he set the fire that killed Lisa and my parents. It was part of a deal with his grandfather. His education would be paid for in return for eliminating our whole family. When he recognized me and realized he had killed the wrong girl, he blackmailed me into marrying him. For almost twenty-four years, he controlled every part of my life with the threat of what would happen if he had his connections take care of me."

"I know this was hard for you, Anna-Marie, but I'm glad you told me everything. You were a good friend to my daughter. No matter what he said, there was only one person to blame for her death—David. It's time to forgive yourself and go on with your life. That is what Lisa would want. Honor her by living a life free from guilt."

Ana hugged Lora, and both of them cried. "I need to call Brosia and let her know I'm all right. I know she's been worried sick since she found my note."

"Who is that?"

"She's the woman the marshal placed me with after the fire. I call her Thea, that's Greek for aunt, but I think of her as a mother."

"Yes, let her know that you're all right and you'll be staying with me until your car is fixed. We can put the demons behind us and remember the good times you girls had together."

The women had lunch and spent the afternoon reminiscing. When Joe called to tell Ana her car wouldn't be ready before the next afternoon, Lora insisted she spend the night. Ana hadn't felt such peace since she realized she had to hide the truth about Lisa's death from the Cutrers.

The next day when Ana got in the car, she thanked Lora and waved goodbye as she drove away. She started to retrace her route back to Eastabutchie County. She was five miles down the road when she realized she wasn't ready to go back to Alabama.

I've depended on Brosia and Raymond too long. I've even been leaning on Bax and Lovie's family. It's time I stand on my own feet. I'll never be whole until I do. She turned left and headed back to Louisiana to exorcize her personal demons.

Closing

Ana felt the chill of anxiety as she turned down the oak-lined street where she and Dave lived. Not surprisingly, their cottage showed signs of neglect. How long had it been since they left for the conference in Tennessee? At least a thoughtful neighbor had occasionally mowed the grass. Even in this neglected state, the outward appearance of their home gave no hint to the nightmare her life there had been.

She went to the overgrown flowerbed and moved a small statue; a key was taped to the bottom. Ana used it to open her front door and stepped back into her past. The odor of stale air mixed with the faded aroma of her favorite potpourri was the only ghost in the long-empty house. She opened all the blinds to let in sunlight.

It was time to get to work. She would not entertain unpleasant memories. There wasn't time for that indulgence, Ana went to the pantry and pulled out a box of extra-large garbage bags and started removing reminders of her life with Dave.

She went through the house dumping photographs. Studio photographs of the two of them portrayed as a loving couple were the first to go. Albums, videos, and compact disks were next. When Ana finished her sweep, there wasn't a trace left of the illusion of a happy marriage Dave had constructed.

Ana methodically went through the house, packing important deeds, documents, and personal information to be taken with her. She called the Salvation Army and made arrangements for them to pick up any furnishings and clothing left in the house the following week.

Next, she called Tony's wife. The phone rang six times before the familiar voice answered.

"Jane, this is Ana."

"Ana, it's wonderful to hear from you. I've been reading about all the things you have been through in the newsletter the college puts out. How are you?"

"I'm fine, but I need to talk to you in person."

"Are you in the state?"

"I'm at my house. May I come over later?"

"Of course, come over. You probably don't know I've moved back to New Orleans. I inherited the house on St. Charles. Tony and I decided to rent it until we retired and moved back. After he died, I had no reason to stay at the house close to campus so I moved back home. I'd love to see you. You and I are the only ones left of our tight little college group. I've really missed you," Jane said.

Ana said, "If I leave here now, I should be at your house by eight o'clock. Will that be too late?"

"Of course not, come on."

The two women did a polite dance around the questions that most concerned them. Did either one really want to bring up what had happened since they last saw each other? They agreed on a convenient time, hung up, and steeled themselves for their meeting.

Ana arrived at her friend's house a few minutes early. She sat in her car planning how to tell Jane what had been on her mind ever since she learned how Tony died. She walked to the door and rang the bell. Jane answered the door and hugged her. "Jane, it's so good to see you again," Ana said.

After a few minutes of exchanging pleasantries, Ana got to the reason she had driven so far to talk to her old friend. "The reason I came back is to tell you in person how sorry I am about what happened to Tony. I blame Dave and Dr. Simmons for everything that happened to him. He recognized a threat and put the evidence in David's hands for safe keeping. The one person Tony thought he could trust was up to his neck in the organization that killed him," Ana said.

"You can't mean Dave was responsible for what happened to Tony. It's hard to reconcile this other version of David with the man I knew. I remember how close Dave and Tony were in school. When they both took teaching positions in the same department at Willow Wood, they remained close. I can't believe the man I knew could've been involved in anything that would put Tony in danger," Jane said.

"Dave was a member of a subversive group called the Vipers. I teasingly asked Dave if he had joined a motorcycle gang. He laughed and said the word Vipers was a crazy acronym for a group of educators whose goal was to reform education. Of course, that was a lie.

"I've found out the core group of the Vipers was made up of some disenchanted scholars and college professors who recruited students who were also unhappy with our government. Those students made up the second level of the organization. The third part of the group consisted of contract killers who were more than willing to do the dirty work for the group. Dave was in the second group when Dr. Simmons recruited him during his undergraduate years at LSU. I believe he was probably in the third group as well. The ultimate goal of the Vipers was to undermine our political system.

"Tony was accidentally slipped some incriminating information intended for Simmons about the group. He was killed for it. Later they kidnapped Dave. The group was so secretive that the men sent to recover it didn't know Dave was part of the group. We believe Dave thought they were undercover agents and was afraid to identify himself as a Viper. He got away, but was later killed by the group's leader.

"The FBI is still making all the connections, but there are a number of deaths and disappearances of people in key government positions that have been tied to the group. Of course, these people were removed so that some of the highly qualified scholars in the organization would be able to take the positions. They spent years laying the groundwork to make one of the Vipers the logical replacement for each person they removed. It worked most of the time," Ana said.

"It's unbelievable that Dave was a part of something that vile. Was that what changed your marriage? You two seemed to be the perfect couple. He was so attentive; he treated you like a queen. I couldn't believe it when I heard one of the top stories on the Alabama news was about David trying to kill you," Jane said.

Ana lowered her head and paused before answering. "We were never a perfect couple, far from it. That was just an illusion Dave went to great pains to create. David Fontaine was a controlling, manipulating monster. He got me to marry him by convincing me he would arrange for someone to kill me if I didn't. He accused me of killing his cousin. Marrying him was the price I had to pay to keep me from the punishment I deserved."

"That's ridiculous, I can't even imagine you as a killer," Jane said.

Ana looked into Jane's eyes and said, "I didn't kill her, but she was killed in a house fire while spending the night at my house. Before he died, Dave told me he was paid to kill my family. He set the fire. Because he failed to kill me, he had to destroy my life in other ways."

"That sounds so sick," Jane said.

"Maybe he was, but I think he was just evil. He had me trapped in a relationship I loathed. You were my best friend, but I envied your life with Tony. It was evident you both loved each other. Even more than that, your husband was an honest, honorable man who respected you as his equal. You two had a real marriage, all I ever wanted, but something I had no hope of ever having." Ana wiped tears from her cheeks.

"I can't believe we didn't see how unhappy you were. I thought your protest when Dave would kiss your ring and say you were his prize was just embarrassment because he was being so silly. He was taunting you, wasn't he?"

Ana said, "Yes, he loved to let me know that I was no more than a possession, something to show off. I felt like a well-trained pet that knows the commands and could do tricks. I hated my life but had no idea how bad it could get."

Jane reached out to her friend and hugged her. "Someday you may find a man who will love you the same way Tony loved me. Don't ever settle for less."

"I doubt that anyone is out there for me, and that's fine. I know I'm better off alone than I have been since my parents died. I have too much baggage. No man in his right mind would want to take a woman with the emotional scars I have." Ana was uncomfortable with the direction the conversation was going. "Let's change the subject. I have to go to back to Willow Wood to get the things we left there. I have no idea what they did with the personal items we left in our offices. I hope they weren't thrown away when everyone thought we were dead."

Jane looked at her watch and said, "Let me go with you. You had a long drive coming here. If you want to know the truth, you look exhausted. We can go in the morning. I have some clothes you can use if you stay."

Ana was exhausted and dreaded going back to her house in the early morning hours. Even more she dreaded being at the house she had shared with Dave. She hated it and all it stood for. Staying with Jane was a good idea.

The next morning the women drove back to Willow Wood College and went to the History Department. When Ana and Jane walked in, Nannette, one of the secretaries, gasped and jumped to her feet to hug them. "It's so good to see you. I can't tell you how sorry we all are about what happened."

Ana said, "Thank you, Nan. It's good to see you, too. I need some help. Dave and I both had personal items in our offices. I would like to pick up our things if you know where they are stored."

"I packed up Dave's and your things and stored them in the basement of the fine arts building. I will call one of the student workers to mind the desk while I go with you to get them. I know just where they are; that will save time."

"Thanks, Nan," Ana said.

When they got to the basement, it didn't take Nan long to find the boxes of personal possessions. The women loaded them in Ana's car.

"Jane, thank you for helping me with this. I'll drive you back home and start back to Eastabuchie County."

"Don't be in such a rush. You don't know what Dave had in his office. Considering what you've told me, you may want to open the boxes here. You may find out other things about his life that could be upsetting. If you should need support, I'm available."

Ana laughed and said, "I doubt there could be anything in the boxes that would be that upsetting. However, I could go through them and discard the things I don't want."

"That's a good idea. When we get back, you can go through the boxes while I make supper for us," Jane said.

When they got back to Jane's house, she went to the kitchen. "I'll just fix a light meal. How does breakfast for supper sound?"

"That would be perfect," Ana said as she opened the first of Dave's boxes. There were books, framed diplomas, and awards, just the typical academic clutter that litters the offices of most college professors. Nothing was out of the ordinary; there was nothing she wanted to keep. The second box was much the same. The third box was filled with personal correspondence, deeds, contracts, and a file of photographs she had never seen.

Ana thought she would have to go through this box more carefully. Maybe she would be through before Jane finished with supper, but she doubted it. She started looking through the file of pictures. It didn't take long to discover why these pictures were kept in the office instead of the house. The eight by ten glossy of the older man was autographed "Job well done. Good luck in your continued education. As I promised, grad school is on me. Love, Grandpa." A chill ran down her back as she read it. As innocent as the note sounded, there was little doubt in her mind as to what the job he had done so well was. The note was dated the week after the fire.

Jane heard the scream from the kitchen and rushed in. "What is it, Ana?"

Ana was ripping the photo into irregular strips. She handed them to Jane. "Look at the note from his loving grandfather."

As Jane pieced together the strips, Ana said, "That date is less than a week from the night of the fire that killed my parents and Dave's cousin Lisa. He was paid off with a free ride in graduate school." Ana continued going through the file. "I wonder how many other thank you notes from Grandpa are in this file."

She recognized some of the faces in the file as missing persons whose pictures had been plastered on billboards and television news reports over the years. Others were strangers with no hint as to why they were included in the file. Were they victims or customers like Grandpa? Then one picture caught her attention.

The photo had been mutilated with pin holes, and the word die was written across the couple. However, the faces in the picture were still recognizable. She had seen them when Lora pulled out the family album. The couple was David's mother with his stepfather who had adopted him. The date stamp in the corner was confusing.

"Look at this picture, Jane. This picture was made after David and I were married. When I met Dave at LSU, he told me his parents died years earlier when he was a boy. This is a picture of them made after we married. I wonder if they are still alive. Lora would know." She picked up her cell phone and called her friend in Blackjack.

"Lora, this is Ana, I need some information. When and how did Dave's parents die?"

"I thought you knew; they were at their fish camp when someone broke in and killed them. It happened about three years ago. Dave came to the funeral. We asked why he didn't bring his wife. He said you were having mental problems, and it wouldn't be wise for you to come."

Ana said, "No, he never mentioned it. He wouldn't because he told me they were dead long before we met. Just for the record, the only mental problem I had was being crazy enough to marry such a dangerous man." She glanced at the photo in her lap again. "Lora, I don't think your brother and sister-in-law's deaths were random killings. I just found a picture of them with die written on it. The picture has been punctured repeatedly. Dave must have been very angry with them. Do you think the police would be interested in seeing it?"

"They might be, but how would it help? With what we know about what he did to our family members, he probably did kill his parents. What good would it do to correct the police records? He's dead now and facing final justice. Do you really want to center your life on the things Dave might have done? My advice is to stop digging in his past and begin work on making a future for you."

"You make sense; I'll think about what you said." Ana hung up and turned to Jane. "I know she's right about moving on, but I feel responsible to the families of the people in the photos. They may not be victims, but there must be some connection to David or he wouldn't have this file. I'm turning it over to the New Orleans Police. I know for a fact that he killed three people in their jurisdiction."

"I'll go with you. I think you're right. We know Dave killed your family and friend. He almost succeeded in killing you. If there's a link between him and the people in the file, the police need to know," Jane said. "I went to high school with a woman who works in the Superintendent of Investigations office. We have kept in touch. I'll call her and see if we should bring in a file of pictures kept by a man we know killed your parents," Jane punched in a number.

"Hello," Jane said after several rings. "Jackson, this is Jane Berry, one of Wanda's friends. I need her work number. My friend, Ana, and I believe we have discovered something that may help with some missing person cases. We're unsure where we should turn in these items."

She waited for an answer, then smiled and nodded to Ana as she wrote down a number. When she got off the phone, she said, "Thanks for your help. Don't have her call me when she gets in. I'll call her at work tomorrow. This is business not personal."

The next morning the exhausted women slept later than usual. After brunch, Jane said, "I'll call Wanda, we can drive in as soon as I get off the phone."

Ana went to the van and reviewed the collection of pictures while she waited for Jane to join her.

When Jane got in, she told Ana, "Wanda is interested in the pictures. She said she would examine the file and talk to us about what we know about Dave's criminal history. After she has the facts, she will make sure the file and the other things in the box get to the appropriate person."

Ana and Jane drove to the police department and went directly to the Superintendent of Investigations office. The women entered the office building with a mixture of excitement and trepidation. They went to the desk. "I'm Jane Berry, and this is Ana Leblanc. We have an appointment with Wanda Dupree."

"One moment, I'll see if she is available." The receptionist called Wanda's extension. "There're two women to see you. They say they have an appointment." There was brief silence then she hung up and said, "She'll be right out."

A statuesque woman in uniform came out to meet them. "Jane, it's so good to see you again. Is this the friend you were telling me about?"

Jane nodded, "Yes, Ana and I have known each other since college. She was married to my husband's co-worker and college friend, David Fontaine. Dave was killed by the same group that killed Tony."

"I no longer use his name; I'm Ana Leblanc now. Thank you for seeing me, Detective Dupree."

"Let's go back to my office where we can get down to business," Wanda said as she guided them down the hall.

Ana noticed the name on the door. Wanda was a chief in the investigation branch, not just a detective as she had supposed. When they were all seated in her office, Wanda asked, "Just what is it you found in your husband's personal effects that you think may give the department some leads?"

"My husband was a killer. He has been identified as a member of a terrorist group. I know for a fact that he has killed for hire. I have no idea how many people he killed, but I know he killed my parents, his cousin, and he tried to kill me. When I was going through his personal effects, I found a file of pictures. Among them was a picture of his parents that had been stabbed with a pin repeatedly. He told me they were dead long before we married, but the picture's date stamp was less than four years ago. I found out they were murdered three years ago, shortly after that picture was taken."

Ana pulled the file from her purse and handed it to Wanda, "There are many more pictures in this file. Some Jane and I recognized as missing persons whose pictures have been in the newspaper. I don't know who they are, but there is a connection to my husband who was a man capable of anything. I thought your department might be able to put the pieces together. I want the families of these people to know why their loved one's pictures were in the personal file of a killer."

"Thank you for bringing the file in. This couldn't have been easy for you. I assure you we will do everything we can to find the connection. You're right to assume some of these pictures are faces I'd recognize from cold cases our department has handled. Others may be cases other departments in the state have worked on. I'll be sure to circulate the information to other police departments. If he did have something to do with the death or disappearance of these people, we will at least be able to tell the families that the man who was responsible is dead and will never hurt anyone else." She stood and extended her hand. Her time was valuable; the meeting was over.

Jane drove Ana back to the house so she could pick up her car and finally return to Alabama. The two friends felt closer than before. They would always be bound by the memories of two men; one each had loved and the other man they hated.

Ana got in Raymond's car and started home. Home, what a comforting concept that was, she thought. For a long time, the cabin in Alabama had felt like the home she had longed for most of her life. For almost as long as she could remember, her life had been a crazy quilt of disguises and identities that were assigned to her for her protection. She was now free to become the person she was meant to be.

All the people she loved the most were there. Her dear Thea Brosia and Raymond, her protective new uncle, were as devoted to her as any parents could be. In addition, she now had an extended family made up of friends who had given her the love and support she needed when she needed it most. Isn't that what home is, a place where you are loved and protected? These were the things that made this place different from other places she had lived.

Even though the trip back to Alabama took a detour through Louisiana, the feeling of relief she was experiencing made it seem shorter and more pleasant than the trip to Blackjack. A lightness she had forgotten existed came over her. She couldn't wait to see Brosia and Raymond and tell them how this time away from Alabama had changed her.

She drove down the familiar road to Bax's cabin. When she rounded the final curve, she could see Brosia and Raymond walking back from the lakeshore. She parked the car and went to meet them. Brosia hugged her and said, "Thank God, you're home. You had me so worried. Where have you been?"

As they walked to the porch and sat down, Ana said, "I've been tying up loose ends, things that have kept me from moving on. Bax told me if I were ever going to be free of the guilt, I've felt all of these years, I needed to find Lisa's parents and let them know what really happened that night after graduation. Her father has been dead for a long time, but I've made peace with her mother. In fact, we have become friends.

"Then I went to see Jane and told her all I knew about how Dave was involved with the group that killed Tony. She was shocked to know that Dave had engaged in criminal activity. Somehow knowing the truth about him brought us closer together. She went with me to get the personal items Dave and I left in our offices. Among the things we found in the boxes of his things was a file of photographs I believe will link Dave to more crimes."

"You have been busy. I hope you achieved what you set out to do," Raymond said.

"At least I've made a start. I'm not the inert victim I'd allowed myself to become. I know I can't rewrite the past, but I will no longer let it control me," Ana said.

"You must be exhausted. Come in the house and rest awhile. I'll make a pot of coffee, and we can catch up." Brosia said as she got up from the swing.

"No, I need to borrow your car a little longer, Raymond. I need to tell Bax I followed his advice, and he was right," Ana said.

"I'm afraid that's not possible, Ana. He's not in Alabama anymore. While you were gone, his father had a stroke. Bax went to Kentucky to be with him," Brosia said.

"Is there anything we can do? I wish we could give him some support the way he supported us when I was in so much trouble," Ana said.

"There isn't anything we can do right now. There is no telling how long he's going to be gone. Brother Martin has taken over his duties at the church until he can come home. He refers to Bax's time away as a sabbatical. However, Hank Wilson said, 'Sabbatical my eye, it's nothing short of Bax abandoning his post. He should be fired on the spot.' No one took him seriously, of course. We all know how Hank is," Brosia said.

"Do you know how serious his father's stroke was?" Ana asked.

"I don't really know. The last I heard he was starting rehabilitation. They say the sooner it's started, the better the results," Raymond said. "Brother Martin sent out an e-mail. He said the rehabilitation could take as long as a year. Of course, it could be a lot shorter."

Brosia added, "Poor man may never be able to resume his ministry. Brother Martin said the effect on his speech has been devastating. Bax took his father's place in the last nights of the Crusade. The revival team and his audience apparently thought he preached every bit as effectively as his father. There was even some talk about him joining the team if his father is unable to continue with his ministry."

The thought of Bax joining his father's organization and preaching all over the world left Ana cold. She couldn't see someone who loved his life as a small-town pastor stepping into that role. He loved being involved in the lives of the people in his church. Being a dynamic evangelist who had no contact with those in the audience after the revival was over didn't match what she knew about Bax. He couldn't be happy taking his father's place. Not only that, she would miss him if he left.

That night while watching the news, Brosia called Ana to the living room. "Ana come here. You'll want to see this."

Ana walked out of her bedroom just in time to see J. B. Alford, Sr. being rolled out of the hospital. The evangelist was followed by Bax and an unidentified woman. The reporter said the earlier rumors that the stroke had left the preacher unable to speak were unconfirmed. However, it had been confirmed Jehu Baxter Alford, Jr. would replace his father in the remaining scheduled revivals.

"Poor man, it must be terrible for him," Brosia began sharing her thoughts on the subject, but Ana didn't hear the rest of what she said. One fact registered with her: Bax was taking his father's place for a series of revivals across the nation. She knew what a powerful preacher he was. With the exposure he would get while filling in for his father, he could have a future in evangelism. It was quite possible he would follow in his father's footsteps as so many sons of evangelists have successfully done. Ana knew she should be happy for her friend, but she felt a pang of regret at the possibility he would no longer be a part of her life.

Brosia's voice had become white noise, but meaning returned. Ana clearly understood when her aunt said, "That woman with them is Cassie McDoniel. I asked Brother Martin if he knew who she was when we first saw her picture with Bax. He told me he met her at Beth's funeral. She introduced herself to him as an old friend of Bax's. Later Brother Martin found out they were sweethearts in college until Bax met Beth. Now she's a speech pathologist and is working with Bax's father. It's funny how the same people turn up in a person's life."

Ana nodded but thought it was not such a funny coincidence. She could imagine that this Cassie called and offered her professional services. Of course, Bax would want a speech pathologist he knew and trusted. What better way for her to get back into her old boyfriend's life than to be the heroine with the skills to rescue his father from the effects of a stroke?

The next morning Brosia brought in the local newspaper. "I thought you might like to see these pictures of Bax and his father." There on the front page were two pictures side by side. The first was a picture of the evangelist, looking older and thinner, being pushed out of the hospital. His eyelids were drooped and his mouth slightly twisted to the side. He looked nothing like the picture that hung in Bax's office. Behind him and slightly out of focus were two people she recognized as Bax and Cassie. The second picture was of Bax speaking before a stadium filled with enraptured listeners. The caption said. "After J.B. Alford, Sr. turned his pulpit over to our local pastor, new vigor has been added to the age-old message." Her heart sank.

છ

Months passed with local news stories on the success of the revivals her only information about Bax. Slowly Ana's life returned to something close to normal. She had never imagined it was possible to miss Bax as much as she did. Someone needed to talk some sense into her. She guessed it might as well be herself because no one else knew how silly she was acting.

Of course, Bax had shown interest in her while she was in trouble; that was his job. She just got so caught up in the euphoria of being relieved of so many fears that she imagined she had slipped into love with Bax.

Slipping into love sounded funny, but she thought that was the right term. Falling in love was fast, exciting, and passionate.

What she had been feeling was gradual, peaceful, and comforting. She was just beginning to discover there was more to her feelings than the warm reassurance that someone really cared about her welfare. Now he was into a new phase of his life, a phase with no place for her.

What was that old song? "Falling in love with love is falling for make believe." That just about summed it up. She should feel lucky; at least she didn't have the opportunity to make a fool out of herself. She folded the newspaper and put it with the others she'd hidden between some unfinished canvases in the closet. That was where she kept her failures; paintings and daydreams she originally thought would work out beautifully but ended in disappointment.

She needed to get away from all the things here that brought back memories. There was no future here for her. At her age she shouldn't continue to live with Brosia and Raymond. They loved it here and had put a contract on the cabin. Before long Bax would be sending someone to remove his personal things before they closed on the little house.

She wondered when he would officially resign from his position at the church. Brother Martin had been there so long that some of the new members didn't even know Bax. Others might be thinking Hank Wilson had it right when he said he'd fire Bax if it were up to him.

Ana found Brosia peeling potatoes in the kitchen. "Brosia, you and Raymond have been wonderful to me, but I've recovered, and it's time I stand on my own feet. I'm going back to Louisiana. Jane will let me stay with her while I look for a job."

"Ana, you don't need another job. You're doing just fine with your painting. You have people clamoring to buy everything you paint. If you miss teaching, why don't you look for a job in Birmingham? There's a branch of The University of Alabama there. I'm sure there are other colleges nearby that could use an artist with your reputation," Brosia rinsed a potato. "Really, dear, you don't need to work unless you want to for personal reasons. You inherited all that money from David. I had no idea he had that much tucked away."

Ana said, "I can't use that money. I know he inherited some of it from his grandfather, the man who ordered my family's death. I suspect some is from other contract killing he's done. I want no part of it. I'm donating it to charities that can help people who've been hurt by people like him. No, I need to get away. I love you and Raymond so much. You've interrupted your lives to help me rebuild mine. But I need to start over in a place without reminders of the horrific things I need to forget."

"I understand what you're saying, but at least stay until Bax gets back. He might be able to help you identify the charities you would want to support," Brosia said.

"I'm not leaving immediately. I have to buy a car and tie up some loose ends, but I might not be here when Bax gets back." Ana thought that she would not be there when he got back if there was any way to avoid it. He was a big part of why she was going. As soon as she got a dependable car, she was leaving.

ᭇ

Bubba pulled up in front of the cabin. Bubba had his short-comings, but he knew more about cars than anyone else in Eastabuchie County. Everyone in the county knew how he babied his limo and kept his mama's truck in top running condition. That made him the logical choice to help her find what she needed at a price she could afford. He honked his horn, and Ana came out and got in the car.

"Are you ready to find that car, Miss Ana?" he said as she slipped into the front seat.

"I am. Do you think you can find a good deal for me?" she asked.

"I've already found a couple over at Warner's Used Car Lot that I think will fit the bill. They're in good shape and priced right." Because he enjoyed a bit of gossip as much as anyone in his family, he couldn't wait to be the first to share the latest news with Ana. "Did you hear Brother Bax got back in town last night? Mama was taking some things over for Maude Harrington to alter to fit her. You know she's gained a little weight lately, Mama, not Miss Maude. Well, Mama passed Bax's house and saw him taking his suitcases in."

As Bubba continued to tell other tidbits of gossip, Ana thought that she was getting the car just in time. She wanted to get away from here before Bax came back to resign.

Bubba pulled into the car lot. She looked over the cars he had previously selected. Both were reasonably new and clean looking. After she test drove them, she picked the one that needed only a few tweaks to be the perfect car for her. "That off-white Buick is just what I'm looking for. Do you think they can pull the dent out of the fender?"

"That's no problem, Ana," he said.

Ana went in and closed the deal. The dent was pulled out and money changed hands. She was satisfied with the deal she'd made and was anxious to show her vehicle to Brosia and Raymond.

As Ana drove the car home later that afternoon, she thought about how she needed to leave the next day. She would call Jane that night to be sure she hadn't changed her mind about letting her stay with her for a while.

When she got home, she called to Brosia and Raymond. "Come outside and see the car Bubba helped me buy."

The couple came out of the back room and followed her outside. "It looks like you made a good choice," Raymond said as he checked out the car.

Brosia said, "Yes, it's nice. I'm glad Bubba went with you. He wouldn't have let you get stuck with a lemon. This is changing the subject, but guess who came by this afternoon. Don't even try; you wouldn't get it right. It was Bax. He came over and stayed for a good, long time. I told him you'd be sorry you missed him. Maybe you can see him before you leave."

"I'm leaving in the morning. I doubt I'll be able to see him before I go."

"That's too bad. He wanted to see you. Bax has been so dedicated to you. Try to go by the church before you go back to Louisiana," Brosia said.

The next morning Ana packed the second-hand car with clothes, paintings, and her art supplies. She kissed Raymond and Brosia good-bye and drove down the curvy dirt road one last time. Brosia was right, there was one more thing she had to do before she left Eastabuchie County and returned to Louisiana. It wouldn't be right to leave without saying good-bye. He was the one person who had been in her corner from the beginning. Bax had listened to her, trusted her, and even after she betrayed his trust, he forgave her. He had been by her side through every life-threatening episode she faced. Bax even put himself in danger of being shot when he tried to tackle David when he had a gun pointed at her.

She touched the silver and jade pendant he had given her. He had changed the way she thought of herself. At the time when she had seen herself as worthless broken pottery, he told her she was precious jade. It had been Bax who convinced her to face her fears by going to Lisa's mother and telling her what had happened to her daughter. Lora had accepted the truth so well that Ana went to Jane and explained why Tony had been killed. The relief she felt after these visits she owed to Bax. No matter that things didn't turn out the way she had begun to hope, she owed Bax so much. It wouldn't be right to go away without thanking him for all he had done for her.

Ana drove to up the church, parked the car and went in the back door. Bax was coming out of his office, reading a letter. He looked up, saw her and smiled. "Ana, it's good to see you. I hope you went to see Lisa's mother when you left Brosia the note."

"I did, Bax. You were right. I used the time I was gone to face the things in my life that have been holding me back. I saw Lisa's mother and Tony's wife; they were wonderful. I turned over some things to the police that may help other people find the peace of mind I have now. I'm not living in the past anymore. I'm ready to go on with my life. In fact, my car is packed, and I'm leaving for Louisiana today. I just had to thank you for all you've done to help me reach this point."

"Don't go," Bax said softly as he took her in his arms and kissed her. As suddenly as it happened, he pulled away. "I'm so sorry, Ana-Grace. I had no right to do that."

What he had done was so unexpected, so out of character, she couldn't help smiling as she said, "I can't think of a reason why you shouldn't." She drew closer and kissed him back. He responded with a tender kiss that became more passionate before they stepped back.

Lovie turned the corner in time to see the kiss and embrace that followed. She couldn't believe what she was seeing with her own eyes. She couldn't wait to tell Sister. She wouldn't believe it. Without a second thought, Lovie pulled her cell phone out of her pocket and was about to hit speed-dial when she remembered the call from God and changed her mind.

ॐ

C O L O P H O N

The text of Shattered Jade *is set in Times New Roman drawn by Stanley Morison and Victor Larednet. The ornaments are Adobe Garamond Pro designed by Robert Slimbach. This book was designed and composed by Kent Mummert, MFA. It was manufactured by Lulu Press Publishing Company, Morrisville, North Carolina using 60# white lead-free, acid-free, buffered paper made from wood-based pulp for the interior and 100# laminated cover stock for the exterior.*

CPSIA information can be obtained
at www.ICGtesting.com
Printed in the USA
LVHW021139260422
717217LV00015B/656